THE SYNDROME

Also by Ridley Pearson

Kingdom Keepers—Disney After Dark
Kingdom Keepers II—Disney at Dawn
Kingdom Keepers III—Disney in Shadow
Kingdom Keepers IV—Power Play
Kingdom Keepers V—Shell Game
Kingdom Keepers VI—Dark Passage
Kingdom Keepers VII—The Insider

Steel Trapp—The Challenge
Steel Trapp—The Academy

Mysteries and thrillers (for grown-ups)

The Risk Agent
Choke Point
The Red Room

A KINGDOM KEEPERS ADVENTURE

THE SYNDROME

RIDLEY PEARSON

With Brooke Muschott (as Jess)
and Elizabeth Hagenlocher (as Mattie)

DISNEP • HYPERION

Los Angeles   New York

Printed in the United States of America

First Edition, March 2015

10 9 8 7 6 5 4 3 2 1
G475-5664-5-14349
ISBN 978-1-4847-2408-8

Library of Congress Cataloging-in-Publication Data
Pearson, Ridley.
  The Syndrome / Ridley Pearson.
      pages cm.—(Kingdom Keepers)
  Summary: Amanda, Jess, and Mattie must use their special abilities to find a missing Kingdom Keeper.
  ISBN 978-1-4847-2408-8
[1. Extrasensory perception—Fiction. 2. Good and evil—Fiction. 3. Walt Disney World (Fla.)—Fiction.] I. Title.
  PZ7.P323314Sy 2015
  [Fic]—dc23   2014038679

Visit www.DisneyBooks.com
www.thekingdomkeepers.com
www.ridleypearson.com
www.kingdomkeepersinsider.com

Special thanks are due to Genevieve Gagne-Hawes and Samantha Frank for their editorial efforts; also, to Wendy Lefkon and Disney Books for keeping the train on the tracks; to Nancy Zastrow and Jen Wood for office management and social media skills; and to all Disney Imagineers for contributing to my research, both on the ground and on the Web.

DEDICATED to everyone with a special skill. Fairlies, all.

DAY 1

AMANDA

I wasn't always this way. Maybe I inherited it, but I don't know because my parents aren't around to ask. I can't say it exactly feels normal. I remember not having it.

The first time it hit me, I was an angry ten-year-old. My mother was still around then and there was a man who could have been my father. I called him Tom. I don't remember him well. My mother was being mean and I stormed into my room—it was actually some kind of closet, I think, off the apartment's only hallway—and I turned and slammed a different door *from across the room. Bang!* The door moved like a hurricane wind had hit it.

From that day on she was afraid of me. What she didn't realize was that it had happened in little ways before that—ways I didn't quite understand but still didn't question. A page of a book would turn on its own as I reached for it; toothpaste would go onto my toothbrush without my squeezing; once, the saltshaker moved across the kitchen table to me—though no one else saw it because I was eating my mac and cheese alone. It may not have made sense to others, but none of the events surprised me.

It felt natural.

* * *

As an escapee from "Barracks 14," a so-called "private school" in Maryland, I did not want to ever go back. Not ever.

My closest friend on earth, Jessica, and I had escaped during Hurricane Cally. In truth, Barracks 14 was a cinder block brick of a building among many others on a military base that had been closed for over a decade. Boarding school, seriously? I don't know what they called us, our so-called instructors, but we called ourselves *Fairlies*, for *fairly human*. Each of us had some sort of strange power. The instructors called them gifts— what a joke! Try telling that to the boy who set his textbook on fire because he became frustrated with his algebra homework; or the girl down the hall who heard people's thoughts the way the rest of us hear people speak. At Barracks 14, she'd worn a set of noise-canceling earbuds to keep her sane. Gifts of coal, if you ask me.

It seemed like one of those "grass is greener" situations: we Fairlies, uncomfortable with the very "gifts" our instructors wanted so badly to understand. Maybe it was mere curiosity, as they claimed, but it looked more like greed, like a hunger to own this private part of us we didn't want to share. They were so annoying with their cameras and their questions.

Once inside that military base, we never left. Barracks 14 was a prison, plain and simple. No matter what they called it, it was a place to poke and test us, physically and mentally. It was invasive, scary, sometimes embarrassing, and often abusive. It was a place from which to run.

So Jess and I did just that. One or two others escaped as well. Most have not been so fortunate.

After finding our way to Orlando, Florida, Jess and I were eventually contacted by five kids our age who were nearly as weird we are—and that's saying something. We all graduated high school last year from different schools in Orlando. The five—two girls and three boys—work for Disney. But not like other interns. The five aren't Cast Members, food service workers, lighting designers, or character handlers. They are in-park guides. Families hire them to tour around the parks, move to the front of lines, meet characters, or get lunch reservations. The weird part: they're holograms. Well, not our friends. Our friends are real. But they modeled for Disney so that their *incredibly* lifelike holograms could be used as park guides. Now the Disney Hosts Interactive—so-called "DHI"—guides are among the most requested service in all of Disney.

Things got crazy. This was Disney and, as Jess and I came to find out, stuff in Disney was a lot more real than we'd known. It was a lot more than fairy tales and princesses. Things happened in the parks after dark. Bad things. Our friends— quickly nicknamed the *Kingdom Keepers*—had become part of the effort to stop the Disney villains—the *Overtakers*—who wanted the good magic replaced by the dark. Jess and I got caught up in that effort.

We'd been hanging around with the Keepers ever since Jess had been taken over—*yes, taken over!*—by Maleficent. If I hadn't seen it, I wouldn't have believed it either—don't worry, you're not alone in that.

* * *

I met Finn Whitman in what I think of as a predetermined moment. And though he did not know it, I did. I'd been expecting him, thanks to an old Disney Imagineer who, I would later come to believe, may have helped with our escape from Barracks 14.

Finn could be annoying and too clever for his own good, but he's also brave, tenacious, irritating, romantic, and heroic. He would never be a jerk. He would never fail to return a text of mine, not ever.

So, when Finn stopped texting me, I knew something was wrong. Very wrong.

I gave it a day. Two. On the third day of silence I rode an hour and a half on a bus to the Walt Disney Pictures studio lot and waited another forty minutes to see a man named Joe Garlington, a highly positioned Disney Imagineer who knew everything that had to do with Finn and the Kingdom Keepers. Jess and I, currently studying with Disney's Imagineers, had every right to meet with Mr. Garlington. Even so, I was intimidated.

We met in a brightly lit conference room. With its fancy black chairs and three conference phones, it had a high-tech feel. One wall, all glass, faced the balcony corridor overlooking the lobby. Joe wore a black Kangol cap over his fuzzy blond hair. He had bright eyes, a big, kind smile, and a gentle voice. He was dressed in a way that made him look like an ad for adventure clothing.

"How's DSI going?" he said, starting the conversation from the chair next to mine. "I hear good things about both you and Jess."

"It's great," I answered. "Unreal. I can't believe we're actually here, that we get paid to do stuff we would pay to do! It's dreamy."

"Glad to hear it. I'm also glad you came up here to visit. You know my door's always open. But honestly, should I be alarmed? It's a long way to travel—from the park to here in Burbank—for a social visit. So let me start by asking what you need. Is there a complaint or situation I need to deal with?"

"Finn's not answering my texts."

"That's it?" He grinned.

"Have you heard from him?" I asked.

Joe looked out the glass as if there was something there to see. "We're trying to respect their return to normalcy. The Keepers, I mean. You know that." He paced. "We've offered them opportunities here as well. I'm sure you're aware of that. They must work that out with their families. We respect that process.

"I'm not sure what you want me to say, Amanda. Friendships can be tricky."

"I want to know why I haven't heard from him. You know something, don't you?" I looked him up and down. "I tried Charlie—Charlene—and Willa, too. Nada!"

"I think we should give it another day or two."

"Give what another day or two?" I demanded, leaning in.

Joe smirked. "Listen, Amanda, the kids went back to Orlando. They probably just need some family time."

"So Finn's too busy having fun to text me?" I wasn't about to cry in front of Joe Garlington, but I felt a lump in my throat the size of a bowling ball. This was not the news I wanted.

"I'm no expert, but sometimes the best approach to these things is to give the other person time."

"You don't know anything about Finn and me."

"True. Do I want to?"

"You're just asking that to keep me from arguing. You think I'm just being a girl."

"Better than the alternative. Now that would scare me."

"Now you're just being rude." I paused, and then added, "You know what happens when I get mad."

"Of course I do, Amanda. Which is why—"

"You'd saying anything to keep me calm."

"That's not what I was going to say. You interrupted me." He pinched his nose, pursed his lips and tested how far back the chair could rock.

"Okay. I'm sorry. Go ahead."

"I've lost my train of thought."

He hadn't lost his train of thought; he'd lost patience. He appraised me, and when he spoke, his warm voice was breathy.

"Let it be."

"Let what be?"

"No good will come of this."

"Then you're saying there is a 'this'? I knew it!"

"I said no such thing. You start chasing rainbows, and all you get is exhausted. He's a boy. Eighteen. Smart. Tired. Home for the first time in many long, grueling weeks. Give it a rest, Amanda. Give Finn a rest."

"Send me back there. Please."

"It's dangerous for you back there. Mrs. Nash . . . we upset her. I upset her. Who knows who she's notified by now? Maybe there's a reward out for you."

"Is there?"

"I said maybe."

"They can't put me and Jess on milk cartons. We're eighteen. They're not going to put us on the FBI's Most Wanted list. What are you so afraid they're going to do?"

"I don't even know who 'they' are. Maybe you do," Joe said, "and maybe you lived with them long enough to not be afraid of them, but if there was someone out there looking for me who had once confined me to a military base, I'd avoid any chance of contact. *Any* chance."

I had nothing to say; only memories that kept me quiet.

"You know how much Jess and I appreciate what you've done for us."

"No more than I'd expect you to do for me," Joe said. "That's the way the world works, right? Or should work, at least."

"Yes," I said. "It should."

"So we're on the same side. I guess that's all I'm saying. Trying to say."

"I know that."

"They're going to sleep most of every day for a while, I imagine. Goof around in the parks when they get the chance. They've probably arranged second semester admittance given that we wrecked their summers and delayed their starting college. Maybe their phones are off so no one can follow them, GPS them, reach them. I'm not saying Finn doesn't want to text you or whatever, but maybe he's just taking a self-imposed break. Or maybe his parents—maybe all their parents—took their phones away so they can't contact each other. I can't pry into their lives. Not anymore. I've already done stuff I shouldn't have done."

"You had a kingdom to save."

"I'm a parent, Amanda. I would never let my kids take personal risks for anything other than service to their country. Do you think their parents, their guardians, care about the kingdom? I would imagine their parents are pretty much done with all of that by now."

I hadn't thought about that. Worse, I knew he was probably right.

Still, I needed to know absolutely. It was Finn, after all.

This was our conversation—as I remembered it. Little did I know how the mind can play tricks on you. How it can distort and misrepresent in order to protect you. The truth was far from what I remembered, what I recalled. It was much harsher and more cruel. More sinister in every way. I would lie, not only to myself, but to others. Those dearest to me. For now, I went with what I knew. I invented a reality, a conversation with Joe, far safer than the one that had really happened.

* * *

By combining Jess's and my money, I had just enough to book a last-minute deal, a red-eye flight to Orlando. With no place to stay, and barely more than bus fare and my phone in my pocket, I ended up on Wanda Kresky's doorstep.

The daughter of Wayne Kresky, the late Disney Legend and creative force behind the DHIs, Wanda was the insider of all insiders. She agreed to put me up, gave me a short lecture about what would have happened if she'd been away on a trip, and lent me fifty dollars that we both knew I was unlikely to repay anytime soon.

"Why would Joe be that way?" I asked across the kitchen counter of her tiny apartment as she fixed me a sandwich.

"Maybe you're reading more into it than was there."

"No one answering their phones? Seriously?"

"Yeah, okay. I don't know, but I think you're right. It's strange. You've got to believe he's protecting them, though, Amanda. I don't doubt that they want some downtime, that they might even spend time in the park together, but not answering their phones is . . . different."

"Right?"

"So where do you start? Can I drive you?"

"I don't want to bother you."

"I hope you're kidding."

"Finn's house. Finn's mom. She's basically one of us at this point." Finn's mother had been put under a horrendous spell by the Overtakers, which left her working against her own son. "If anyone's going to be honest, it's her."

"Then that's where we start."

* * *

Mrs. Whitman looked pale and sickly. She stepped outside their one-and-half story ranch home instead of asking me to come in. Wanda waited in the car, her head turned toward us. It was dusk, but the heat caused my skin to prickle with sweat. The palm fronds stood motionless, looking plastic. A few red flowers dared to test the heat. They weren't winning.

We'd already said our hellos and how-are-yous by the time Mrs. Whitman decided to let me in, closing the door quietly behind her.

"I'd heard you're enjoying it out there," she said.

"Yes! It's going great. Thank you! Is Finn home? Could I see him please?"

"He's . . . no . . . I mean, he's not here. He's . . . He's away . . . trying to work out the whole college thing. We're so proud of him. He was accepted by four schools! Did he tell you that? Isn't that wonderful?"

With so much to be happy about, why had she been crying recently? Why was she several shades paler than I'd ever seen her look? Why shut the door so quietly if only Finn's sister was home? I knew Finn's room was one of the windows facing the garage; we'd all heard the stories of his best friend, Dillard, or the dreaded Greg Luowski coming and going by climbing up on the roof. I felt so tempted to just run down the length of the house and try to sneak a peak.

But I didn't have to. A thin rim of light outlined a drawn shade in the window closest to the garage. If it was Finn's room—and it made sense that it would be—and he was away, why leave the light on?

She caught me looking in that direction.

"I'm sorry, Amanda. I wish you'd—" She caught herself.

"I did. Remember? I called Finn and Philby, Maybeck, Willa, and Charlene. All of them. I left messages for all of them." I lowered my voice. "You can tell me. You know that. I'm here to help."

I watched her eyes fill to overflowing, but she managed to hold back the tears.

"I want to help." I saw no reason not to push. I was only

going to meet with more resistance from the other Keepers' parents. "Mrs. Whitman, of everybody, I thought you . . . I thought I could . . . that we knew each other. We've been through this together. You, me, Finn, the other Keepers. Let me, please let me help."

"I think it's best if you leave now, Amanda. If they call . . . if Finn should call, I'll ask him to get in touch with you."

"That would be nice," I said. "Thank you." Though I felt so foolish playing along with her game, I offered her my phone number. She told me she could remember it, and I didn't doubt she was telling the truth. Mrs. Whitman had been a rocket scientist with NASA. For real.

But when I recited my number, she showed no sign of hearing it. I'd lost her. She'd gone off someplace all her own. We had a short staring contest. I was clearly going to win, so I looked away, back toward the lighted window.

"You might want to save yourself some money," I said.

"How's that?" I'd surprised her. Like shaking her awake.

"Finn left his light on. Seeing how he's away doing his college thing . . ."

"Did he? Oh, how silly of me not to notice. Thank you, Amanda. You're right: what a waste."

"Yeah," I said. "What a waste."

* * *

Maybeck—the Keeper most likely to exaggerate—had once told me about a rumor concerning Mattie Weaver, another escapee from Barracks 14, who had joined the Kingdom Keepers on the Disney Cruise Line ship, the *Dream*, during its Panama Canal cruise. Jess and I had put her up to it, and Mattie had come through for us in a big way. Her "ability"—as the researchers at Barracks 14 referred to what we thought of as our "weirdness"—was what Mattie called "reading." Not the reading taught in school, of course. As a child, she'd been petting her godmother's dog and had sensed he was sick. She went ballistic until her godmother finally agreed to take him to the vet. The dog was diagnosed with a benign tumor on the stomach, *exactly where Mattie had said it was.*

Over the next few months, things only got weirder. Now Mattie wore gloves, long-sleeve shirts, and long pants at all times. If someone tried to touch her, she would move out of reach. Her life outside Barracks 14 was all about hiding from and avoiding people. Of the three of us, I considered her the most likely to voluntarily return to the facility outside Baltimore; at least there she could walk freely down a hallway or attend a lecture. Here in "the real world," she found herself in an exile of her own choosing. The burden that came with incidental contact—handing a salesperson money, shaking hands, touching a waiter or waitress—was not worth it. She didn't want to sense illness or grief, desire or addiction. She wanted no part of a stranger's internal thoughts. As Mattie had explained it to me: priests and psychiatrists have training. The rest of us do not.

Maybeck had told me that Mattie was in Orlando, squatting in the same old church where Jess and I had once lived in secret, a place so familiar to me I could have reached it blindfolded. Afraid of scaring her away if I came up the stairs, I approached from the roof—one of two possible escape routes from the abandoned apartment. I knocked twice on the window, paused, and then knocked twice more, making my face visible.

Nothing. After a moment, I opened the window and pushed past a faded curtain. The interior was clean but spare— some inverted milk crates, a bed made of couch cushions secured by a rope around their perimeters. A stack of water-warped paperbacks teetered by the bed. A towel, still damp, was hung to dry. I shuddered, knowing what it was like taking cold showers.

Despite the signs, there was no Mattie. I left a note on the pillow, asking her to meet me at a nearby Starbucks. Nine A.M. or nine P.M. I'd be there regardless.

* * *

Later, I would wonder how I could have missed the significance of it all, but miss it I did.

One of the church walls held a dozen photos thumbtacked in the shape of an inverted pyramid. The shots were of the same three people—four, if you counted the driver. Three men and one woman. All adults. To study them, you would think them out of place, each the kind of person who'd stand in the corner alone at a party. The quiet type.

I would eventually realize I should have paid that wall

more attention. Because it turned out that they weren't the silent type. They were the dangerous type instead.

JESS

I wasn't always this way. Maybe I inherited it, but I don't know because my parents aren't around to ask. I can't exactly say it feels normal. I remember not having it.

It started out with little things. I never gave them a second thought. I think my mom knew something was up, but back then I didn't realize it was anything more than my imagination.

Everything changed with the pink bunny. I saw it on the shelves of the gas station after the car broke down and I decided I needed it, that I had to have it. But when I told my mom we had to go back and get it, she wouldn't go. She claimed it wasn't real, that I was making it all up.

I was so angry with her for that. Every morning I reminded her about the bunny. Every morning she'd claim she didn't know what I was talking about. That made me even angrier. My mother, faking confusion to avoid buying me another gift? Why?

I didn't realize that the event at the gas station hadn't happened . . . *yet*.

A few days later, we broke down on a road we'd never taken. It was all new to my mom, but from my car seat, I told her exactly what would happen next. The more it did happen, the more freaked out she got. When we reached the gas station, she saw the pink bunny, the one I hadn't been able to stop talking about. That was the last straw. My mom ran out of the gas station's mini market, pulling me along behind her. I saw fear in her eyes when she looked at me. She wanted to know how I could possibly have known three days ago what would happen today. But she was afraid to ask.

In that brief exchange, I gained this weird sense of importance. And of guilt, for making my mom afraid. Of excitement. We rode in the tow truck in silence. I couldn't understand how I'd scared her; I only knew that I had. To me, my dreams just seemed to repeat themselves sometimes. I didn't know then how familiar it would become to see fear in people's eyes.

My powers got stronger as I got older; the dreams became more vivid. As I neared the end of elementary school, I woke up screaming every night. It was often the same dream: my parents being dragged off by bad guys while on a trip, me being sent to foster care. The doctors called them night terrors and told my parents they were common in kids my age.

When my parents left on a trip to South America, I begged them not to go. I told them I'd dreamed a hundred times about something awful that was going to happen. Even with my mother's obvious desire to believe me and stay, my father told me I'd be fine for two weeks, and off they went.

Two days after they left, the nightmare stopped abruptly. Hushed phone calls and pitying looks from my sitter followed. When child protective services showed up at the door to take me away, I was waiting for them. I'd seen them coming. I even knew their names.

Every kid thinks they're "different" or "special," but this was the first time I *knew*. I had dreams like everyone else; the difference was that mine had a tendency to come true. I didn't tell people about them, but eventually they found out and a few years later, I was sent to a place in Baltimore.

* * *

The dreams grew more and more powerful. Sometimes I'd get a break for a few days, a week, even a month. I'd start wondering if they were gone for good—but then they'd come back stronger than ever.

Eight years later, Amanda and I were rooming together in Burbank. One summer night, I had a dream so forceful it made my head throb. I found it hard to hear myself think through the barrage of images in my head. It wasn't a movie of the future playing out in my mind. It was more like a bunch of snapshots being thrown at me and me trying to catch them before they were gone—without getting hit by them.

Habit guided my hand to the journal, pen, and book light tucked between my mattress and the bed frame. Before I even had the light on, before I was fully awake, I had the pen on paper, racing to get the image in my mind down before it disappeared.

I sketched quick, feathery strokes. A thin rectangle became a door opposite a small window with lace curtains. Framed in the window was an antique lamp. I added the vague outline of a twin bed with a train set on the shelf above it, a couch like something out of a grandmother's house in a movie, and dark, thick lines that became the outlines of three men, menacing in their stance, blocking the main door. Their clothing was identical, standard army fatigues, except for the number 14 embroidered on their shoulders. A number whose significance Amanda and I knew all too well. These men weren't average foot soldiers; they were the "military" from Barracks 14, and I could think of only one reason I would be dreaming about them.

There was light coming through the door on the left, silhouetting the central figure, the object of their pursuit, a girl crouched in the dim light. Her back was turned to me, but I didn't need to see her face.

It wasn't the first time I'd dreamed this scene. The chances of it not coming true were disappointingly slim. My drawing was only a vague sketch, and the girl in it was looking away. But the girl was Amanda. Even if we weren't blood relatives, we considered ourselves sisters. If my dreams told me Amanda was in danger, we *both* had a problem.

Still, I couldn't exactly call her up on a hunch. Amanda was generally accepting of my so-called gift, as she had one of her own, but we both knew I could get it wrong when I was attempting to come to grips with what the dreams represented. I had no evidence the faceless girl was Amanda, only a gut feeling expanding from a pit in my stomach. Calling her in the middle of the night, Eastern time, me being all paranoid, would only freak her out. Hardly fair. If she'd been across my room in the bed where she belonged, she would have likely flashed me an eye roll and mumbled, "Go back to sleep."

I tried to heed that advice, but the more I thought about my dream—the girl, the uniforms—the more jittery I got. It was like I'd had a triple-shot espresso. And though the barrage of images—"visions" still sounded too strange—had subsided, I felt like my heart was going to burst. My dreams rarely came with an indication of *when* (or even if) they were going to take place. For all I knew, what I'd just seen could be happening right now. Or it might never happen at all.

My stomach was knotted and tight. After everything we'd been through in the past eight years, Amanda was the closest thing I had to family. I missed her. I hoped she was safe.

I knew she'd only gone to Orlando for a few days, a week at most, but in light of the dream, it felt like forever.

Sitting in the dark, empty room, I felt alone in a way I hadn't felt in years. Amanda and I had been together longer than we'd been with anyone else. Amanda-and-Jess, Jess-and-Amanda. The team. Like twins, one and the same, never without the other. While that connection could feel smothering at times, it was also reassuring to know that she was there for me.

Now she was off in Orlando on an adventure of her own. I felt the panic set in. Every wind was Maleficent's chill blast; the trees outside seemed bewitched to grab me from my bed. In my overactive imagination, even the jovial kids downstairs were OTKs plotting evil deeds.

I understood the signs of paranoia. I also knew when I was right.

MATTIE

I wasn't always this way. Maybe I inherited it, but I don't know because my parents aren't around to ask. I can't exactly say it feels normal. I remember not having it.

The first time it happened was strange because everything seemed so . . . normal. My godmother didn't understand, or she didn't want to. At the time I truly thought I was being helpful. We both loved her dog, so why was helping him wrong? Those were the sentiments of a young girl, innocent feelings before things took a turn for the worse. I was running my hands over Rex's glossy fur, and strange thoughts trickled in. The mix of emotions was hard to place, but hidden beneath it, I sensed that something was gravely wrong. Rex peered at me with sad brown eyes, and I realized with a start that they were *his* thoughts. His stomach hurt.

My frantic pleas didn't seem to sway my godmother; she only seemed concerned for me. She didn't believe me when I told her that her dog was sick. I begged and begged until she came to her senses, and sure enough, the vet diagnosed Rex with a benign tumor. It was on his stomach. Until that point, I just assumed I was naturally intuitive. But I could see the way people looked at me when I touched them. Confused and lost, like there was something they needed to remember but couldn't. It was even worse for me. Sometimes the thoughts were happy, but more often they were filled with pain and greed and lust. Very human things. And I couldn't turn it off. My abilities were only growing, so I made sure to limit all contact. The gloves and long sleeves I could handle, but it was much harder to keep my distance from people.

* * *

Jess and Amanda used to squat in this old building when they first came to Orlando. That's how I knew it would be safe for me to stay for a while. We had been close at Barracks 14. I showed up not too long after I discovered my powers on the pretense that I wanted to be with other kids like me. That much was true, but aside from that, the place was a nightmare. Jess and Amanda helped. They were tightly knit, but they accepted me, and I trusted them.

In the formerly reconstructed attic of the abandoned church, I had tried to arrange what furniture—if you could call it that—there was to make the space comfier. Even so, it was just a bunch of couch cushions and milk crates. When I returned from some errands, I knew right away that someone had been there. I'd been squatting for months, after a harrowing series of adventures on my way back into the United States from Mexico. I'd spent time in Los Angeles, Denver, and St. Louis in between. The attic space had grown to be a part of me. There were no clear signs of disturbance, but something was off.

I scanned the room, and my eyes landed on a small scrap of paper on my makeshift bed. It was in Amanda's hand-writing, which I knew all too well. She wanted to meet, and soon.

Wasting no time, I ran down the stairs to the back door of the former church. The fewer people who saw me, the better.

AMANDA

The difference between paranoia and remaining alert is how you let your fear affect you.

I worked hard to not to cross the line into Paranoiaville, to play it safe, stay aware, and not see danger in every shadow. The working-hard part came without much effort—nothing had come easily for me, ever. But I'd struggled enough to know I didn't want to dwell on it, to celebrate the victories and tolerate the losses. The world was a random place. Abnormality ruled.

Something happening twice was a flag for me. Walking along the sidewalk at a brisk pace at night, a noise to my right could easily be a lizard darting about in the ground cover. Even so, I'd learned techniques of personal safety. Most of them had rubbed off from being around my fellow "inmates" at Barracks 14 or spending time with the Kingdom Keepers. I knew how to use the reflections off vehicles and buildings to see behind me without turning fully around; I could vary my speed in order to distinguish between someone walking at their own pace or copying mine; I knew how to subtly use my phone to take a photo behind me or in front of me; to cross at a crosswalk, change my mind, and return to the corner I'd just stepped off; to cross at the very end of the permitted time to see who dared challenge traffic to stay with me. Dozens, maybe hundreds of little tricks of timing and posturing that could help me identify possible surveillance. I didn't live this way—that was the definition of paranoia—but I possessed these tools for when they were needed.

Tonight, I was likely being followed. Though I couldn't say for sure. Being sure was another boundary between precaution and paranoia. I didn't freak out, just went through my routine safety checks to find out if I was right or wrong.

I was right. There was someone following me by a block or more—enough distance to make it hard to confirm and harder still to identify. Enough distance to leave the next move up to me. I also knew ways to "lose a tail" as Philby called it—some were common sense, others a little trickier. Losing a tail while also identifying the spy was far more complex, though—easier if one worked with a partner.

Mind whirling, I called Wanda without telling her exactly what I needed. I didn't like the idea of inconveniencing her. Despite what she said to the contrary, I never got around to asking her for help because I could tell she was working late. I fumbled through some lame discussion of dinner, and hung up.

I was going to have to fly solo. I'd gotten so attached to Jess that I suppose the only time I allowed myself to be more than "half a friendship" was when I was with Finn. Of course, then

I was another half of a friendship. I wanted—no, needed—to prove to myself that I was capable of flying solo, thinking for myself and being by myself. You spend too much time around others and you begin to depend on them. That didn't feel so healthy all of a sudden. It made me feel needy. One thing I'd learned growing up was that no matter who claimed you, you had to first claim yourself.

I walked past my intended bus stop and picked up speed. I didn't want to look like I was running, but I needed to reach a different bus line. This particular route briefly ran east, providing me with a shortcut—one stop past the one at which I assumed Mattie would board.

If I hurried, I had a chance.

MATTIE

If Amanda had come to Orlando from Imagineering School, it had to be urgent. My feet carried me quickly, and I made it to the stop just as the bus was pulling up. At the last minute, I quickly slipped off my gloves. It was a necessary task, but I dreaded it all the same.

As I boarded, I made a point to slip so that I could fall onto the driver. He reached out; we touched. A stream of faces flashed in front of my eyes; each passenger who had boarded ahead of me. I thought it would be an inconsequential stream of people I didn't know, but it seemed worth a try. And right as I made a move to pull my hand away, I saw something.

Not a good something.

Panting and out of breath, the Overtaker boy I knew from the cruise ship had boarded the bus. *Louis . . . no, Luowski! Greg Luowski!*

I yanked my hand back, ignoring the dazed look on the driver's face. I would never forget Luowski's piercing green eyes, a trademark of Maleficent's zombified army. She was responsible for the turmoil in Jess's and Amanda's lives, and she wanted to take over the Disney parks. But she was long dead; Finn Whitman and the other Kingdom Keepers had seen to that.

So why were this boy's eyes still that alarming shade of green?

I passed the bus driver and peered over the heads of the other passengers, trying to locate Luowski. Just ahead of me, I could see his strong frame and distinctive red hair. Something told me that I needed to get to him and read him. "Reading" was the term I used for my visions of people's thoughts.

Dropping my shoulder, I muscled through the crowd of bodies. Time was flying, but I wanted to be subtle, so I pretended to stumble and catch his hand. As my powers had grown, I'd learned to narrow down what I was able to read. Upon contact, I immediately honed in on thoughts relating to Finn Whitman.

Finn's face flashed before my eyes, and what I saw wasn't good. It seemed like Luowski spent a lot of time planning his revenge. When I gripped his hand, he tensed, and I knew that he sensed me. On the Disney *Dream* cruise ship, I had tried to read him; even then, he was aware that something was amiss. Now he was familiar with my abilities. He started to turn, and I ducked into one of the rows and sank down into a seat. He scanned the bus, but he couldn't seem to find me. I knew I would be safe as long as he didn't link me to the sensation; he hadn't seen my face the first time I'd read him, either.

I mulled over what I'd seen for a long time. There was a good chance that this was what Amanda had wanted me to do: to have me spy for her. But why would she be so cryptic? My anger simmered. Was she testing me? If so, it wasn't fair. I'd been through plenty on the ship, certainly enough to prove my trustworthiness.

But what else could she want?

AMANDA

I reached South Lakemont and waited for the 313 bus to the Corners. Boarding came down to timing. And as I was the only one waiting at the stop, my plan was compromised from the start.

"You coming?" the bus driver said.

I'd wanted to wait until the very last moment to board, steal a peek out the window, and catch a glimpse of my pursuer. "Yes, sir." I tried miserably to contain my defeated tone as I boarded and used my elevated position next to the driver to look down Summerfield Road.

"You done sightseeing? I got passengers, you know?"

"Sorry." I still had my Youth ID pass, which lowered my rate.

I was halfway toward the back door when I spotted Mattie Weaver—first in profile, then I made out her face off the glass of the window. Her eyes told me in no uncertain terms that I did not know her, was not to come anywhere near her. That look of hers rattled me.

MATTIE

Engulfed in my thoughts, I hardly noticed Amanda board the bus. She seemed disheveled and distant, but I knew that I couldn't reach out to her. Not with Luowski lurking on board.

Amanda was glancing out the window when she caught my reflection. Our eyes met and hers widened in surprise, but I couldn't acknowledge her. Instead I gave her a sharp look of rebuke to keep her from making contact. It worked. She slipped into a seat across from mine. My whole body tensed. I hoped there wouldn't be a scene.

When Amanda got off at Mizell Avenue, I finally breathed a sigh of relief. Best for me to stay on board, I decided, since Luowski also remained on board.

We were supposed to meet at Starbucks. I could still make that happen.

AMANDA

I got off at Mizell Avenue, before the hospital, way before the Corners. Had to walk five more long blocks because of it.

I went from thinking someone was behind me to discovering Mattie was ahead of me.

Disoriented, disturbed, and still unable to stop thinking about Finn, I headed for the Corners. The Starbucks there had practically been part of Winter Park High our senior year. They could have renamed it the Caffeine Lab. I arrived and took a table.

Mattie showed up a few minutes later. She didn't look happy.

* * *

"Hi, there!" I said, decaf mocha in hand. "What was that about on the bus?"

"You were five feet away from Luowski," she said.

"Not possible."

"For real. I promise. And if this is this some kind of test or something, I don't appreciate it!" Mattie glanced around, making sure no one could overhear us, paying special attention to those outside.

"No test," I groaned. "He was on the bus?"

"He got on the stop before yours. He was out of breath, like he'd been running hard. Why the note? Why'd you want me here?"

"I came all the way from Burbank to find Finn. I need your help. This has nothing to do with Luowski!" As I said his name, my chest tightened. I was either going to cough or throw up. I coughed. "To be sure: Luowski? Greg Luowski?"

"That's the one. He was on there when you saw me."

"No way!"

"Way."

I'd allowed spotting Mattie to distract me. You don't survive mistakes like that. "Come on!"

"What?" she asked, pulling away.

I tugged her T-shirt. It read: NO HOPE? GOOD LUCK! "We're going. Now."

I walked her east, taking several precautions to make sure Luowski wasn't following us.

"We're good," I said from inside the lobby of a bank. I led her out the back door into a parking lot, through a connecting parking lot, and across the street to a bus stop. We boarded, and I picked a bench seat by the back door. We needed to be able to get off quickly.

"He was running to make sure he caught your bus, wasn't he?" Mattie asked.

I shared my sense that someone had been following me.

"Yeah, well, I think he outsmarted you. He figured out you were heading for the bus and raced to board ahead of you."

"Trouble is," I said, "that's not like him. There is nothing subtle or stealthy about Greg Luowski. He's completely in your face. An imbecile of the first order. But he can and will hurt anyone he feels like hurting. He's no one to mess with."

Mattie was silent, but she had an air of secrecy about her.

"What?" I said. "I know the guy, believe me."

Mattie's confident expression didn't change. "I read him," she said.

I gasped, looking down at her gloved hands. "And?"

"I think he remembered me."

"Meaning?"

"From the ship. Remember? I read him on the Disney *Dream*. The first time I read someone, most people have no idea what's happening. The second time is different. I've never experienced it myself, of course, but from the looks I've seen, it's like that sensation of losing your phone or wallet, like something's missing and you can't figure out what it is. Most people check their purse, or tap their pockets, reviewing a list of the most important things they carry. An internal inventory, kind of.

"Well, with Greg, I didn't give him the chance to see me," she continued, "but I felt his reaction. There were enough people trying to get off the bus that he wouldn't have known exactly who touched him, but I have a feeling that this time he knew it had happened."

"And?"

"If I tell you, you have to promise you won't scream or freak out."

"If? Of course you're going to tell me." I waited. She waited. "Okay," I said, "I promise."

"He was stronger than that time on the ship. Not

physically. I don't mean that. Stronger inside. More determined, you could say."

"But Finn said Luowski expressed misgivings, said maybe he'd changed his mind about the whole OTK thing."

"OTK?"

"Overtaker Kid. The green eyes. There are a bunch of them. We think the OTs put them under some kind of spell."

"But she's dead, right?"

"Right," I said.

"Doesn't that mean there's no one to remove the spell? Maybe the longer you're under it, the more intense it grows."

"It's been three years," I said.

"So it's a lot more intense," Mattie said.

The bus passed over some bumps in the road. It was a surprisingly quiet, comfortable ride. I realized all the discomfort was coming from inside me.

"How long have you been on the East Coast?" I asked.

"I came out here chasing rainbows, but we can catch up another time." She looked away, out the window, and I sensed her distance had more to do with the past few years than the suburban landscape. After a moment, she said, "It was more than his intensity, Amanda. I read for Finn. I can target that way. Otherwise, it's like you've been let into a gymnasium of five hundred sixth graders. You can't believe how noisy it is inside most people. Noisy is the norm. Noisy is good. Others are super quiet. There's good quiet and bad, scary quiet."

"Luowski was quiet," I said.

"Like I said, I read him for Finn. Targeting blocks out most of the noise. Whatever it is that passes between us, and believe me, I have no idea how this works, it stays with me for a few seconds."

"Pushing is like that for me. It lingers."

"Yes! It lingers. It takes me over. It goes dark; I see and hear stuff—" Her voice caught. She stopped talking.

I said nothing. I knew she wanted to tell me something, but had been avoiding it for a few minutes now. I gave her time, hoping my silence would force her to fill the void. It worked.

"His daydream . . . the image inside him that he wants to see . . . like how as a kid you could see a particular present under the tree—"

"I get it! Come on, Mattie, tell me what you saw?"

She knitted her forehead, forcing her eyebrows toward the bridge of her nose. Mattie was a simple looking girl, but as I was learning, she was full of facial expressions. This was a girl who was horribly upset, ruinously troubled. It was as if she were divulging a truth while sworn to secrecy.

"He plans . . . I think he plans to kill him."

JESS

Lying in bed, staring at the ceiling, was making me crazy. Amanda had barely been gone for twenty-four hours but I could barely stand it. I needed to do something. To act.

Tracing my recurring dreams through a Disney park last

year had helped me make sense of them, so it seemed logical that I should start my search for answers at the source: Disneyland. My dream of Amanda being caught by the Barracks 14ers included glimpses of an antique lamp, a big bed, and a long toy train on a high shelf. I knew intuitively I should start in Disneyland. By seeking out these images, I thought maybe I'd see or dream more. Maybe I'd be able to determine if what I'd dreamed had been fact or fiction.

Rolling out of bed, I grabbed the first T-shirt and black jeggings I laid my hands on. I slipped on running shoes and a black hoodie and was out the door and into the cool LA night in a matter of minutes. I couldn't plan what I was about to do, or I knew I'd talk myself out of it.

The parks were open until midnight during the summer. By breaking into a light jog, I managed to make it onto the last shuttle.

"Disneyland?" the driver asked as I boarded. "You know it closes in ten minutes? You'll get there too late."

"I'm meeting a friend at Downtown Disney," I lied smoothly. The driver shrugged. I took a seat near the back, squinting against the harsh fluorescent lighting.

The short ride gave me time to process my dream. I recognized the location, or at least a piece of it. The room was distinctly fancy, something you wouldn't find in a hotel, no matter how nice. The lamp was the key. Something about it seemed familiar. Even in my dream, I could tell it was an antique, but more than anything, its placement in the window was what

33

seemed familiar. I had seen it before, I was sure. Not in Walt Disney World, though. After all our adventures there, the seven of us knew the Florida parks like our own homes, maybe better. So I knew I was on the right track with Disneyland.

My task was made easier, too, by the fact that at Disney everything was completely themed, down to the smallest chair or lamp. Nothing in one part of the park would ever be found in another, and by the looks of it, the lamp from my drawing only fit on Main Street, USA.

The shuttle pulled into the bus station opposite the central plaza from Downtown Disney. After disembarking, I turned immediately right, avoiding the late-night crowds spilling out of the park, and used my newly issued Cast Member ID to cut backstage through the Cast Member entrance. I'd only had it for a few weeks, and I felt a slight pang of guilt at abusing it already. But I reassured myself with the thought that if I was caught by security, Joe or Brad—the Imagineers overseeing the Keepers—would come to my aid. They knew everything we'd done to save the Kingdom, knew that sometimes we had to do things that might seem strange, things we weren't allowed to explain until much later.

Unfortunately, I also knew security was not the only obstacle I had to worry about. The buddy system was the first rule of the Keepers; and while we had all broken that rule at one time or another, it had been put in place for a reason. I thought about texting Amanda, even though she was thousands of miles away, just to let her know I was here. But I wasn't prepared to answer the questions I would get in response.

I cut across the open backstage, running in a crouch below a row of shuttered windows in a building behind Space Mountain; I passed a set of lockers, and slipped through the backstage door of the Opera House. Silently, I moved into an empty exhibition room. In the dim lighting I made out a model of the United States Capitol. Through the windows of the room ahead, I saw the faint light of Main Street. I'd timed it just right, I realized. The shuttle ride had taken long enough that the last of the guests were being shuffled out the front gates by security.

I stayed in the shadows, crouched near a roped-off antique park bench. Fifteen minutes later, the gates were closed, the lights were out, and the security guards had dispersed to the rest of the park.

Town Square glowed under the crescent moon. The flagpole stood tall; the train station and streets were empty—the guests had gone home, and the vehicles had been taken backstage for the night.

Most of the buildings' decorative lights had been turned off, part of an effort to conserve energy, and as enchanted as the park may seem during the day, at this hour it felt haunted. All the windows stood dark, save the one directly across the square, above the firehouse.

Recognition hit me hard. Although my dream sketch showed the whole lamp, and therefore from a location inside, there was no mistaking the antique lamp. It shined from the other side of a small window above the firehouse, a place I knew to be Walt Disney's private apartment.

I cut straight through the center of the square, dodging flower beds and benches, not pausing until I reached the shadows of the Emporium opposite. I slipped through a narrow door that took me off limits. I climbed the back staircase to Walt's famous apartment.

I tried the handle. Locked. Peeking through a window, I could see a short hallway and the corner of the room. The couch from my dream was there, too, along with the lamp on the end table: enough to convince me I was in the right place, or at least one of the right places. But no matter how tightly I squeezed my eyes shut and willed a dream to come, I didn't even get a flicker. I slumped on the top step, defeated. Something about my dream didn't add up. I couldn't see any train set running across a high shelf, nor could I see a large bed.

But the lamp was definitely the lamp.

I sat on the step, and let my mind drift, hoping for an image. Opening my eyes, I saw someone tumbling down these very stairs. Amanda? There were Barracks 14ers in crisp suits. I lost it. Gone. Only then did I actually open my eyes: they'd been shut all along.

I'd dreamed!

The Keepers had demonstrated time and again that puzzles were better solved by a team. I had none. Philby would've been able to search his encyclopedic memory, or Maybeck's artist's eye would've noticed a detail I'd missed in my sketch.

I had my phone in my pocket; I could call one of them . . . except Amanda had tried that, which is why she'd left in the first place.

My phone! Of course. I almost laughed out loud: the solution had been with me all along.

Careful to avoid screen glare revealing me, I conducted an Internet search for "Disneyland, train set," only turned up kids' toys for sale on Amazon, and "Disneyland park model train set" brought up stories about Walt Disney's personal model train collection. Getting frustrated again, I cleared the search box and started over, this time adding one word to the search. I did it out of desperation and spite. There was no reason it should help, but I was out of ideas, and I really was searching for a dream.

I began typing "Disneyland Park Dream" . . . and to my relief, Google had one search suggestion—"Disneyland Park Dream Suite." I went with it and clicked the first result.

First intended as Walt's second apartment in the late 1960s, this space above the entrance to Pirates of the Caribbean had been remodeled as the Disney Gallery after Walt's death. It wasn't until the Year of a Million Dreams celebration in 2006 that the space was transformed into the apartment Walt had originally imagined. During the Year of a Million Dreams, one park guest was randomly chosen every day to spend the night in the apartment, now called the Dream Suite. Since then, it had been mostly vacant, only opened on occasion for special events.

I scrolled through the pictures. Cinderella's glass slipper

in the living room, lanterns over a terrace, an Adventureland-themed bedroom . . . and a Frontierland-themed bedroom complete with *a train track around the top of the room*. My second perfect match of the night.

Time to move.

My tiptoeing footsteps echoed off the doorway to the Bazaar to my left as I neared New Orleans Square. Passing the entrance to the Jungle Cruise, every shadow looked like a lurking villain. *The Overtakers are gone*, I reminded myself. *The battle's over. Mickey's back. You saw their defeat.*

But if the Overtakers were really defeated, a doubting voice in the back of my mind whispered, why hadn't we heard from any of the Keepers in days? Why was Amanda on the opposite side of the country? Why was I still dreaming about the parks?

Passing Indiana Jones Adventure, I shuddered at a piercing memory: "It all ends in lightning." I'd dreamed that in there. Finn's defeat of Chernabog had come via a bolt of lightning. Now I'd dreamed Amanda would be captured and returned to Baltimore. I shuddered. My feet moved faster.

I heard a rustle in the bushes along with big, heavy breathing—and I then I glimpsed two eyes glowing in the dark. I took off like a shot.

I reminded myself there weren't wild animals in Disneyland. The Jungle Cruise creatures were plastic. So if there was a large animal after me, it could only mean that I was its intended prey.

The entrance to Pirates loomed ahead of me, just beyond

Adventureland. Above it was the main entrance to the Dream Suite, where I expected to find the toy train set. At the same time, I realized that, like Walt's apartment above the firehouse, it would be kept locked to keep curious guests out during the day. There was a chance it might be unlocked, but if it wasn't, I would be mincemeat.

I dared to steal a glance behind me and caught a flash of orange and black stripes, and a curled grin on a gaping maw. Another glance confirmed my suspicions: Shere Khan. The Bengal tiger from *The Jungle Book*; the ruler of the jungle. I'd only seen the movie once, but it had been terrifying enough to stick with me. My pursuer was coming fast, was already dishearteningly close.

As I passed Tarzan's Treehouse, I shot my arm out at the last second, grabbed the railing, and pulled myself around the tree. Shere Khan flew by me, and I doubled back and ran up the stairs, taking them two at a time. Below me, the tiger's claws skidded against the pavement, trying to find purchase to turn around. I had bought myself what could be a lifesaving lead, but would it be enough?

Running across the rope bridge, I was no longer concerned with the noise I was making. I climbed the stairs past the first scene. I remembered Finn's story of fighting a jaguar up here, and made a mental note not to dawdle. Not that I was taking a leisurely stroll.

Below me, Shere Khan turned, now coming toward me faster than ever.

I had come into the park to try to identify where and how the Barracks 14ers intended to go after Mandy. Shere Khan was clearly acting like an Overtaker—the group of Disney villains we were certain were no longer operating in the parks. Was Shere Khan a loner who hadn't gotten the message the OTs were over, or was something else going on that none of us knew about? If the OTs were back—I shuddered at the thought!—I tried to identify what I'd done to incite their wrath. I'd sneaked around the park; I'd peered in some windows. Big deal! Confused, out of breath, and working to recall how I might have triggered the attack, I cleared my thoughts and confronted the situation before me.

The tree house was set up in two parts. In the first half, guests climbed through scenes in the treetops; in the second, they explored the ground in the research camp. The tree house afforded good views of the camp, and through the foliage, I could barely see a building beyond. A path led behind the Dream Suite stairs to an elevator. Handicapped access, I realized.

The second level, a bit lower than the one I was at now, featured a wraparound porch with a rustic but sturdy looking wood railing.

Behind me, the rope bridge shook. Shere Khan was only seconds behind.

Though not the sportiest person, I considered myself athletic enough. My time with the Keepers had kept me in shape, and taught me running and climbing skills. I'd been working with martial arts YouTube videos, though they weren't going to help me against a man-eating cat. What could a human like me do that a cat couldn't—other than brush my teeth and comb my hair?

I looked out over the tree house. Vines hung from the branches, and below me a canvas tent covered a pile of camping gear. I wasn't one for stunts, but as I heard Shere Khan's claws ripping into the wood deck, I decided taking a risk was the better option. Grabbing a branch, I pulled myself up to balance on the guardrail. I reached out and found a nice thick vine, one sturdy enough to support me—provided the other end was actually attached to something.

I couldn't be sure.

Shere Khan rounded the corner onto my level, and jumped.

I closed my eyes and jumped too, clenching my teeth to keep from screaming. My stomach took a trip on the Tower of Terror. I turned, my face stinging as the wind whipped my hair against it. Nine feet from the ground, I reached the end of the vine. My momentum almost wrenched it from my hands, but I held on for dear life. I bounced twice on the end of the vine—it was made of some stretchy material—and caught my breath briefly.

Then the vine snapped, unable to support my weight from the fall, and I hit the canvas, hard. I'd be bruised in the morning, but it was nothing too serious.

On the platform above me, Shere Khan roared in frustration. He'd be forced to go through the rest of the tree house to catch up, hopefully giving me enough time. I gathered the vine in my arms and jumped to the ground from the canvas tent. I raced through the undergrowth, across a small stream that left my feet swimming in my tennis shoes. Then I threw the vine up, looping it over the railing. I pulled the ends even and tied it off like Charlene had taught me.

Shere Khan had reached the ground impossibly fast, and he was racing across the camp toward me, knocking over the heavy crates like they were made of nothing but Styrofoam. I pulled myself up the vine hand over hand, heart in my throat, painfully aware of how close I was to becoming kitty chow. Shere Khan leaped, paw swiping the air inches below my left tennis shoe. I celebrated my small success as I pulled myself up and onto the porch.

Below me, the tiger batted at the vine like a cat toying with a length of yarn, giving me one last snarl before sauntering away.

Struggling to catch my breath, I followed the porch to the back of the building, entering through a back door. If I could see more of my dream by being here, I felt convinced I could actually *change the future* by keeping Amanda away from whatever place the Barracks 14ers planned to capture her.

* * *

Inside, the suite was as gorgeous as the Web site had described. Even with the lights out, I could see a small patio through the wall of floor-to-ceiling windows on my left, and a bedroom through the windows on the right. The Web site had called it the Adventureland bedroom, with a jungle-themed canopy bed and a Peter Pan landscape.

The hallway led to the living room. A French-style couch and matching chairs took up most of the room. A carousel horse stood between the two windows, one of many distinctive Disney touches sprinkled throughout the room. Two paintings of castles hung opposite the fireplace, which was also adorned with a castle silhouette. A display case held a glass slipper and vintage clock. I wished I had time to absorb it all, but I was interested in only one thing: a train on a shelf.

I walked to the front of the room and peered out the window. Shere Khan paced the area below. For whatever reason, he didn't try to enter the Dream Suite. He simply patrolled the exits, serving effectively as a jail guard.

Sighing, I let the curtain fall and moved on to the next room, the kids' room. This one featured not one but two full-size beds, both matching the one in my dream.

And there it was: a toy train up high on a shelf that ran completely around the bedroom.

I sagged down onto the bed. At last I'd found it, this small image from my sketch of my dream. I pondered its significance. Maybe Amanda was to be snatched up in this room. Maybe it represented the Disneyland Railroad that ran around the park. If I could calm myself and slip into a partial daydream, I thought I might see more of the elusive scene and save my sister.

I thought back to Shere Khan pacing outside. The park would be reopen at eight or nine A.M., possibly earlier for Magic Hours. The big cat would have to be in hiding by then. These beds, this gorgeous suite, seemed as good a place as any to spend the night. I carefully removed my shoes and climbed onto one, not daring to slip under the covers. The less I disturbed the room, the better. I set my phone's alarm for six A.M. and curled up on the foot of the bed.

As I lay there, eyes closed, I considered the consequences if it turned out that the OTs had never left, only hidden themselves. We *all* thought it was over, the Overtakers defeated. But Shere Khan hadn't decided to attack me on a whim.

With that reassuring thought, I drifted off into a fitful sleep.

* * *

A dimly lit room. Board games. A yellow squash with a horn.

I swirled in and out of a nightmarish voyage. *Train set. Clocks. Horses.* I saw rich brown wood and a fireplace. My eyes fluttered opened and shut, leaving me no real idea what was this room and what was dream.

I jolted awake, disoriented, no idea where I was. Next to me, my phone blared the first few bars of Taylor Swift's "Long Live." My alarm, I realized. Confused, I fumbled with it, dropping it twice before finally shutting it off.

Blinking, I sat up on the bed, took in the red walls, the memorabilia scattered on the shelf around the top of the room:

old books, decorative plates, a train, a Disneyland map over the dresser. The events of the previous night came flooding back. My first dream; visiting Walt's apartment; Shere Khan; my escape to the Dream Suite; and my latest dream.

My dream. I needed to draw it. Now, before I lost the memory. I jumped up and poured the contents of my pockets onto the floor, finding a pen with a little ink left and an old Chick-fil-A receipt. I sat down at the desk; trying to recall the different images, to separate them from what I saw around me.

I drew the horn player. Some vegetables. Kids' blocks spelling out CAT. Green mouse ears—of course! A board game, possibly of Main Street USA. I disregarded the clocks and the fireplace because they were right there in front of me in the room.

Just to be safe, I took a picture of the sketch using my phone. I headed toward the back door, thankful the rear entrance to the Dream Suite was placed so far back in the trees. By the time I made it out, the park was crawling with Cast Members. Shere Khan was gone.

I crouched and waited for a break in the constant flow of Cast Members before climbing over the rail, hanging from the ledge by my fingertips, and dropping to the ground. Though it stung, I managed to stick the landing, absorbing most of the impact with the balls of my feet.

I kept to the shadows on my way toward the exit, aware that anyone not in a Cast Member uniform would stick out. Plus my black hoodie, messy ponytail, and jeggings didn't exactly conform to the Disney look. Luckily, I made it to the Main Street door without incident. At this early hour, the Cast Members were both too groggy and too busy to notice a lone black shadow on the other side of the street.

As I neared the end of Main, I couldn't resist the temptation to try Walt's apartment one more time. I had come all this way, and having enough time off to come to the parks on my own was rare. Above all, I had come for answers and only found another puzzling dream. I still held out hope that the apartment could be the clue I was searching for to help me stave off Mandy's abduction.

I approached the entrance to the apartment from backstage, well aware that it might have been my visit here that had prompted Shere Khan's attack. The path was narrow and mostly empty, and I was painfully aware of how much I stood out. Shots sounded from the Jungle Cruise; Cast Members were doing an early morning training run.

As I drew closer, I saw I was not the only visitor to the apartment that morning. A man kneeled in front of the apartment door with a toolbox, working on the doorknob. He wasn't dressed in the standard maintenance uniform, and I recognized the familiar Sorcerer Mickey emblem on his magenta hardhat.

An Imagineer.

He picked up a piece of shiny brass hardware before sensing me and turning toward me. Our eyes met briefly. My breath caught in my throat. I smiled and waved. He nodded.

I moved along, not wanting to draw any more attention than I already had.

The man had been changing the lock on Walt Disney's apartment. And not just any maintenance man, but an Imagineer. Given that my original Mandy dream connected to the lamp in the apartment, that changing of the lock needed explaining.

I added it to my long list of things that needed explaining, my head thumping. I'd filled in another sketch, drawn closer to the truth of Amanda's confrontation with the Barracks 14ers. But currently, not close enough to save her.

DAY 2

AMANDA

Mrs. Whitman showed no enthusiasm for my second visit.

"I have nothing more to add, Amanda."

"This is a friend of mine and Finn's," I said, and introduced Mattie by name. Mrs. Whitman didn't know Mattie, so she didn't know how odd it was that Mattie wasn't wearing gloves. Nodding, Mrs. Whitman said it was nice to meet her—at which point my plan dissolved. Mattie had taken too long to offer her hand to shake. Shaking hands would have meant making contact, which would have given Mattie the chance to read Mrs. Whitman.

I stood my ground, having no idea what to do next.

"Guests?"

A man's voice. Mr. Whitman pulled the door open farther, much to his wife's dismay.

"You're back from your trip!" I said.

He looked puzzled.

"Your trip to drop Finn off at Vanderbilt," Mrs. Whitman said. They had not rehearsed. Both were bad at improvising.

"I . . . yes!"

"So Finn's here?"

"No, Finn's not here," Mrs. Whitman said quickly. "He—"

"I left him," Mr. Whitman added.

"At Vanderbilt," I proposed, trying to help them. At this point I'd determined that nothing they were going to say would be the truth. I'd been around adult liars most of my life. These two were nowhere close to good.

"Amanda, come in, for heaven's sake," Mr. Whitman said. His wife's disapproving look caused him to shrink back slightly.

Mrs. Whitman seemed to punch him.

I reintroduced Mattie. This time she took her cue, sticking her hand out so fast it looked wrong. She and Mr. Whitman shook hands. Mattie's reads took fractionally longer than a casual brush or shaking of hands, so there was a second or two during which the other person felt socially uncomfortable. Knowing this, I made a point of trying to get past Mattie and through the door, pushing her slightly forward and buying her a few extra seconds.

MATTIE

As we entered the Whitman house, the tension wafted off Mrs. Whitman in waves. I had missed my first and easiest opportunity to read her—a handshake—and Amanda was working a little too hard to create another opportunity.

Mrs. Whitman directed a curt nod my way; her gaze was

withering. I didn't know the lady, but I didn't need to know her to sense her unease. Her hair was frazzled. A dark blue-gray shadow draped below her eyes, hinting at too little sleep. I didn't gather my courage until it was too late to offer my hand.

Still, Amanda remained unfazed. I had to give her props for that. Of course, she had more experience around the Whitman family being that she and Finn were an item.

I could understand why Mrs. Whitman's earlier dismissal had hurt her. When I'd told Amanda about Luowski's plan, I wasn't expecting us to go the parental route. Frankly, I was expecting some sort of attack on Luowski. But Amanda seemed to think we now had the perfect excuse to pry into Finn's life. More than anything, I think Amanda just wanted to see Finn again. But I couldn't say that out loud—I didn't need to make life more difficult by upsetting her.

AMANDA

Mrs. Whitman looked feverish by the time her husband showed us to the living room couch.

The living room was painted rose white. A large gilded mirror didn't belong, though the upright piano and wooden furniture made the room inviting and comfortable. A grouping of studio family photos surrounded a hand-painted sign that read HOME SWEET HOME. The photos were posed and dorky. Poor Finn, to endure that every day, and yet I felt jealous. I realized I'd judged too quickly—I'd have traded nearly anything to have a wall like that with me in the photos.

Mattie gave me a slight shake of the head: she wasn't satisfied with her read of Mr. Whitman. At the same time, I could tell that it hadn't been a total bust.

"How 'bout some popcorn?" Mr. Whitman asked. "I think we're all out of cookies."

I elbowed Mattie as Mrs. Whitman stood.

"Please, let me help," Mattie said.

"That's all right," Mrs. Whitman said. "Thank you, but I've got it."

"No, really, I'd love to."

Mrs. Whitman was too polite to outright refuse. She grimaced and led the way.

MATTIE

All in all, I knew, Amanda was right. I was the only one who could help find Finn, and we had to help him before someone else could harm him. I had faith that his parents wouldn't mind us prying if they knew Finn was on some mind-controlled teen's hit list.

The Whitman's living room was quaint; it reminded me of my grandmother's from so many years ago. But then again, any living room with a couch and a piano would probably invoke the same feelings. Photos of the Whitmans in rigid poses and similarly hued outfits plastered the wall. Finn's parents avoided looking at them.

Mr. Whitman cleared his throat and suggested popcorn. It wasn't what I was expecting, but anything was better than the silence we endured. Mrs. Whitman frowned at her husband, but rose anyway. Amanda thrust an elbow into my rib cage. I stifled a gasp and glared, but took the not-so-subtle hint.

"Please, let me help," I wheezed.

"That's all right," Mrs. Whitman said. "Thank you, but I've got it."

"No, *really*, I'd love to."

Mrs. Whitman flashed me a smile, but it was stretched so tightly I thought her head might pop off. I had a feeling that, on any other day, the offer would have earned major brownie points with Finn's mom, but this woman was on a mission to keep Amanda in the dark.

AMANDA

I made small talk with Mr. Whitman. It took me a minute to realize he was just as upset by our visit as was his wife, but he was far less confrontational. We both knew his lame excuse for Finn's absence had failed miserably.

"How long are you back in Orlando?" he asked.

"For as long as it takes," I answered.

He didn't have a comeback, but I could hear his brain screaming.

Dropping a bombshell is all about timing. I tried to wait just the right amount of time. I said, "For as long as it takes to see Finn." I think he stopped breathing. "And the other Keepers, too. They've all stopped communicating. Did you know that?"

"Finn isn't answering your texts?" He said it so convincingly. "I can hardly believe that."

"No. It's complicated."

"Sounds like it." He wormed his hands between his knees. "Maybe the others are all together somewhere without cell coverage. If he lied to me about spending time at the college and is instead off with the Keepers, he won't like it. . . ." His voice trailed off.

"Mr. Whitman, you know I'm on your side, right? That I'd do just about anything to make sure they're all okay? And if they're not okay, then I'd get the Imagineers or whoever's necessary to help make it right. You know that, don't you? You trust me?" I came off whiny, gave myself a C-. I could have done much better if I'd kept my feelings out of it and gone with a more analytical approach. But it was me, and it was Finn, and there was no way to act beyond a certain point.

"You're what, seventeen, eighteen, Amanda?"

It was rhetorical and I felt no obligation to respond.

"You mean well. Duly noted. Sometimes things that start one way end another. Finn's going off to college. This Disney thing? It's over. I'm sure he made some wonderful new friends, including you, but you'll look back someday and realize you only remember, you only talk with two or three of your friends from high school. Maybe a dozen from college. It doesn't seem like that now, I know. Finn is moving on. I suggest you consider doing the same."

"Are you trying to break up with me for him? What exactly are you saying? That Finn's done with me? That friends forget each other that quickly? Do you have any idea how close we are? All of us? Do you know what we've been through?"

MATTIE

I followed Mrs. Whitman into the kitchen. Without a glance in my direction, she pawed through the pantry for some bags of popcorn, reappearing with two bags of "movie theater butter" style. I nodded in approval. At least she knew how to shop.

"Can you just pop these in the microwave?" Mrs. Whitman said with feigned cheeriness.

I was growing more anxious by the second. I'd have to read her soon, but I suspected the news would be more difficult to bear than a normal reading. What else would have a former rocket scientist at wit's end?

I took the bag from Mrs. Whitman's outstretched hand and tried to brush fingers, but she pulled her hand away quickly. She didn't know my secret, so I chalked the gesture up to nerves. Quickly shucking the plastic wrapper, I put the bag in the microwave on the popcorn setting, turned to face Mrs.

Whitman, and cleared my throat. It's easy to make a connection when the target is distracted by conversation.

"So, college? That's a big deal." I mentally smacked myself for the lame conversation starter, but I had to go with it now.

"Well, yes it is," Mrs. Whitman said.

From the brief snippets that Amanda had told me, I knew his parents were more involved than most. Not in the breathing-down-your-neck kind of way, but Finn had a good relationship with his family. He either would have shared his experiences or his mom would have grilled him about them.

"Must be hard on all of you." I racked my brain for more questions, but none surfaced. Mrs. Whitman was not making conversation easy; it was like bobbing for apples. I chose to believe that she didn't always act this way. Amanda had said Finn had a cool family. I rocked back and forth on my heels and avoided looking at Mrs. Whitman.

Just as another question formed in my mind, Mrs. Whitman turned her attention elsewhere, away from me. She opened a drawer roughly and scanned its contents and took out two bowls. She inspected them, probably for dust, and decided they needed a rinse. I crossed the distance of the room and tried to grab the bowls from her, mumbling something about helping, hoping we would brush fingers. No such luck. The loud, persistent beeps of the microwave drew Mrs. Whitman away. She muttered something about the popcorn being burned, but when she opened it, it was perfect. I sighed, realizing this was going to be more difficult than expected.

AMANDA

Mattie and Mrs. Whitman appeared from the kitchen. Finn and Philby had been in this house once, plotting out how Mrs. Whitman could aid the Keepers. Something had changed all that. Mattie and I were pariahs.

Mattie did a brilliant job of shooting me a look to let me know she had not read Mrs. Whitman. Although Mrs. Whitman brought out two bowls of popcorn, she didn't appear interested in the food. Connecting her hand with Mattie's was apparently up to me.

So I played the klutz. It wasn't much of a stretch; when I'd been about thirteen I couldn't move without breaking something. I sat forward to grab some popcorn and knocked the bowl to the carpet. I hated doing it.

Mattie was right on it. She waited for Mrs. Whitman to lunge to catch the bowl and then she grabbed her wrist. Popcorn and bowl did a slow motion dance, spilling. Mrs. Whitman's head snapped toward Mattie at the moment of contact.

Some people are more sensitive than others. I should have suspected that a woman as brilliant as Finn's mom would have heightened sensitivity.

She looked at Mattie as if Mattie had cussed. Horrified. Angry. Unforgiving. If they'd been boys, a fight would have broken out.

One of the things that prevented that fight was that Mrs. Whitman could have no way of knowing what had just happened to her. She only knew that *something* had happened. She'd been robbed, her mental pocket picked, yet she had no idea what had happened or what, if anything, the thief had taken.

Mattie, an experienced reader, gave no indication that any of Mrs. Whitman's defensiveness was justified. The three of us shoveled the popcorn back into the bowl. Mrs. Whitman went for a Dustbuster. Mr. Whitman was munching away nervously.

We took the hint, said our good-byes, and left. We were barely to the street when Mattie said, "It's bad. Really bad."

MATTIE

A dozen unsuccessful attempts later, Mrs. Whitman and I returned to the living room. We were greeted by a very rigid Mr. Whitman and a very red-faced Amanda. I sucked in air and widened my eyes at Amanda. I hoped that it looked more like a signal and less like an agitated puffer fish. We couldn't leave until we uncovered the truth about Finn, but the odds of that happening were decreasing by the second. The longer we stayed, the weirder things got.

Amanda tilted her head down a fraction of an inch, and I knew she understood. Popcorn went flying.

I was done with subtle. It was now or never. When Mrs. Whitman made a move to catch the popcorn, I reached out and grabbed her wrist.

Finn, I thought, homing in on what I was about to see.

Images and sounds swirled around in my mind before I ironed them out and made sense of the jumble. Memories began to play before me like snippets of a slideshow. Finn lying in bed, his face pale. Creases that had not been on the Whitmans' faces before, now etched permanently into their skin as they argued. Mr. Whitman yelling things about doctors and comas while Mrs. Whitman tried to convince him that she knew better.

And she did. This was not a coma. Grief snaked around my heart, and then pulled tight. Weighing it down was sadness and anger and fear. They were Mrs. Whitman's emotions, but they felt as real as if they were my own.

The images slowed. My entire body felt drained. Feeling another person's emotions takes its toll. When I am reading someone, my eyes may be open, but I can only see the target's thoughts.

As my sight returned, I saw the horror plain on Mrs. Whitman's face. She might not have understood, but she knew something was up. I had to give her credit for being sharp.

But there was no time to worry. The truth was worse than anything Amanda or I had suspected—or even imagined.

Finn was suspended in Sleeping Beauty Syndrome.

AMANDA

Mattie and I were soon to go different ways—I would head to Wanda's; she, to the apartment above the church—and were therefore headed to different bus stops. As I walked her through a park to reach her stop, we discussed her reads of Mr. and Mrs. Whitman.

"You know when you're afraid to tell somebody something because you have no idea how they'll react?" She sounded genuinely concerned.

"That is not a good way to start this discussion," I said. "Out with it, Mattie."

"Finn is in a coma. The Syndrome."

I stopped walking, catching Mattie by surprise. She took a couple steps back to rejoin me.

She said, "His mom knows it's Sleeping Beauty Syndrome. His dad has argued with her. He wants to take him to the hospital."

"No!" When a DHI is stuck in a crossed-over state, the effects of any medical treatment performed on the sleeping subject are transferred to the DHI. Pain. Stimulation. Drowsiness.

Mattie jumped back. "Hey! Easy."

I couldn't catch my breath. I felt like I had a food bubble in my throat. I'd been anticipating something bad, yet I was unprepared for the awfulness of the truth.

"How long?" I asked.

"It's not like I interrogated them! When I read, I catch a few glimpses. I saw Finn in bed. I heard some arguments. It happens so fast—no, I've never been able to explain this to anyone. I don't know why I bother."

"A couple days at least," I said. "He stopped answering my texts."

"Mr. Whitman wants the doctors. Wants him fed, whatever it is they do to coma people."

"They can't do that. I'll have Wanda call the Whitmans," I said.

"Yeah, and say what?"

It wasn't Mattie's voice. It was deep—but trying to sound deeper than it actually was. I spun around. There on the path, the three of us surrounded by only trees and benches, stood a boy.

Greg Luowski had grown, which I would have said was impossible. Were there bigger physical specimens than Greg? Of course. But Greg had filled out; he looked like a different kid. Or not a kid at all. A giant of a human being. His upper arms were probably the size of my thighs. I'd heard he was getting a full ride at Florida State. Looking at him, there was no reason to doubt it. A guy his size wouldn't need much athletic skill to tackle his opponents, and yet Luowski had the reactions of a cat and the speed of a jackrabbit.

I'd wondered why he'd stayed on the bus after Mattie read him. Now I was betting he'd only gone one more stop, had watched us heading into the Starbucks, and had likely been following us ever since. Part of me didn't believe that, because I'd taken precautions and I was good at taking precautions. Then I realized Luowski had been watching Finn's house. How thrilled he must have been when we came along.

"Get lost, Greg." At one point I'd been certain he was

crushing on me, had hated Finn because of it. I didn't know if I still possessed that kind of pull or power over him, but I had to try.

"You two are the ones looking lost."

In fact, there was a lane bisecting the park. Mattie and I backed up to get closer to it. There were no cars on it, but if one came along we could cry out for help.

Greg was no National Merit Scholar. He tended to quote the latest villain from the newest action film. He learned their lines, practiced their postures, and then allowed them to inhabit him. A person could almost not take him seriously, except for his size and the dramatic green eyes Maleficent had bestowed upon him. The Keepers had thought the green eyes were contact lenses—Greg wasn't the only kid in school to suddenly change his original eye color. Maybe they started out as lenses; maybe they still were, but they didn't look it. They looked terrifyingly real, and his green gaze sent both Mattie and me stumbling back in fear.

"We're fine, thank you," Mattie said.

"Stop where you are!"

"No," I said, continuing to back toward the park lane.

Lousy Luowski dared not come too close. He understood my ability to push. If he made a move, it would be on me to stop him. He didn't know Mattie well. Didn't know whether or not to fear her.

"We need to have a little talk," he said in his best cinematic tone.

"I've always liked talking to you, Greg. You know that." Back to testing him, seeing if any fragment of the crush remained. Boys get bigger. Boys grow up. But many carry their crushes with them, just like girls do.

"Tell me what's up with Witless."

"You know I don't like you calling him that." I could charge him and push as I ran. Risky, but if I was successful he'd sail away like a grocery bag in the wind.

"I don't care what you like."

So much for the old crush. He struck me as an old, ornery dog—one with all had its teeth. I had no desire to tangle with him.

Mattie took several steps back. He looked at her with a flicker of recognition, but it was gone just as quickly.

"I haven't seen him, Greg. Haven't spoken to him, either. I can't believe you'd hurt us, hurt a pair of girls, but bring it on. I haven't seen Finn. Period."

"I don't much mind hurting anything or anyone," he said. "Whitless included."

"It's over," Mattie said. "You know that, right? You know what happened in Disneyland? You're not like one of those soldiers who think the war's still going, are you?"

A disturbing snarl twisted his face. A secretive, perverse smile, full of contempt.

"Finn said you had changed," I blurted. "That you'd figured stuff out. That you'd realized the things they were asking of you—"

62

"Shut it!" He took a step forward, a mistake that delighted me. One or two more, please. I had to use his anger as bait. "He can't change things."

"He said you, the real Greg, was still in there somewhere, trying to get past the green-eyed Greg. We can help with that, you know. The magic in the Kingdom is only stronger now. Since the victory."

A nearly identical self-confident snarl blinked across his face. I felt cold. Nauseated. I had no idea what he meant about Finn not being able to change things, but combined with his claim that he wanted to hurt Finn, it struck a chord of panic in me.

"I know what you're doing." He took another step. Actually, he was confirming my hunch that he had no idea.

"Talking?" I said.

"Trying to communicate?" said Mattie.

He moved with astonishing speed, grabbed Mattie in a chokehold, and dragged her back a step. "Do your thing," he said to me, "and she goes with me."

I looked around. "Greg. This is a public sidewalk. Two cars just went by. Three. How smart is this?"

He wore a T-shirt, meaning his inner elbow was touching Mattie's neck. I hoped that explained her strangely fluttering eyelids. She was reading him—not a touch-read, but a long, deep read. Like settling in with a good book.

A car drove by too fast on the deserted park lane. I turned. It screeched to a stop. Two college boys jumped out.

"Hey!" the driver hollered, running down the path.

Luowski dumped Mattie, turned, and sprinted away. The boys slowed as they reached us.

"You okay?" the driver asked.

"We are now. Thank you!" I nodded vigorously.

The other boy was holding Mattie by the shoulders. "Did he hurt you? Do you need to go to the hospital? We can take you to the emergency room."

"I'm good," she said, rubbing her neck.

"You sure?"

She nodded.

"Do you know him?" the driver asked. He pulled out his phone, presumably to call the police.

"I do. I'd rather not," I said, looking at his phone.

"Because?"

I considered my words carefully. "I have issues with the authorities."

"Me too," Mattie said.

The driver smirked and chuckled. "Yeah. Well, me too, for that matter. But you just got mugged. That should be reported."

"We were in school together a couple years ago," I said. "He was the class bully. He plays tough, but he's harmless." I wasn't a terrific liar.

"He didn't look harmless."

"Not at all," the other boy said.

"Can we take you somewhere? Drop you off?"

"Could you? I mean, are you sure?" said Mattie.

"No, thank you," I said. "We're good."

Mattie wasn't going to challenge me. Neither, it turned out, was this boy.

"So, you live around here?" he said.

"Thanks for helping," I said. "I really mean it. You saved us."

"No problem." At least he could take a hint.

Mattie and I thanked them repeatedly. They asked for our phone numbers. We declined.

As soon as they'd driven off, Mattie turned to me, ashen as a ghost.

"He—" she began, struggling to speak.

"Did he hurt you?" I stepped toward her. She shook her head.

"The whole time he was choking me, I was reading him. He believes Finn and the others are trying to change something. Amanda . . ." Her eyes were pleading. "He's going to hurt Finn, really hurt Finn. I mean, really! After running into us, he was panicked, because he'd planned to do it tonight."

I stumbled. Mattie caught me, and I pulled gently away—I didn't want her reading me, too. I had my privacy to protect.

"We have to warn everyone," I muttered. "Wanda and I can do it. We'll meet tomorrow—you and me. We'll get through this."

"The thing is . . . he's on orders. Luowski's on orders."

I stared at her, long and hard. "That can't be. You must

have read him wrong. He's just never been fully deprogrammed like we thought."

Mattie shook her head slowly. Defiantly. "No, Mandy. He's on orders. He believes Maleficent told him to do this."

"But that's impossible. She's dead. Maleficent is *dead*."

"Yeah. That's what I thought, too."

LUOWSKI

I paced in back of the old apartment buildings near the abandoned church. I didn't have to think about it anymore. I'd come here so many times already. Spying on Weaver, hoping to gain information about Whitman and the Kingdom Losers.

Every time I laid an eye on Weaver I wondered what she'd done to me on that ship. I could destroy her easily. I'd been given the powers. But she was far more useful as a link to the others.

I felt impatient. Something was up. Something was different. I forced myself to shake off the unease, but it wouldn't leave me.

"Maintain control," I muttered.

"But you aren't in control, Greg . . . You've never been in control," whispered the cold voice of a woman.

Not just any woman. *Her!*

I whipped around. And around. Nowhere. She was in my head. No, she was in the glass of the window in front of me. A pair of icy green eyes. I went as cold as that voice before staggering forward and falling onto my knees. Maleficent. Inescapable.

I squeezed my eyes shut, expecting her snarl. She'd gone silent. It's own kind of torture.

"I . . . I'm trying," I gasped like a crazy man. "I have a plan! Tonight, I'll crush him tonight. He will be no more. This girl will help me. I will make her help me."

Again: the dreaded silence.

Where the eyes had been I saw a massive boy of eighteen with red hair and alien green eyes. Me. I stood, glancing around to make sure no one else had seen me. Furious, I glared at my own eyes and they mocked me. I felt slightly unglued. What was happening to me?

I swung out and punched the reflection with my full force. Glass shattered. Shards rained to the concrete, sounding like broken icicles.

A mother and her child hurried past on the sidewalk. The little girl tugged on her mom's hand and pointed at me.

"Look away now, Mia. He's . . . crazy!" She thought she'd whispered to her daughter, but I'd heard. She was lucky I didn't make her pay for that comment.

I let my hatred of Whitman own me instead. Ever since freshman year, I'd despised him. He made Amanda like him without even trying. No matter how I pushed him, he didn't give. Not like the other kids. He always gave me the feeling he thought he was better than me. And then his superhero image with the Kingdom Losers made him a big deal all over school.

I joined Maleficent because of him—to put Finn in his place. Her YouTube was genius. Impossible to resist.

The YouTube videos had proven irresistible. Her glowing green eyes she gave to me. The promise and delivery of unexpected powers. Later, after I'd let her put her spell on me and a few others, people had feared us. I no longer felt pain the same way. What Maleficent promised, she followed through with, unlike a million other grown-ups I knew.

I recalled her words to us, before she'd been taken by them. *"The end is near. The beginning is only a beginning."*

Whatever that meant.

The sound of a door opening caught my attention. I narrowed my eyes and backed into the shadow of the church dome. I hoped no one had heard the window shatter.

A shadow came closer, stretched and thin. A girl. Weaver, I could tell by her silhouette; I had followed her so many times. Too many times. I knew she was my ticket to the Losers, that she was all I had, but the voice and the eyes in the glass and my bloody hand told me it was time to do something, not just follow.

I jumped out. She screamed, but I cupped her mouth and heaved her against the brick wall of the church.

"Where is he?" I demanded, pressing her harder against the apartment wall.

"I don't know."

"You'd better." I grabbed her bare elbow as she tried to swing at me. I suddenly felt—empty. Drained. I released her.

She tried to escape but I threw her to the wall.

I heard a thud. Her head on the brick.

She sagged slowly to the burned grass and folded down into a heap.

"Get up!"

She wasn't moving.

"I said: Get up!" I kicked her. Hard enough she'd remember it.

She didn't move.

"No one's going to save you now, Weaver. No one's going to save Whitman either! You hear me?"

I didn't think she did. I was beginning to freak.

"Hey! What are you doing there?" A short, slender girl approached with a boy on her arm. They started running toward me.

I took off. People didn't take kindly to boys hurting girls, even for the right reason.

They didn't know Greg Luowski, the boy with the green eyes. They didn't know me.

DAY 3

AMANDA

"I can come in with you, if you like?" Wanda spoke from behind the wheel of her car. We were back at the Whitman's house. My third visit in three days.

"You've helped so much already. Jelly says we should keep Finn hydrated. Wet sponges in his mouth. She says when Terry was in SBS he even drank from a straw once or twice despite being totally out . . ." I trailed off, fingering invisible figures onto the faux-suede car interior. My stupid eyes released tears at the same time, making my feelings impossible to hide.

"Hang in there. We know this is bigger than Finn. We can assume by the fact they aren't answering that it involves them all. We're doing the right thing. One at a time." Wanda pulled me toward her, battling the seat belt. We did an awkward hug, me with my head on her shoulder.

"I'm so scared for him," I said. "For them all! It's been days!"

"Go on. Talk to her. I'll wait here. I'm right here."

"Thank you!" I gathered the plastic bag from the car floor. I was off.

* * *

Knowingly repeating a mistake is one definition of insanity and was not something I felt comfortable doing. Maybe it was because of my different (think: lost) childhood, my being forced to grow up so quickly, but I'd also learned mistakes were a useful, even necessary, part of figuring things out. Approaching the Whitmans' front door for the third time was no cakewalk for me.

It was up to me to negotiate a truce with the Whitmans.

I had stopped trusting *all* adults a long time ago. Wayne and Wanda weren't exactly exceptions, but I trusted them more than I would admit.

Finn's parents were *not* exceptions. For me, knocking on this door was asking for trouble. The question wasn't *if*, but *how much*.

"Please, Amanda!" Mrs. Whitman greeted me with a look of disdain. "We've had enough."

"He might drink from a straw if you offer it. Gatorade is best." I handed her the bag. It contained two bottles of red Gatorade and a box of flex-straws. "He needs a damp sponge, water; you run it around his lips and over his tongue every hour. It's best if you put bright bulbs in all the lamps of his room, maybe bring in extras and leave them on at all times. It helps stimulate rapid eye movement."

Tears sprang to Mrs. Whitman's eyes. She showed me inside.

I whispered to Mrs. Whitman in order to keep Mr. Whitman from overhearing. "Which floor?" Finn had moved rooms a couple of times, but I didn't want to seem presumptuous to know that.

"Upstairs."

"Your daughter?"

"She's terribly upset. Her room is also upstairs."

"She needs to leave the house tonight. Can you have her stay with a friend?"

Mrs. Whitman turned sharply. "What's that mean?"

"I think you know. I think it happened before."

"That beast of a boy, force-feeding . . ." She half sat, half collapsed onto the living room couch. She sank her head into her hands, her back shaking with the force of her sobs. Maybe she'd been waiting to get that out, because she continued for several long minutes.

"Why is this happening to us?" She lifted her head.

I took her literally. A mistake. "There's some evidence that the boy, Greg Luowski, is under a spell again."

She glared at me. An affront. It felt like she'd punched me.

"Sorry," I said.

"I do not need all the voodoo-hoodoo you kids are so obsessed with."

"I understand."

"No. You have no idea. *None.*" She took a moment.

Gathered herself. "Amanda, I'm sorry. That was unfair and uncalled for on my part. I apologize. I know you care."

"Very much," I said.

"But at your age . . . never mind."

"All I want . . . *all I want*, is to help Finn. To help him get better. To protect him. To keep him out of the hospital."

Her eyes brimmed with more tears. "That won't be good for him, will it?"

"If your husband could talk to Philby's mother, his parents, I think he might believe them more than me."

"I'm not sure he'll do that."

"He has to!"

"That's a matter of opinion, young lady. He's Finn's father. You can't understand the agony of sitting, waiting. It gets worse, too. There are . . . unspeakable things. But you need to earn my trust if you hope to be included in any of that. Believe me, we are terrified of what's happening."

"A sponge. A glass. Maybe some ice?"

"I have to talk to my husband first. He's not going to like this."

"I would offer to leave, but you need me. I can help you. I have . . . well, I'm strong. I know I don't look it, but I'm very strong. Greg Luowski is afraid of me, and he's not expecting me to be here. That's our advantage."

"You make it sound like a battle, Amanda."

"If there was time, I'd try to sugarcoat it," I said. "But there isn't, and this *is* a battle. Or it will be. And it's coming tonight."

* * *

I climbed the stairs timidly. Finn was up there. Vulnerable. Half dead. Stuck in a limbo that no one, not even the Imagineers, fully understood. There was no science to explain the transfer of consciousness. I couldn't scare Mrs. Whitman with talk of such things, but I wore the knowledge like a stone around my neck.

"He's not happy about this," Mrs. Whitman said. She didn't mean Finn.

"But I can stay?"

"I wasn't about to tell him about that boy. And we can't call the police until he actually does something. Do you have proof of any of this? Anything at all?"

"No. I could be wrong, but I'm not. If that makes any sense."

"Not to me, it doesn't."

"No. I didn't expect it would."

She swung open the door. I'd seen this upstairs bedroom before—there had been meetings here. We would huddle around his computer or talk strategy, sometimes for hours. Always with the door open, always with Mrs. Whitman bringing snacks and making conversation. So I knew what to expect. I knew what I'd see.

And still I fell to the floor, bawling. Nothing had prepared me for seeing Finn in SBS. I felt like a baby. An idiot. A fool. But I couldn't stop sobbing. Mrs. Whitman placed her hand on my back, and I cried all the harder. No one ever gave me sympathy like that. Jess could console me, and did, but she was my age, my friend. Having an adult like Wanda or Mrs. Whitman actually care devastated me.

Taking big, shuddering breaths, I pulled myself together and drew closer.

Finn looked peaceful, but too still. I knew him; he was always filled with energy and determination. Always moving, he epitomized the deep thinking, overly aware leader he'd proven himself to be. Wayne had molded him, starting with a quiet, introverted boy who had a love of Disney, a little sister he adored, and parents from whom he felt himself growing away. We'd talked for hours about all this—and more. I knew him in ways Mrs. Whitman never would, and she knew him as only a mother could.

It explained why, when I looked over at her, she was crying, too. Then we both started laughing nervously, self-consciously. Two people cherishing the same boy, made sad by his present state.

We worked as a team after that, Mrs. Whitman's animosity washed away by our shared tears. My inbred suspicion of adults melted away, too. While Mrs. Whitman dabbed Finn's lips and tried to provoke the sleeping boy to open his mouth, I held a face towel below his chin, collecting the runoff. At first, our effort was a failure. The water cascading down Finn's chin made him look pitiful, infantile. I closed my eyes, unable to watch.

It wasn't until Mrs. Whitman pulled the sponge away that

we had our first real success: Finn's lips twitched and kissed, as if reaching for the fresh water. His mother stabbed the sponge into his mouth, but then backed off, barely wetting his lips. Bit by bit, drop by drop, the slumbering Finn took to the idea of water. Within minutes, the sponge was making sucking noises.

I prepared the Gatorade. We slipped him a substitute. I provoked him to "Sip!" and eventually, after a good number of tries and another fifteen minutes, Finn drank an ounce or two of the red lifesaver. It wasn't much, probably not enough, but I was elated and Mrs. Whitman was beside herself with joy.

It was late and getting later by the time she could no longer contain her delight and sought out her husband to share the news.

"You'll watch him. Just watch him, yes?" she said. I got the message. She didn't want me stealing any solo moments watching him drink.

"Yeah. Sure."

"What is it?"

"I didn't say anything," I protested.

"I can hear it in your voice."

"It's late," I said. "That's all."

"The boy." She wasn't asking.

"Yes."

"You are not to open any windows." Again, an order, not a suggestion.

"Of course not!" I said.

"I've locked all the doors. I don't see how he's supposed to pull this off."

"No. But I'm pretty sure he will. He's not a deep thinker, Mrs. Whitman, if you know what I mean."

"I know exactly what you mean!"

"We could outwit him, but more likely we need to beat him, defeat him."

"Win," Finn's mother said. She looked at me for a long moment. "You said you're strong."

"I am. I can be."

"Can you fight?" Mrs. Whitman asked.

I didn't answer right away. She took that as uncertainty, which it was not.

"Your strength," she said, trying to give me confidence I didn't need. "My brains. Hey, I'm a real-life rocket scientist. What chance does this Luowski have?"

"Not much," I said, feeling better in spite of myself.

"I'll double check the doors," she said.

"Couldn't hurt."

* * *

Waiting for Luowski slowed the clock to a crawl.

Mrs. Whitman said something to herself about being "home alone," which I didn't understand. There were three of us, four, counting Finn. But after that, she brightened and put me to work. We strung Mr. Whitman's fishing line across the staircase, leaving a tennis ball on the carpet to mark the invisible line for ourselves. She loaded the room with a variety of sporting equipment, from baseball bats to golf clubs. As it was dark out, I stood guard while she poured what remained of a five-gallon bucket of black sealant for the driveway around the base of the tree below Finn's window. Returning inside, she had me hold her feet while she worked with a handsaw on the only limb that neared the window.

Inside the front door, she taped down two layers of black garbage bags, making sure the door would swing open without disturbing them. She seeded flakes of laundry detergent between the layers; the combination had to be the slipperiest surface on earth. More fishing line made a second trip wire, which we tied to the plug of the only lamp left on downstairs. The family's vintage video camera, with its mounted spotlight, was positioned on the top landing with Mrs. Whitman, while I was left in possession of the newer digital camera.

Mr. Whitman got into the act, too, by agreeing to be the radio man. At the first sign of any trouble, he would phone 911. He was also in possession of the only real weapon at our disposal. Mrs. Whitman had cannibalized parts of a dog-training device for a dog the family no longer owned. Originally it had consisted of a shock collar and remote control button with which to activate it. Now it took the form of a lacrosse stick with a barbecue fork duct taped to the end; the remote was taped on the stick's handle. "Poke, stick, zap," was how Mrs. Whitman told her husband to operate it. She repeated the commands several times. Mr. Whitman practiced a lunge like the fencing champion he was not.

The preparations brought him around. Instead of battling a coma, he had a real enemy to fight, and Mr. Whitman came to life, getting into it.

It was approaching midnight by the time Mrs. Whitman brewed a stiff pot of tea for the team. We clinked cups—and then we waited.

"If he doesn't come," Mr. Whitman said, his face alight with mirth, "we're going to look like a sorry bunch of paranoid idiots."

As it turned out, that was the last time anyone laughed that night.

* * *

The first suggestion of trouble came as I heard the snap of a tree branch outside Finn's window. It was followed by the sound of a thud, some groaning—and silence.

Downstairs, Mr. Whitman was poised behind a couch halfway between the front door and the staircase, his thumb ready over his phone's call button. From above, I watched Mrs. Whiman gesticulating wildly as she sought to keep him in place.

"We don't want him for trespassing. We want him for breaking and entering. We want him caught and locked up, not wrist slapped! Oh . . . my . . . gosh!"

Mrs. Whitman was interrupted by the sound of someone kicking sharply.

"The dog door!" Mr. Whitman called upstairs. "I'm not sure it's going to hold!"

"Good! Then we can have them arrested!"

A slender girl crawled through the dog door that entered the house from the Florida room.

"Stupid, cheap thing!" Mrs. Whitman complained. "I locked it!"

Mr. Whitman overreacted, charging into action and activating the lighting trip wire. My heart clenched as the living room went dark. The sound of him falling, followed by the sound of a lacrosse stick tumbling across the floor, pretty much established that Mr. Whitman had lost any advantage with which he might have started.

The girl sprinted for the front door. In too great a hurry and with too little light to see by, she hit the greased garbage bags and collided with the door at full speed. Dazed, she somehow still managed to twist the doorknob while falling backward, unlocking the front door.

The door swung open. What looked like a black bear charged through, banging the door into the girl and knocking her down for a second time as she struggled to stand. The intruder hit the plastic bags too, slipped, and fell, smacking the back of his head on the door's threshold.

Coming to his feet, Greg Luowski, dripping cold, black driveway sealant, froze. An apparition had emerged from the dark of the family room. It looked like a prehistoric fish with silver fangs.

Turned out it was the lacrosse stick. Mr. Whitman jabbed the device into Luowski's leg. The boy hollered. Mr. Whitman pressed the dog collar remote. The boy did an awkward puppet dance, imitating a robot with its control software scrambled: his neck twitched, his arms straightened, and he broke wind sharply, like a car backfiring.

But Mr. Whitman hesitated a fraction of a second too long. He didn't notice that the girl had reclaimed her footing. From behind, seeing her partner in trouble, she shoved Mr. Whitman through the open door and the screen door beyond. She slammed the front door, locking it.

"We're in!" she said. "Out through the terrace!"

"Noooo! Waaaait!" Luowski sounded like a slowed down recording.

The girl fanned the air. "Was that you?"

"There's time," Luowski said. "We have to end him."

* * *

We heard his words from our position at the top of the stairs. At her feet, Mrs. Whitman had her husband's steel barbell; we'd put twin twenty-fives on either end, bringing the total weight to seventy-five pounds. He'd had it forever, and had probably used it three times since, but he refused to allow her to remove it from the bedroom, claiming he intended to work out. Now it would finally serve a purpose.

Standing inside the bedroom door, representing the last line of defense, I waited with my heart in my throat. Behind me, Finn slept peacefully. I ached for him to sense the danger and awaken. Wherever his DHI hologram might be, I urged him to press the Return and come back to us. At the thought that we would be incapable of holding off the enchanted Luowski and his banshee girlfriend, I resorted to a desperate plea for divine intervention.

"Can't see a thing." Luowski's groggy whisper came from downstairs.

"Maybe if you got that goo out of your eyes," the girl wheezed.

"It's drying or something. I can barely move. Wait! Here's the stairs."

I held my breath. Only the sound of the tarry substance smacking the carpeted steps could be heard as Swamp Thing climbed the stairs.

From outside the house, we heard Mr. Whitman reporting the intrusion to the police.

My breath caught in my throat. A police response would certainly include questions about Finn's state of health and could very well lead to an ambulance and doctors—the last thing Finn or his parents could afford if his DHI was to remain functional, wherever it was. Calling 911 had the undesired effect of summoning a second enemy.

The only light in Finn's room came from a pulsing white LED on his laptop; it grew incrementally to a strong flare, and then receded to a dim glow, like a dormant animal breathing. It cast my shadow onto the wall, then faded it out in slow motion.

"I . . . can't . . . see . . . a . . . thing," said the girl.

"Shh!" But it was Luowski's sticky trudging that was making the noise.

My heart pounded, threatening to break through my rib cage. Finn, Luowski, the police. Suddenly the odds seemed insurmountable. I took a step back toward the bed, wanting to be closer to Finn, to protect him. But memory drove me forward again. The Kingdom Keepers did not step back and let trouble come to them. They teamed up and aggressively fought to stop it. The early DHI technology—version 1.6 and earlier—had failed to account for the power of fear. By giving into fear, the Keepers found their holograms more material, more vulnerable to injury. They quickly learned to push the feeling away, to overcome its material claim and thus protect themselves from attack. I wouldn't do Finn any favors by retreating. Desperation required action.

I stepped to the open door and mentally declared myself a force impossible to pass.

In the soupy black gloom before her, the girl could just make out Mrs. Whitman, standing tall at the top of the stairs. Mrs. Whitman stood her ground defiantly.

"Go away," she said. "Go away and we won't hurt you."

The sloshing stopped.

"Last warning," Mrs. Whitman said.

"I've called the police!" Mr. Whitman shouted from outside the house.

"You'd better move, lady," Luowski said in a growl.

"You were warned," said Mrs. Whitman. Her foot pushed the barbell, which rolled like an axle and sent the weights careening down the stairs.

But she turned on the lights a moment too soon. A half-second more of darkness, and Luowski would have been mowed down at the shins by seventy-five pounds of steel and iron. He might have broken both ankles, been knocked to the bottom of the stairs. No matter what, his advance upstairs would have been halted.

Instead, the high school state all-star in both football and track vaulted the barbell. It slipped beneath him and took the girl down like a bowling pin. She fell, face forward, screaming. Tangled in the barbell, she flew back down the stairs, thumping her way to the ground floor.

Luowski was horrific, covered in black tar, wood splinters, and grass clippings. Still, he directed his vengeful, defiant green gaze at Mrs. Whitman. Taking two stairs at a time, he arrived at the top and swung his mitt of a hand at her.

I hip-checked Mrs. Whitman off her feet and down the hall, taking her place as Luowski's blow connected with my arm. *Whoosh!* I flew to the side and into Mrs. Whitman, clearing the way into Finn's bedroom for Luowski.

The beast reached the landing, glanced in our direction with fiery eyes, and turned towards the comatose Finn. I leaned against the banister for support. Then, overcome by rage, driven by . . . love, I pushed.

There: I admitted it. Jess had been arguing with me for

months now. "It doesn't have to mean romantic love," she said, "but it's a depth of care and concern that goes beyond simple friendship." She was right. This push was like no other. I knew that the moment my arms extended, knew that as the post behind me cracked, unable to support the force of my effort.

Luowski lifted off his feet and hit the wall like a truck. The door to Finn's room crashed open further—then tore from its hinges. Finn's bed moved. A lamp flew off and smashed into the same wall as Luowski.

"You will not hurt him!" I screamed, coming to my feet. Something else was new, too: I didn't feel tired, just energized. A first. I was just getting started.

Luowski sagged to the floor, but somehow he collected himself and stood. The wallboard was cracked from the impact of his body. He had to be under a spell to still be moving.

He glowered. "You shouldn't have done that."

I moved toward the doorway, brought my hands up, and hit him again. The bedcovers lifted like sails, covering Luowski as he slammed into the wall, fracturing it further. Glass blew out of both windows. I thought I heard Mrs. Whitman call out to me, but the wind I'd generated drowned out whatever she'd said.

Another two steps closer. I could crush him now, collapse his rib cage into his lungs, kill him. My power no longer had an on-off switch; rather, it had an accelerator pedal. I had *control*. And I had to control myself.

Luowski staggered toward Finn's bed. He looked as if he

was on cruise control, a marionette controlled by a puppeteer. No human boy could go through what he'd just gone through and come back for more.

"No," I said in an eerily calm voice. "Not now. Not ever."

I lifted my hands, stepped to the left and said good-bye.

Luowski flew backward through the open window. Gone.

* * *

Finn, dressed unusually grown-up for him in a button down shirt and khaki chinos, lay on the unmade bed, the blankets thrown off, only a sheet caught at his ankles. His shirt had come untucked at the waist. It bunched at his collarbone. The shirt's chest pocket stood up, unnaturally rigid.

I eased closer, wary. The gentle curve of a red piece of paper protruded from the pocket. I felt Mrs. Whitman behind me but didn't turn, my full attention on Finn. Drawn hypnotically to the pocket, I reached the side of the bed and pulled Finn's shirt down to smooth the fabric. In doing so, the red curve of construction paper slipped further out of the pocket. I could see the curve; it was attached to another similar curve.

A red heart.

From downstairs came the anxiety-ridden voice of Mr. Whitman. "She's gone! She ran away!"

In the bedroom, Mrs. Whitman nodded, granting permission to my unspoken request. I reached out tenderly and slipped the paper heart from Finn's pocket.

"How did I miss that?"

I wasn't sure if I'd actually heard Mrs. Whitman say that, or if I imagined it.

The lopsided heart had been cut crudely with a pair of dull scissors. But I thought it looked perfect, because I knew it was intended for me. I turned it over and recognized Finn's awkward handwriting.

My favorite Fairlie:
Our time in MK could fill a jar to overflowing.
Should I be stuck, it's yours for the knowing.

Mrs. Whitman's chin nearly rested on my shoulder as she read from behind.

"What's it mean?" asked the all-knowing rocket scientist.

Wiping the tears from my eyes, I collected myself. "It means he needs us."

DAY 4

JESS

I reread the message on my phone. It had come through moments before.

> Please meet me in my office at your earliest convenience. I have something I need to discuss with you.
> JG

I sighed. I'd been half-hoping it would have magically changed. But magic didn't work that way. I should know.

JG for Joe Garlington, the Imagineer responsible for the Keepers. If they'd discovered I'd been sneaking out at night, or worse, *into Disneyland* at night, I was probably about to be fired or expelled from Imagineering school.

I hadn't talked to Mr. Garlington in over a month.

I had to think I'd been seen on security footage or that the guy installing the lock had recognized me somehow. I'd blown it. I was about to lose everything I loved.

Best-case scenario, I'd be given the chance to explain that I was helping the Keepers and be let off with a warning. That didn't make me feel any better.

At least Amanda wasn't involved. Maybe she'd be able to stay in the school.

The butterflies in my stomach didn't listen.

I hopped a dorm shuttle over to the Disney campus, absentmindedly staring out the window, only vaguely aware of my tapping foot and wringing hands.

Too soon, the ride came to an end, leaving only the short walk to Joe's office between me and my fate. *Deep breaths*, I instructed myself.

As I raised my knuckles to the wood Joe's face appeared. He'd swung open the door, startling me.

"Jess!" he greeted me. "Come in! Sit down!"

I forced a smile and made my way inside. Joe's office was a brightly lit room, nicely sized and fairly tidy—except for a large stack of papers on the desk, which were piled close to avalanche heights. I noticed subtle hints of Disney everywhere: a Vinylmation stood next to the desk lamp; concept art of the latest Disney parks hung on three of the walls. The fourth was entirely windows.

I sat down on the edge of the leather desk chair opposite Joe. In spite of the air conditioning, I could feel myself sweating like a kid in the principal's office. I caught myself fidgeting and sat on my hands. I wasn't about to convict myself by acting guilty.

Joe leaned back in his chair, apparently far more comfortable with the situation than I was. "Jess, there's something I need to talk to you about."

I forced a polite smile, though it came out more as a grimace. "Oh really, what's that?" I did my best to match his laid-back tone, hoping he couldn't hear my voice shake.

"I promised to protect you and Amanda from Mrs. Nash, but I've had an inquiry." He paused, allowing this to sink in. Brought his hands and fingers together as if in prayer. "You and Amanda mentioned the government's involvement. What gave you that impression?"

For a moment, I was too stunned to answer. I'd been convinced my world was about to end, and here it appeared that Joe didn't even *know* about my latest adventure. My grimace transformed into an outright grin. Waves of relief washed over me, leaving me light-headed.

Joe leaned forward, confused by my strange reaction. "Mrs. Nash is one thing; she was breaking the rules anyway, but . . ." He trailed off, wanting me to finish the sentence.

I did my best to quit smiling like a maniac. My elation was dimmed somewhat as Joe's question registered. Amanda's and my past had always been something to run from. I was suspicious of Joe's sudden curiosity, worried by his implication that the questions were coming from someone else. I had done my best to put my history behind me; wasn't that the point of the Imagineering school, our move cross-country?

I studied the curtains as I thought, finding hidden Mickeys

in the elegant spiral pattern, making Joe wait as I carefully composed my answer to be as vague as possible.

"Well, there were scientists. We were told that we were doing a great service to our country, so we assumed it was the government. It seemed like something they would say." I stopped, wanting to share nothing more.

Joe continued staring at me expectantly.

"Umm, yeah." I added lamely, hoping to signal that I was done.

Joe studied me a few seconds longer, letting me squirm under his gaze before leaning back in his chair. "That's all. Thank you."

I practically skipped toward the door. I wasn't about to press my luck.

My hand on the knob, I thought back to Barracks 14, to my latest dream. Now Joe was asking about our past. I'd been searching all over Disneyland for answers, but perhaps I'd been looking in the wrong places. I didn't believe in coincidences, and when it concerned Amanda and Barracks 14, I couldn't leave any stone unturned.

I sighed internally and turned around.

"Joe?" I called out.

"Uh-huh?" He'd already buried himself in the stack of papers at his desk.

"A dream I've had . . ."

Joe looked up sharply. He knew the power of my dreams.

"Guys from Barracks 14 were capturing Amanda." Now I

had his full attention. "I want to help her. I *need* to help her. But I don't know how."

Joe was out of his seat before I finished my sentence, shoving his phone in his pocket, pushing handfuls of papers into his briefcase.

"We have to act quickly. Have you ever flown on a private jet?"

MATTIE

At first, there was darkness and silence. But as my consciousness returned, I heard all sorts of other noises—beeping, humming, the distinctive buzz of overhead tube lights.

When I opened my eyes, I was on my back looking straight up. Blue drapes hung around me, forming partitions. Most of the beeping and humming came from the digital displays on nearby machines.

I was in a hospital. The emergency room.

Images and memories trickled back into me. Luowski had hit me, smacked my head against some bricks. He had found me, figured out my power. He'd hurt me. My body felt like one giant bruise. It hurt to move, to breathe, but those were the least of my concerns.

Despite my muddled memory, I scrambled to remember what I'd learned from touching him. A threat of some kind . . . but I couldn't place it.

The sounds of hurried footsteps brought me back to the

present. Voices rose as they approached. I shut my eyes, pretending to sleep. Eavesdropping on the doctors might be easier if they thought I couldn't hear.

Someone took my wrist. I continued to play possum, hoping my pulse—if that was being taken—wouldn't give me away.

The grip was rough for a nurse. It felt more like a pro-wrestling move.

The voices grew closer.

The person next me took hold of my forearm. My skin. I was suddenly reading this guy. Definitely not Luowski. Older, but not old. A strong thinker. Determined. *On a mission!*

This last thought woke me up more quickly. It was as if I'd jumped onto one of the moving sidewalks in an airport, but heading the wrong way. I had to speed up to stay even. If I ran, I could beat the speed of the belt under me.

I let my thoughts ramble forward, into this guy's immediate past. He'd traveled here. He knew me by name.

He was Barracks 14.

The beeping of the monitor, loud and fast, kept time with my suddenly speeding heart. *Baltimore.* I could see the guy's image of carrying me out of here. A white van. He envisioned handing me off to someone in the back of that van.

The chattering voices out in the hall arrived to my area. The hand let go of my wrist. I heard the side curtain flutter and I struggled to force open an eyelid

Here came a doctor and two nurses, the source of the

voices. When they saw I was awake, they began asking me questions. They waved a light in my eyes. More questions. How many fingers were they holding up? The doctor felt under my chin. He listened to my chest.

I couldn't speak. It had nothing to do with my physical condition. The only thing I could think of was escape. I had been discovered, and I needed to get out of here.

I was not going back to Barracks 14!

I yawned pointedly and rolled over; I ignored the rest of their queries and pretended to sleep until the last nurse left the room.

As soon as I heard the curtain whistle on its track, I shot out of bed, wincing at my pounding head and sore muscles. I was partially clothed; I searched for and found my shirt, jeans, and running shoes. Getting into the skinny jeans tested my patience. Finally, I spotted behind me a row of horizontal windows much wider than they were high. All had levers for opening. I climbed up, using the machines as my ladder, and quietly moved the nearest lever. The window lifted up from the top, and was hinged to only open partially. I struggled to fit through the small space available to me; it forced me to lie down into it in order to slip out. I rolled, dropped, and landed hard on a ridged metal roof.

Biting back the scream that wanted to burst from my lungs, I crawled along the edge until I found the hospital's fire escape, checked for anyone below who might see me, and climbed down the fire ladder. Dropping to the pavement, I ran hard and fast, ignoring my aching, stinging limbs. Barracks 14 was here and they were coming for us.

We needed to leave, to cover our tracks and never come back. Our escape would have to be carefully planned. We could ill afford more attention.

The running cleared my head. My earlier reading of Luowski came back to me. His internal struggle against outside control. His fear of the trouble he would be in if he followed his present orders. I knew those orders as well.

Luowski was about to destroy everything.

AMANDA

Luowski's raid the previous night had ended with the police arriving at the Whitman house. Insurance adjusters would follow the next day, but that night, the police were told about the pair of teens who'd been caught entering the house, "presumably to rob us," as Mrs. Whitman put it.

I was told that Mr. Whitman did a decent acting job, claiming that a blow to the head, the result of a fall, left the exact events unclear. This allowed Mrs. Whitman to do all the reporting, and ensured that their stories didn't contradict.

Wanda was my source here. She and Mrs. Whitman rescued the comatose Finn just prior to the arrival of the police; they carried him into the carport and placed him in the backseat of Wanda's car, so he was gone by the time the badges came knocking.

It was not safe for Finn to be returned home. He would remain at Wanda's for the short term.

I slept fitfully that night. I felt sad, afraid, and alone. I wanted desperately to see Jess. We texted until late my time and I fell asleep in the glow of my phone's screen.

Re-reading the texts, I wondered if Joe was up to something. Maybe Jess understood it, maybe not. Her messages were too cryptic for me to get much out of them, and I didn't want to push her to tell me more. For the first time in forever, our relationship felt strained, like we were pulling on the same rope from different ends—and each claiming to do it for the sake of the other. It was maddening. If I pushed for more information, I'd be seen as prying; if I didn't, uncaring.

I remembered seeing a massive tree once that, on inspection, turned out to be two separate trunks entwined. At the top, the trunks split off into separate crowns. It was a spectacular sight. Now I begged whatever powers were out there not to let Jess and me grow apart like those trunks. I had zero desire to be my own crown of limbs and leaves; I refused to believe that the time had come to grow apart. But that's what it felt like. And it was solely our own doing.

That was a strange, dreamless night. I woke repeatedly, wondering at my surroundings. Finally, I awoke in tears. Wanda sat on the bed, shaking me gently.

"You've had a nightmare," she said.

"No," I said. "I don't think so. More like reality. But I'm glad you woke me."

Hearing my concern, she hugged me.

"I lied to him," I said, crying again in the safety of her embrace.

"Who, Finn?"

I nodded, my chin striking her collarbone. "When we first met. I told him I had passes because of my family. I mentioned my mom. None of it was true. Your dad got me in there. Your dad basically put us together, told me what to say so Finn would go into the park with me. Your dad planned it all, didn't he?" I eased back so I could see her face.

"I don't know," Wanda said. "I honestly don't."

"I think you do."

"He always seemed to be several steps ahead of everyone else, so I wouldn't be surprised. But I have no firsthand knowledge. Honestly. I never knew much about what he was doing."

"I'm going to fix it," I told her. "With Finn like this, it's like I suddenly know all the stuff I want to tell him—need to tell him. I never thought . . . you never think something like this can happen, you know? But here it is. And how long can he last like this? How long can he make it?"

"The Gatorade, the fluids, that was brilliant," Wanda said. "You may have saved him right there. There are probably other things we can do, without drugs, without medicating him. I have a close friend who's a registered nurse. I can trust her. *We* can trust her." She hugged me again. "We're a team now, okay?" I heard her voice tighten. She was hugging me so I wouldn't see her cry. "You, me, Finn, the others. We're a team, just like Dad planned."

I returned the embrace, partly because I thought I was supposed to, but mostly because I never got hugged and it felt insanely good. This, I thought, is what families do. This is what I've missed my whole life. This is what I want more of.

"Sounds good," I whispered.

And then it was time.

* * *

I waited for nightfall to enter the Magic Kingdom. Faces were more difficult to see in the dark, and I didn't want to be seen.

Greg Luowski had escaped Finn's front yard after smashing through the second-story bedroom window and falling to the ground. At the time, it struck us as an impossible feat. I had pushed him hard, possibly injuring him even before he'd landed. Combined with a fall of at least fifteen feet, he should have at least twisted, sprained, or fractured something—if not broken bones. But people in general and grown-ups in particular resist the notion of magic and spells, so I didn't tell Mrs. Whitman the reason Luowski was still able to move after that "freak fall," as she called it. Even a woman, a mother whose son was immersed in a world of black magic, relied more on her training as a physicist than her own experiences.

It was strange, though. Mrs. Whitman had been placed under a horrible spell for the better part of two weeks. She of all people should have believed me. But time is an eraser.

Memories are repressed and bad memories forgotten. Her analysis of Luowski's "freak fall" explained his escape. Enough said.

Once inside the Magic Kingdom, though, I felt otherwise. A million eyes seemed to bore into me from all directions. Among them? Greg Luowski's. I could imagine him following me, the same way he'd clearly tracked Mattie and me. I could sense him lurking. Waiting to pounce. I felt sick to my stomach.

On the ground, I approached the first line of Finn's riddle in reverse, mostly out of sentimentality. I wanted to save my best memory with him for last.

Our time in MK could fill a jar to overflowing

The Keepers had taught Jess and me about codes, riddles, and clues. Wayne had communicated with them in these forms in order to slip a message past the Overtakers. Finn had done the same, and I knew to pay strict attention to his choice of words, and any possible underlying meanings.

Our, could be the Keepers, or Finn and me.

Time could mean something more, like "running out."

In MK was straightforward: in the Magic Kingdom. Which was why I was here.

Could fill a jar might be an expression, or I might be looking for a particular jar that would be significant to anything else mentioned or implied in the message. This was a tricky one.

To overflowing? A water attraction, fountain, and food service all came to mind.

The Keepers had covered every inch of the park over the course of their many battles with the Overtakers. If Finn was talking about the Keepers in the park, I was in trouble; it might take weeks to cover all the spots. But in my heart I believed he meant the two of us. Filling the jar to overflowing was a reference to how we'd grown together as friends. The expression had a touch of romance, too, that gave me chills. He'd anticipated how that might affect me.

I approached each stop—I could think of three in particular—keeping in mind my memories of what had happened there and how the present-day Finn would want me to think about it.

Should I be stuck, it's yours for the knowing.

Finn was stuck in SBS. That needed no translation. *Yours for the knowing* proved more challenging. I wasn't sure if I would know, if I had to figure something out, if whatever I was supposed to know would then reveal something else. I'd keep alert for anything.

I found the Cast Member backstage entrance in Tomorrowland, which accessed that area's trash chute. Wayne had told all of us that Disney didn't cart or carry the trash out of the Magic Kingdom; they sucked it out through negative-pressurized tubes housed in the underground network of tunnels known to Cast Members as the Utilidor. The tube system was accessed through a variety of backstage chutes. The chutes themselves looked like submarine hatches—heavily weighted, hinged lids sitting atop a wide metal tube rising up through concrete in a specially designated trash station.

Here I had held the lid open, allowing Finn to jump *into* the trash system. Had he not been able to attain All Clear and turn himself into a hologram, Maleficent, who'd entered behind, might have killed him. I thought about "time" and how quickly Finn had been sucked out of the park through the trash tubes in matter of minutes. I thought about "time" in terms of his battle with Maleficent, which had pulled Jess back from a deep, dark curse that made her Maleficent's daughter-slave. I searched the area for a clock. I wandered from trash can to trash can, wondering if the "overflowing" reference had to do with trash. I searched for any kind of jar. I came away frustrated, impatient, and angry, having found nothing of significance.

Fresh in my mind's eye, a boy lay in bed, fully dressed, occasionally twitching, only able to drink from a straw. My boy, a boy I'd come to cherish and think about constantly. A boy who mattered to me. So far I seemed incapable of helping him. Defending him was only going to get more difficult; Mr. Whitman's determination to take him to doctors would soon win out. Finn was out of "time" in more ways than he'd probably imagined.

Time was running out for me as well. I'd spent far too much of it searching Tomorrowland. I had to get to the Haunted Mansion before the park closed for the night.

Waiting in line, memories played before my eyes like videos. Hurrying into the attraction with a seventh-grade boy I barely knew, a boy I'd lied to in order to share his company. Working to avoid security Cast Members in pursuit of Finn.

I snapped out of my daydream as the spot on the back of my neck, beneath my hair, began to overheat. A barometer I'd come to trust, it meant danger. Not the kind of warning system involved with decision-making, but an alarm that signaled hostile intent. People or animals or Overtaker *villains* were either in my vicinity or spying on me.

I knew better than to immediately turn to look. As long as whoever, whatever, was out there believed I was oblivious to their presence, they'd be in less of a hurry. Surveillance was an art form. Maybe they wanted to capture or harm me; maybe they were merely curious about what I was doing in the park alone. I suspected I would discover Greg Luowski or the girl with the vivid green eyes back there. I wanted so badly to look that my neck tensed.

The standby line steered us into an interactive area of graves and tombstones, pieces of which moved or reacted to each guest, their tremors enhancing my already excessive paranoia. However, interacting with the set pieces allowed me to finally get a look back at the line.

I nearly screamed.

Two women, both too old for college. One wore a white knit polo shirt. Shirts like those were part of the costume for Cast Members who worked the merchandise shops. The woman next to her, who had dark hair and wore too much makeup, had on a blue T-shirt. I couldn't see more than their heads and shoulders. They struck me as Cast Members or security guards, but I couldn't rule out Overtakers.

Every kind of person might be in a Disney park at any given hour. People of all nationalities, faiths, and levels of income. Yet, somehow, I knew that these two were here looking for me.

Using a tomb as a screen, I moved away from them, advancing forward in line. All the while, I was thinking that the graveyard represented the end of "time," that cremation jars, carrying the ashes of the dead, might be "filled to overflowing." Finn's words haunted me in a place that didn't need any help being creepy; the cemetery reminded me viscerally of Finn's and my efforts to avoid past pursuers.

I made myself unpopular by slipping around families and paired-up guests, excusing myself softly as I went. I didn't need to look back when I heard the distant complaints. My pursuers had lost sight of me and were hurrying, trying to fix the problem. As long as I kept my patience and didn't anger those around me too much, I might achieve my goal—get locked in the Stretching Room without them.

I entered the welcome room. So far, so good. Glancing back, I saw the top of the dark-haired woman's head moving as rudely as I had, cutting the line by pushing her way forward.

The dark-haired head pushed closer. My right leg shook nervously, the way it sometimes did before math tests. Instinctively, I moved toward the doors, which I knew were about to open. As we were admitted, I crossed the octagonal chamber to the panel that would lead to the Doom Buggies.

Our Cast Member host told us to stay away from the walls. The doors closed. I didn't see the security woman. She hadn't made it inside the Stretching Room.

For the first time in several long minutes, I felt myself relax. I enjoyed the voice of the ghost, the puns, and the story-line. But then I screamed the loudest as, in the midst of total darkness, a booming, evil voice called out, "Of course, there's always *my* way!"

The guests looked up. A few let out muffled screams.

The lights came on. Instructions were spoken. The wall panel slid open. The crowd surged forward.

The dark-haired woman stood mere feet away from me. She'd been in the room all along. She'd used the darkness and my distraction to sneak up on me. She reached out . . .

I shoved her back. Other guests complained "Cut it out!" "Stop it!"

My plan had been to take the "chicken door," an emer-gency exit that allowed frightened guests to skip the Doom Buggies, but that door moved just slightly as I was about to push through. It breathed open and closed, alerting me to another door on the same hallway that had just opened. *The gift-shop woman was inside.*

Clearly, their plan was to grab me up in the privacy of the chicken door hallway, away from the prying eyes of curious guests. The dark-haired woman's sole purpose was to scare me into using the exit.

So I didn't. My plan required bold action, luck, and perfect timing—

Which made me think of Finn's message.

"Sorry," I said, barging my way through the crowd, giving no thought to being polite. The line narrowed to single file and funneled into path lines that turned back on themselves. No way I could get stuck in there.

A velvet rope chain blocked off the handicap access. As I jumped the chain, I tried something I'd never tried before. "I'm with the Kingdom Keepers! Don't stop the buggies!" I ran down the moving belt and slipped in unexpectedly on a mother and her son just as the bar was about to lower. I kept my legs over the bar, so I wouldn't be trapped, and held my breath, not yet saying so much as hello, expecting the ride to stop. Expecting to be caught.

The ride did not stop.

"Hi," I said, addressing the mother. "Sorry!" To the boy I asked, "Have you ever heard of the Kingdom Keepers?"

"Are you kidding me!?"

That was an affirmative.

"If you see a woman—blue shirt, dark hair—if you see her, I need you to scream as loud as you can. Will do that?"

The mother objected, horrified by the intrusion. But the boy said, "Be quiet, Mom! This is important." She clucked her tongue, as if shocked by her son's rudeness, but didn't say anything.

It was dark now. We were in a tunnel. I jumped, using

the safety bar as a springboard. Hooking my fingers over the clamshell back of the next Doom Buggy in line, I swung my feet around the side. Two young girls screamed. The nice thing about the Haunted Mansion, I realized with a rush of joy, was that such reactions were expected. People could scream as loud as they liked, and nothing would seem out of the ordinary.

We slid past changing wall art, then entered and passed through the ghost story library. I clambered ahead through two more buggies. A lot more screaming. The ghostly dining room was below. I strained to look for glass jars, knowing how important this scene had been to Finn and Jess. Nothing.

When I heard a young boy's piercing, bloodcurdling scream from behind me, I took it as the signal that my scout had come through: the security Cast Member was close behind.

I saw strobe lights, chandeliers, and the infinity hallway. Leading out of the hallway were doors.

I jumped off. The ride immediately stopped, as if I'd thrown a switch (and of course, I had, by tripping a sensor!). If I'd planned correctly, my attacker would be caught in the library while I fled down the infinity hallway. The first door did not open—a prop. The one immediately across from it, the same. The next . . .

The handle turned.

I stepped inside, pulled it shut behind me, and turned the small nub on the handle.

Locked.

* * *

I was in a world unto itself. The Keepers had shared dozens of hair-raising stories about the backstage areas in Disney World; they'd told me these secret places defied understanding. One in particular, a subterranean catacomb beneath Pirates of the Caribbean, was a place I never wanted to see in person. A place I was no longer welcome.

Faced with oddly positioned doors and a hallway that wandered left and right without logic, I decided I'd entered a haunted house, not the Haunted Mansion. Between the brightly colored doors were floor to ceiling mirrors, which distorted my image into fat, thin, tall, short reflections. Cobwebs clouded the overhead light fixtures, turning the space murky; a line of ants bisected the path before me. This seemed to be the work of whoever had designed Escher's Keep, a place the Keepers had spoken of often. I'd finally seen it for myself. The mirrors reflected parts of the opposite walls.

When a ghoul appeared over my shoulder, I screamed and jumped. The lights flickered on and off. Nearby, someone moaned. I'd seen these effects on the main attraction before, but here they felt far less like special effects and far more *real*.

I touched a doorknob. Cold. I elected not to open that one. Maleficent was constantly cold—and though dead, I wanted no look into her afterlife. I cracked open the next, a royal blue door, and peered through. An empty black space as dark and void of light as if I were buried. I wasn't going in there. A brown-green door inside of which was a flooded floor. I wasn't going in there either.

I tried a door across the hall, unable to look at my stretched visage, which gave me the head and immense eyes of an alien. I was beginning to imagine this hallway as some kind of purgatory, a place the one thousand souls the Haunted Mansion meant to claim had to pass through to be accepted as the final piece of the puzzle. How many people, living or dead, had wandered this hall in search of a "way out"? Was I condemned to try door after door and never escape the mansion's clutches?

Threatened by tears, I closed my eyes, trying to collect myself, but I was too scared to keep them shut. I shuddered. Gooseflesh rippled up my arms. I felt like I might throw up.

Think like a Keeper, I scolded myself. I pushed away the fear—step one. Told myself the moaning girl's voice, the bizarre, ugly images of me in the mirrors—all these were nothing but illusion. I worked feverishly to set aside emotion, clear my head, and focus on the positive.

The security woman had not followed me here. I wanted desperately to take that as a positive, but what if she'd stopped because she'd known where I was headed? The same swirling head and sick stomach sensation overcame me. I fell to my knees along with the wobbly figure-eight-headed Amanda in the mirror.

"Go away!" I shouted at my image. It shouted back at me though a mouth that looked like it belonged on a Halloween pumpkin. Only then did I feel a tickling sensation on the fingers of both my hands; only then did I see the ants swarming over me.

The first bit into my skin. Then the second. I shook my hands. Ants flew off, but some landed in my hair, on my face. Fifteen, twenty stinging bites. My cheek. My right eyelid swelled. My vision blurred.

This wasn't purgatory. This was where the attraction claimed its victims. The ants would blind me, swell my tongue and lips. Then who knew what they'd do, what the haunted house would send? Rats? Feral cats? Snakes?

Water! The ants would not survive water. Crawling on hands and knees, seeing out of only one eye, swatting desperately, brushing the ants off, pinching my lips shut tightly so they wouldn't get inside, I made my way to the brown-green door. I reached up, turned the knob, and rolled inside. Thankfully, the water turned out to be only inches deep. Facedown, I squirmed like an alligator. I felt the ants fall off, felt the stinging subside. It was as if—was it possible?—the water was some kind of solvent for the bites.

As I rolled and sat up, splashing water all over me and rubbing my arms and my face, the swelling lessened, the pain vanished. The door had swung closed shutting out all light. I did not want to go back out there with the ants.

I did not like the dark. Never had. In Barracks 14, one of the tests they'd put us through involved subjecting us to total darkness. They placed me in a pitch-black room and told me I'd be there for two hours, or until I found the way out. I was there seven minutes. I *pushed* in four directions. The last push threw open a trapdoor in the floor, and I climbed down and out. They'd tricked me into using my "gift," something I'd resisted doing. I wasn't the only one.

Poor Jess couldn't use her gift in a place like that. She stayed in the dark for the full duration. I'm not sure she was ever the same after that.

Of course, a solution for one problem is not always right for another, similar problem. But try convincing the human brain of that. Recalling my experience at Barracks 14, reliving the sense of panic the dark room instilled in me, I turned *away* from the hallway door, and I *pushed*.

That insight about one solution not fitting all problems revisited me a little late. I'd acted on instinct before allowing my brain had time to catch up, something the Keepers always listed as a rule not to violate. *Don't let your emotions dictate your actions.* But panic owned me.

I heard an unfamiliar and unwanted sound. I couldn't identify it because it was foreign to me. The unfamiliarity spiked adrenaline in my limbs and the center of my chest—it was a threatening sound. It was bad. It was coming at me.

It was water.

My *push* had unleashed a wave, apparently driving all the water away from me to where it struck an obstacle—a wall—and came crashing back. I was lifted off my feet. Thrown into a slow motion backflip, water roiling over me, I mistakenly released air through my nose. Simultaneously, I spit out water and clamped my lips tight, swimming frantically up—or at least I hoped it was up.

As it passed, the wave dropped out from under me and slammed me onto my hands and knees on a rubbery, slimy floor. I gasped for breath, coughing.

Then it hit me from behind, tumbling me forward into an unexpected somersault and threatening to drown me once more. My toes hit the rubber; I got my feet under me and leaped. My head broke the surface; I sucked in air. The wave passed, throwing me to the floor again, this time onto my back, knocking the wind out of me.

Now I knew the pattern. I rolled and turned headfirst into the expected wave. It came. In a diving position, I glided through and settled back onto the slime, as though I was body-surfing. With each pass, the force of the wave lessened until it was just sloshing, like when you move back and forth in the bathtub too fast. The rubber floor was certainly not hiding a trapdoor, and searching the walls, I found nothing to give me hope. At last, I ventured meekly back out into the horror hallway. The ants were gone, but that was hardly reassuring.

Fourth door to the right: a graveyard. My first instinct: slam the door shut. But this gave way to eager curiosity. Near the end of the ride, a living graveyard presented some chills and scares. I had to test whether these graveyards were one and the same. If true, I'd just found my way out.

Venturing into the gray space, I took a moment to identify my door. It was disguised as a panel on the side of a large tomb, and fit perfectly with the set. I didn't dare pull it shut until I could figure out how to open it from this side. Carefully, I located its latch, an angel's wing.

Surrounded by tombstones, ghouls, and statues of the dead, I tiptoed quietly, keeping my head low, afraid I might come into view of the Doom Buggies.

All I wanted was out. Away from this place.

When I spotted the red eyes of the raven above the door to the hitchhiking ghosts' room, it signaled the end. I practically let out a shriek of relief! The problem now was that by trying to get *to* the Doom Buggies, I would inadvertently trip the emergency stop again. I needed another way out. If I stopped the ride for a second time, I'd certainly be caught and captured.

The answer lay below me: a red, glowing exit sign angled so that the guests could not see it. I lowered myself to hands and knees and scrambled from tombstone to tombstone. The exit led to the hallway accessed by the chicken door, which I recognized immediately. Cracking it open, I waited. And waited. Finally, a mother and her two crying sons came down the hall. I slipped through and followed them outside, head down.

Only one location left to check: the place Finn where had won my heart for good.

* * *

The raft ride to Tom Sawyer Island passed peacefully. The only thing I found disturbing was the awful mixture of smells—

suntan lotion, turkey legs, and popcorn. Once on the island, my chest ached from the pains of memory. Walking slowly toward the fort, crossing the rope bridge, reliving the powerful feeling of *friendship* that had only grown stronger with time. I missed Finn. And I was tired of the word "friend"; it felt so limiting to me now. Ours was more a bond of innocence mixed with commitment. A tad Taylor Swift's "Love Story," a bit Olaf-and-the-fireplace. In the absence of that connection, I felt like I was walking to a funeral.

Maybe it was a holdover from the mansion.

Given the earlier pursuit, I remained on high alert. I couldn't let my emotions take me out of the present moment. But so many images were flooding me that I might as well have been Jess. Going off the path, I moved inexorably forward, like a toy pulled by a string. This place was where Finn had kissed me for the first time. Just a peck, but a real kiss, too. Something he'd meant to stay with me. It had.

The tree near where we'd been standing had grown, or I had shrunk, but things were different, a condition I found unsettling. My right knee locked, sending intense pain shooting through me. I shook it loose. I could see him. I could hear him. Did I dare admit, I could feel him?

I studied the open tunnel entrance that led into the fort. I considered the tree for a second time. I submerged myself in a roiling tsunami of loss and expectation, of regret and encouragement. I'd either lost Finn completely, or I was about to find him. I'd exhausted every possible location for "our time in MK," and found no jar to fill. Nothing was mine for the knowing.

"Finn," I moaned softly.

Then I saw it.

JESS

Even from inside the small, climate-controlled Kissimmee air terminal that housed private planes, I could feel the Florida heat coming through the windows. I sat with Joe and the two Imagineers who'd been on the plane with us in an empty corner of the luxury lounge, awaiting the driver who'd take us to Walt Disney World.

Joe seemed increasingly impatient. He and the Imagineers were engaged in hushed conversation. I was definitely unwanted, but being the outsider I was used to that.

Apparently invisible, I set my backpack, my only luggage, on my lap and pulled out my phone. I mindlessly scrolled through Tumblr, pretending to be distracted while I strained to hear their conversation. They were obviously working on some kind of project they didn't want me to know about. That only made me want to know about it more.

Joe turned to me suddenly. "Want something to drink, Jessica? Why don't you go get something to drink?"

"I'm good," I said, returning to my phone, feigning disinterest.

"For me then. How about an orange soda?" Joe checked

with the others. They declined. He handed me some money. "There's a vending machine over there." He pointed to the far end of the building.

I could take a hint, though I snarled involuntarily. I headed for the far wall.

As a confidante of the Keepers, I knew things that likely qualified as Disney company secrets. I'd agreed to keep all such information confidential when I'd been admitted into Imagineering school. If I violated that agreement, they'd expel me. So their secrecy didn't make a lot of sense to me. Not unless it was super secret. That possibility left me all the more curious.

Returning from the vending machine, I took the long way around, approaching Joe and the others from the opposite side, keeping my head down while trying to eavesdrop. One of the men with Joe was speaking. "The DNA came back as reptilian, possibly prehistor—"

Joe interrupted, cutting him off. "Hey Jessica, find it for me?" He must have had eyes in the back of his head.

I handed him the orange soda.

Joe shifted on his feet. He and the others looked seriously uncomfortable. "We were just talking about . . . what's next. We suggest you contact Amanda and arrange for me to meet with her."

Keeping secrets was one thing. It was understandable on many levels. Outright lies cut me to the core. The Keepers, Amanda, and I had done so much to help the Kingdom. Being lied to was almost too much to take.

Almost.

"Ah, of course. Sure thing," I pursed my lips and offered a tight smile. The resulting silence was awkward, and was only broken by the arrival of the black SUV.

The car ride into the parks thrilled me. I had so many memories here—most wonderful, some scary. Disney World was so much more than an amusement park. It was a kingdom. A place where my life had started over in so many ways. A place I'd made real friends. Friends that were real keepers. I giggled to myself, excited as we passed beneath the welcoming sign that spanned the road.

Home.

When the car turned into the entrance to the Grand Floridian, I practically squealed aloud. What a place. All white antebellum-Victorian architecture. A carriage out front. We'd passed the Wedding Pavilion on the way.

"We've got to pick up the Magic Bands from the front desk. You can wait in the front lobby with Bob," Joe said.

Stepping through the doors overwhelmed me. An open atrium reached five stories up; gingerbread trim and delicate railings lined the balconies. Across the enormous room, a live band played. High above, two chandeliers hung from the ceiling; higher still were a set of domed stained-glass skylights. Palm fronds dotted the lobby floor, interspersed with chairs and couches. It was to one of those couches that Joe walked me, hand on my shoulder, apparently feeling obligated to ensure that I made it safely.

"I'll be right back," he said.

I resented being treated like a five-year-old. I nodded, but with difficulty. Something wasn't right. Joe's patronizing tone and actions were an affront to me.

He caught the eyes of the VIP receptionist accompanying us. His look said *Watch her.*

I shuddered.

Joe joined the two Imagineers at the front desk. Turning to the VIP hostess, I put on my best innocent-teenager face and asked for the nearest restroom. The receptionist pointed away from Joe and the others.

I excused myself.

The lobby's design worked in my favor. In front of the door to the ladies' room, I was shielded from view by a giant decorative birdcage. I stopped for only a second to pull a sweatshirt from my backpack, slipping it on and pulling up the hood in spite of the heat. Then I power-walked, keeping my head down. Seconds later, out the back door of the lobby, I broke into a run, past the pool, past Narcoossee's restaurant, down to the dock from which water ferries shuttled guests across the lagoon to the Magic Kingdom.

"You just barely made it," the captain of the ferry said, smiling as she closed the rail gate behind me.

"Thanks for waiting!"

I took a seat in the back of the small boat. It pulled away, leaving Joe and his secrets behind.

AMANDA

Strapped neatly around an upper branch of the tree outside Fort Langhorn was Finn's wristwatch.

I climbed up, eager to confirm it was his. I knew everything about it, down to the black band's rough outer edge, worn away from constant use. I fought the tightness in my throat; swallowed back my fears for Finn and shoved away the self-pity.

I saw a heart carved into the tree. It was a deep old scar left long ago. Framed within the heart were the initials: *F + A*. My heart did a somersault. How had Finn found this spot where two lovers carved their initials twenty, thirty, forty years ago? I wondered if discovering the carving had spurred him to kiss me for the first time here, near this tree. Finn knew so much about the parks, though he had been aided by Wayne's mentoring. How incredible to have found such a spot. The carved heart matched the paper one he'd left in his pocket for me. Finn planned everything, dreamed everything, believed everything. I missed him now more than ever.

Our time, he had written, and he'd hidden his wristwatch on a tree limb in an area of the park only I would know to search. Finn was acting more like Wayne than ever. I dropped back to the dirt with a thump and tried to work out whatever message he'd intended for me.

Time. A tree. A fort. A kiss. Again, my heart felt like it was riding the Rock 'n' Roller Coaster. I struggled against the thought that Finn was trying to say good-bye, was trying to leave a message, a reminder of our best times. Please, no!

A jar to overflowing . . .

Time. A watch. A tree. A fort. A kiss. A jar.

A kiss. A fort. A tree. A watch. A jar.

A watch.

A jar.

Maybe it was desperation. Maybe Finn and I had a connection that transcended time and trees and the fort. But standing there, staring at the tree, trying to make sense of it all, I took Finn's watch as a landmark. He'd wanted me to find it, of course. I knew that much. It meant something. It marked something.

I climbed back up to the branch and felt around for any carving, for a note, for anything I might have missed. Nothing. On the ground, I inspected the watch. The only thing wrong was that the day of the week on the face was incorrect. It read Monday, which wasn't the kind of mistake Finn would make. It might have been intentional, but I didn't see how or why.

About to give up, I stepped closer to the tree and studied the precise spot at which the watch had been strapped to the limb. I couldn't see well in the dark, but I was hoping for something I might have missed. An arrow? Initials?

My eyes drew a line down the trunk, past another branch, farther down to the soil at the base of the tree. Maybe the dark helped, or maybe it was Finn's work, but I suddenly saw that the dirt at the base of the tree was different colors. In the soil, I made out four shoe prints. Four.

The dark disturbance in the soil had nothing to do with me.

I dropped to my knees and started to dig, throwing soil and wood chips to either side. My fingers traced a circle of soft soil about as wide as a Frisbee. The rest of the dirt, compacted and hard, gave up nothing, but the softer circle yielded to my quickening scoops. The hole had been dug with a trowel or shovel, its interior edges sculpted vertically. The soil was damp and smelled like a rich spring garden.

My fingers struck something solid. Not a rock. My heart practically stopped. Finn. The watch. Buried treasure. It drummed under my touch, and I knew at once it was a plastic lid. Something inside me, deep inside, understood the significance of the find, the secrecy of it. I took a moment to look around, to see if anyone was watching. I was alone. It was safe to continue digging.

I worked more methodically, my thoughts struggling to catch up with my actions. Finn had knowingly crossed over into the DHI state, but still, something had provoked him to leave a cryptic message and emotional scavenger hunt intended only for me. I thrilled at the trust this implied even as part of me recoiled at the responsibility. I felt protective, even a little angry. I was a mess.

Literally, a mess—dirt and wood chips covered me. Sighing, I used the dim light of my phone to reveal the hallowed treasure. Protruding from the remaining dirt in the hole was the top of a blue and white soy protein powder container.

New and undamaged, it clearly had not been in the ground long. I took one last look around and pulled it free. I couldn't resist opening it, though my internal voice warned me not to.

Inside were a few small toys, a rubber ball, and a picture I couldn't make out. No note.

I didn't want to spend time here, kneeling in the grass on Tom Sawyer's Island. I returned the lid to the canister, kicked dirt into the hole and stomped it down, then double-checked that I had pocketed Finn's watch. In my heart, I told myself, *When he returns, he's going to want that back.*

In my hand, I carried the item I feared would explain why that might never happen.

* * *

I rode a city bus from the Transportation and Ticket Center to downtown Orlando, and took another bus in the direction of Wanda's apartment. One of its stops came close to the old church. I got off, in part because I was closer to Finn's house, too, though I doubted his parents would appreciate yet another visit—especially one this late. And I got off in part to connect with Mattie and tell her about the can.

A trick for getting in and out of the church attic involved using the side basement entrance to the Alcoholics Anonymous meeting, which was held as late as midnight on some nights. A regular in the program, Joyce, came bounding over to me the moment I entered. We hugged, having not seen one another for a long, long time. As always, she offered me juice and a pastry. I gobbled down both and wiped down the outside of the tall blue can I was carrying.

Then I took the building's middle stairs to the upper reaches and knocked lightly on a door that felt like home. Nothing. I knocked more loudly.

"Mattie? It's me!"

When she failed to answer, I tried to open the door, which could be "locked" from the inside by turning a piece of wood mounted to the jamb. To my surprise, it opened, suggesting Mattie wasn't home. That shattered my plan to examine the can with her, and sent a small shiver of fear darting through me. Where would she be this late?

She didn't own a phone that I knew of. I stood in the dingy apartment, trying to think how or where I'd find her.

"Knock knock!" Joyce was standing at the door.

"Hi."

"Listen, honey," Joyce said, "I came in late tonight to the meeting and . . . well, just now one of the girls saw me with you, and I thought you should know that Mattie was hurt two days ago. There was an ambulance."

"What!?"

"She's okay, I guess. Said she fell and hit her head."

"Police?"

"I don't know, Amanda."

"An ambulance?"

"I'm sure it was just a precaution."

I could barely hear her. My hands shook. I hadn't realized

I was crying until Joyce wrapped me in a hug and told me everything was okay.

"Can I take you somewhere?"

I nodded, my shoulders shaking.

"Mattie'll be fine. You'll see."

I looked at her through blurry eyes. My voice croaked as I said, "I'm not so sure."

DAY 5

AMANDA

Fifteen minutes later, past midnight, I trudged up the outside stairs to Wanda's apartment. I used the key she'd given me, worried I might wake either her or Mattie, if Mattie was actually inside.

I swung the door open slowly—and immediately heard voices. A girl's voice. I hadn't realized how tired I was because to me it sounded like—

"Jess?"

I sprinted across the room and dove on top of her. We hugged and laughed. In that moment, no one else existed. Just Jess. Wonderful Jess. I must have told her a hundred times how much I'd missed her.

When I emerged from my adrenaline rush, I looked up at the smiling faces of Wanda and Mattie.

"Mattie, Mattie," I said, crawling my way across the carpet and past the coffee table to the sofa. We hugged. I asked her if she was all right; to my horror, I learned that Luowski had brutally attacked her and left her unconscious.

I settled into one of the chairs, still overcome with

giddiness at the sight of Jess. I couldn't take my eyes off her. Wanda asked me about the soy protein canister and I laughed, releasing what felt like days' worth of pent-up tension.

"Never mind that! What about Luowski attacking you?" I asked Mattie.

Mattie told me about the horrible visit to the emergency room and the encounter with the Barracks 14er.

"You're sure you're okay?" I said.

"Yes."

"And that he was Barracks 14?"

"Positive," Mattie said. "You'd have recognized him immediately. He used to hang around the guy we called the general. Remember the guy with graying hair?"

"Flat Top?"

"That's him."

"Flat Top is here in Orlando?"

"I was pretty much out. I didn't see him, but I saw him in the thoughts of whoever touched me."

"I should have told you," Jess blurted out.

Whatever she was talking about was clearly news to the others. We all focused on her.

She spoke softly and apologetically. "I had one of my dreams. I didn't sketch all of it; I couldn't sketch. But . . . Mandy, the Barracks 14 people captured you. I think it was you. It felt like you to me."

"Where?" I asked, swallowing hard. I didn't take Jess's dreams lightly.

"Here, I think. That's why Joe let me come along."

"Joe's here?"

Jess nodded.

"And it gets worse, I'm afraid," Wanda said. "Tell her."

Jess's whole body seemed to tighten. "I overheard Joe say something about DNA, about bones. I wasn't supposed to hear it. I'm swearing you to secrecy, too. Only the four of us can ever talk about this."

"No problem," I said. "But why? What's going on?"

"Something's obviously afoot," Wanda said, "and I can promise you: if it's something to do with Finn and the Keepers, if Joe finds out Finn's stuck in SBS—if the others are stuck in SBS, too—I mean, that could be what it's about. Philby wasn't supposed to cross them over. What they're doing has got to be against every rule at this point."

I looked at Wanda, asking a silent question. She faintly shook her head.

"I think we should," I said. "Show them."

"Show us what?" Mattie asked.

I stood, Jess rising with me. Together, we gently helped Mattie off the couch. I picked up the blue can and carried it with me as Wanda led the way.

She opened one of the guest bedroom doors quietly and, when the three of us were poised in the doorway, turned on the light.

Jess and Mattie gasped.

Finn lay comfortably in the bed, fully clothed. Sleeping.

"We have to get the others," Wanda said, "before Joe finds them."

"Or Greg Luowski," said Mattie.

"And we have to figure out this," I said, kneeling on the carpet alongside Finn's bed. I peeled the plastic lid off the treasure I'd unearthed and spilled the contents out onto the floor.

MATTIE

Studying Finn's blue can with Amanda and Jess felt oddly alienating. A photo. Jacks. A glove. All sorts of seemingly unrelated stuff. The experience reminded me that I hadn't been part of so many of their shared adventures. We had our time in the Barracks together, but thankfully, that now felt like another world.

After all I'd learned in the past few days, I hoped we could keep it that way.

It was strange: being alone and by myself actually felt better than being alone with others around. The connection between Jess and Amanda would never be matched. When they were together, there was no way not to feel like a third wheel.

"When you touch this stuff, do you get anything?" It took me a second to realize Amanda was talking to both Jess and me.

I shook my head. "It's only living creatures for me. I'd love to be able to read a deck of cards, but I can't."

"I'm not having any flashes," Jess said. "I've had more of

those lately, but not now. Maybe I'll dream something at some point."

"He left this for you, right?" I asked Amanda.

She nodded. "Pretty sure."

"But it doesn't mean anything?"

"I'm sure it does," she said, "but not to me. I'm not getting it."

"Knowing Finn," Wanda said. "It's something very clever. It won't be any one part, but all the pieces together, just like the Keepers."

"Well," Amanda said, "all the pieces together are a lot of junk."

We all laughed in spite of ourselves.

"Keep trying," Jess said. She grabbed my elbow and pulled me aside as Amanda turned over the items on the floor. "I need your help," she whispered.

"Sure. If I can!" I felt less alone already.

"I need you to read an Imagineer. He's the guy who flew me out here, the guy who started the DHIs. There's something off about him. I need to know if he's still on our side."

"Yeah. I mean, I can try." I hesitated, but decided not to tell her that I didn't like to read people unless it was absolutely necessary. Seeing so many private thoughts took its toll. Crawling around inside the heads of others could be frightening.

"I know it's hard, Mattie," Jess said. "It's important, or I wouldn't ask."

I nodded, and we hugged. "Tell me where to find him."

"You can get backstage using my pass. It won't take long."

"Right," I said. "All I need to do is figure out how make physical contact with a complete stranger, an adult who's one of the most important people in Disney."

The last part never came out of my mouth, but it swirled around in my head the following day, when I was on my way to Disney's Hollywood Studios.

DAY 6

MATTIE

I arrived backstage at Disney's Hollywood beneath a tall water tower that had ears. Definitely Disney. Nearby, a trolley drove park visitors around. In and among some warehouse-like buildings were nested a few one-story bungalows. The second of these, according to its sign, was the building Jess had described to me as Imagineer's headquarters.

I wasn't about to go in and face some receptionist who'd just tell me to get lost, so I sat down and waited—for a long time. A few people came and went, but not much happened. I began to grow impatient.

Worse, not far from me, two attractions beckoned: Rock 'n' Roller Coaster and Tower of Terror. I had gotten in for free! I had no desire to waste my entire morning on what seemed like a hopeless mission. Jess wanted me to read Joe and find out what he knew about Barracks 14. Even the mention of our former prison stirred unease in me. I'd never go back. I couldn't.

"Can I help you?" The man's voice startled me.

"Oh, I, uh . . ." I stammered, turning quickly.

Two men. One of them was Joe Garlington. "I . . . ah . . . well, I was . . . Aren't you Mr. Garlington?"

"Yes? And you are?" Joe studied me. He exuded naturally pleasant curiosity. Not a creep. Not a person hiding something.

"Excited!" I answered.

"Are you one of our inter—?" Joe cut himself off, his eyes on my ID tag. I should have thought to turn it over or hide it after using it to gain entrance. "Would you excuse me a moment, Alex? I'll catch up to you."

The other man nodded to me, patted Joe on the back, and headed toward the building I'd been staking out so poorly.

"That's Jess's ID," he said, his voice lowered.

"I'm Mattie. Mattie Weaver. A friend of hers and Amanda's."

We were about to shake hands, giving me two options: I could keep an open mind and read his surface thoughts, or I could mentally name either the Barracks, the Keepers, or Amanda, and Jess and see what came at me.

The contact would happen fast. I reached out, already naming Jess and Amanda.

As he took my hand in his, Joe stood up a little straighter. I should have guessed a person with so much creativity would be a Reacher. They're as rare as four-leaf clovers—the handful of people who can use the door I open between us to read me. Thankfully, most Reachers don't know what they possess. For them, it must be like stepping from the dark of a tunnel into the light; they see, but not clearly.

My reading for Jess and Amanda connected and came back at me in a mass of confusion. Joe's confusion. Like radio wave interference, both of us saw static.

"Do you work here?" Joe asked as he released my hand. He definitely seemed more interested.

I smiled and relaxed my shoulders, attempting to look natural.

"You're a Fairlie," Joe continued, his voice sincere. He returned the smile.

"Yes."

Bombarded with thoughts—his thoughts—as the static lifted, I wondered if he was experiencing mine as well. I didn't know what I was looking for, what exactly Jess was after. But I read concern, sincerity, admiration, curiosity, and determination. All these feelings centered on the girls, but I failed to pinpoint any specific information.

There were pieces of sentences he'd spoken. "Social Services." "Pixar." "Archives." "Fairlies." "Inside Out." "Prehistoric scales." But I also saw images of a dozen different park attractions, including Avatar Land in Animal Kingdom.

With a start, I realized some of the images had to be before-and-after scenes. It was all too jumbled. I couldn't trust the read of a Reacher.

He had an appointment. I was holding him up.

"I don't mean to keep you," I blurted out.

"You're a mind reader!" he said playfully. "As a matter of fact, I do have a meeting to get to."

I swallowed what felt like a golf ball.

"Well, it was nice to meet you," I mumbled. The sooner I got away, the better. If he came to realize he'd read my thoughts, he would sense that I was predatory. I couldn't be sure how someone so important might react to that.

I turned to leave.

"You're right to be concerned," Joe said. Had he read my mind?

"Excuse me?" I couldn't help myself—I looked back at him.

"It's dangerous for you three."

I took off running.

JESS

Park lights glowed through a futuristic landscape. The Carousel of Progress, a time capsule of sorts, one of only a couple of attractions older than the park itself. Something drew me to it, through the queue, and into the theater, a force as unexplainable as a dream—

The realization that I was dreaming woke me up, and I shot bolt upright in bed, drenched in sweat, my heart pounding.

The Orlando weather was going to take some adjustment, I realized. I felt as though I could hardly breathe through the humidity. A year ago I'd been able to run around in this blast furnace without a second thought! Clearly the SoCal weather had spoiled me. If only Wanda had AC.

As it was, the humidity was making it hard to sleep, too; something I didn't appreciate. I'd faced enough sleepless nights in the past week. And now yet another dream, one in which I recognized the attraction. That required investigation.

Three middle-of-the-night bus rides later, I was showing my Disney ID to a toll booth security guard at the back of the Magic Kingdom. He swiped the ID. I was admitted, but I was also in the system now, which couldn't be good.

Walking down Main Street, I felt an overwhelming sense of déjà vu. I had done this exact same thing on the opposite coast. The week of snooping around the parks was wearing on me.

Reaching the Central Plaza, I turned toward Tomorrowland.

Unlike my visit to Disneyland, I reached my destination without incident, something I celebrated as a small victory. Nothing seemed out of place. Slowly, I reached out and touched the oversized cogwheel that displayed the attraction's name.

It hit me hard, flashes behind my eyelids so forceful that I sank to my knees, frightfully aware I was locked in a daydream.

I saw a man, here, on this very spot. The angle of view changed and more men appeared behind him, not one man but three, all eerily similar. Two, dressed in costume. Though barely conscious, I reached and found my sketchbook and pen in my back pocket and I began drawing.

As the vision ended, I slumped against the wall. Yet

another mystery to solve. But one thing was clear; whoever these men were, they were bad news, and they were after the same thing we were.

My first dream of the night had led me here, looking for something that I suspected had to do with Finn's apparent disappearance. If I'd told Amanda about my dream, she'd have wanted to come, to investigate the area. But it would benefit no one if our paths were to cross those of the men I'd seen.

Would Amanda be led here by something other than my dream? I wasn't sure. All I knew was that I needed to keep her away. She was an adult now, like me, and could take care of herself, but after all we'd been through I felt responsible for her well-being.

I studied the sketch in my hand, weighing my options. I didn't fully trust Joe. Actually, I flat-out did *not* trust Joe, and I was sure my flight from the Grand Floridian hadn't exactly earned me brownie points with him, either. The Keepers were MIA; I wasn't ready to explain this to Amanda, who was with Wanda. The man I'd gone to with these kinds of questions for the past six years was dead. I didn't know what was going on, and I needed help.

I needed to think outside the box.

The Box! The nickname of a weekly live video podcast by a Disney connoisseur named . . . Louis? Lucious? Lou! Mongello of WDW Radio.

Lou knew everything about Disney. Perhaps he would know one or more of the faces I'd just dreamed.

To my delight, an Internet search revealed that he would be filming an interview with an Imagineer at Disney's Hollywood Studios in the morning. It felt like a sign.

I took the time to explore the Carousel of Progress, having only my dream to go on. Nothing else surfaced, and I left thirty minutes later feeling defeated.

The park buses had long since stopped running, so I walked to the Contemporary Resort hotel and hopped a Cast Member bus to the Boardwalk. I relaxed enough to enjoy the warm night as I walked toward Disney's Hollywood Studios. I'd gotten a late start, waking up from my dream at three A.M. It was now nearing seven. The sun shone above the horizon, and I knew Lou's filming would start within the hour.

Backstage at Disney's Hollywood Studios, I had no idea of where to go while I waited for the park to open and Lou Mongello to arrive.

The Imagineers worked backstage here. Lou's interview would probably bring him to their offices. Why not?

Eight o'clock. Things picking up.

I passed a group of women in professional clothing, not costumes, with the Sorcerer Mickey name tags worn by the Imagineers. I was in the right place. Not wanting to draw attention to myself, I let them pass and stopped the next costumed Cast Member to ask for directions.

As I walked backstage, I spotted Joe's name on an office door. I had time, and I wanted answers. While I was not about to march into his office and ask him what was going on, I wasn't above a few minutes of basic surveillance.

I stood off in the corner, watching Joe's door.

A man in a suit knocked. The door opened. He and Joe stood outside the office, talking in hushed tones. I moved to get a closer look—and caught sight of the tie worn by Joe's guest.

I nearly fainted. I knew the pattern on the man's tie. Knew it only too well.

The only time I'd ever seen it, I'd been in Barracks 14.

With no idea where I was going, I ran, Lou Mongello long forgotten. The park was open now, and I entered through a door at the end of Streets of America. I pushed my way through groups of guests, mumbling apologies over my shoulder. Frantic, I looked for an escape. Gasping, I slipped into Writer's Stop, a small store on the corner, and sat down on a couch in the back, shielded from the windows by a long line of caffeine-deprived parents.

No one gave a second glance to a girl who looked like she was in desperate need of coffee. And I did my best to stay composed on the outside. Cheery, groggy, just another girl waiting for a friend at an hour far too early for a teen to be up anywhere except Disney.

Inside, my world was falling apart. I tried desperately to explain away what I had just seen. The signs were all there, but I didn't want to admit it. There had to be some reason, I told myself, but inside, I was screaming. Was Joe in league with Barracks 14? Had I put us all in danger by going to him and believing him when he offered help? I felt betrayed, but worse, I felt stupid. I had learned over and over not to trust anyone but myself. First with my parents, then with the Barracks and Maleficent. Only Amanda had earned my trust, in the same way I'd earned hers. With the Keepers and the Imagineers, I had felt too secure. I had let my guard down. I'd started trusting again.

Look where that had gotten me. Amanda and I were trying to help the Keepers, but it suddenly seemed that Joe had other plans for us. Plans he wasn't willing to share.

DAY 7

AMANDA

So there we were on Wanda's living room floor arguing if the Imagineers would possibly try to lure us into being captured by the Barracks 14ers.

"It just doesn't make sense, Jess," I said. "Joe has worked so hard to keep them away from us."

"This guy was meeting with Joe. I saw him."

Mattie stayed quiet.

Wanda said, "I know people who know people. Let me chase this one down."

"Sounds good to me," I said, not needing anything extra to worry about.

Eyeing the odd and irreconcilable contents of a blue soy protein powder can between us, I once again felt angry at Finn for making his secret message so difficult to decode.

"Let's try this. What do you see, Amanda?" Wanda asked, sounding like a teacher in science lab.

I studied the stuff carefully. "A very old black-and-white photo of a big crowd either in Disneyland or Disney World. It's slightly blurry—only slightly—and, I think could have been shot with a phone camera given the shape. In the corner, there's some kind of weird moon shape. It might be the reflection of a piece of a face. The person taking the photo? Hard to see."

"What else?"

"One white glove," I said, turning it over in my hand. "A hard, black rubber ball. A bag of some metal jacks and a smaller red rubber ball." I picked up the small metal rectangle, the top third of which hinged open. "I've never seen one of these, whatever it is." I picked up the one item specifically intended for me. "And an empty envelope with my name on it, but no note inside."

MATTIE

While Amanda described the objects, I had an idea. I picked up the rubber ball off the floor and squeezed my eyes shut. I knew better, though: I could only read things that lived and breathed. Only darkness and disappointment. I kept trying with the next closest item, a white glove. Again, zilch.

Reading living things had become second nature to me. All it took was a touch. My inability to contribute to the group's efforts now frustrated me.

I was interrupted out of my daze when Wanda called my name.

"Mattie, what do you see?" she prompted.

"I've tried reading a bunch of this stuff," I said. "But it's no use. It has to be living and breathing."

"Any ideas?" Jess was trying hard to include me. I loved her for it.

"Well, I guess a white glove could have been used for any-thing—cold weather, part of a staff uniform, fashion. No dirty work. And the ball is obviously a toy. I've seen sports balls—squash, I think—pretty much like it, but they hardly bounce. This thing is insane the way it bounces. Then there's the game of jacks, but that's pretty obvious." I looked at Wanda, who nodded for me to continue. "The photo . . . People take pictures, keep pictures, to remember things, and this one's old, so someone wanted to remember something from a long time ago. Something in one of the parks. The cigarette lighter. I've seen them in movies. Never up close. It's interesting."

No one spoke, so I continued. "It's not like I can see any hidden meanings. They're just a bunch of random objects in a can. Right? The only items that have any real significance—at least to me—are the empty envelope and the photo. But you guys are the Wayne experts, not me."

"Excellent!" Wanda said. "That's terrific input."

"Really?" The word escaped my mouth, though I hadn't meant to speak it. Just minutes earlier, I'd felt like such a dud.

"Hugely helpful," she said.

JESS

The four of us sat on Wanda's living room floor, the contents of the mysterious blue can between us. We all agreed that Finn had left this for us to find. Somehow it conveyed a message that we had yet to figure out.

Wanda asked each of us to describe the objects in turn. Each of us brought our own interpretations to the table. Amanda described the objects' physical appearance, whereas Mattie, after lamenting that she couldn't "read" them as she could people, talked about their practical uses.

Wanda turned to me. "Thoughts, Jess?"

I took in the assortment in front of me, picking up the red rubber ball and metal jacks before speaking, "An old-fashioned kid's game. Make that two games; I forgot about the other ball." I examined the black ball, cracked and hardened with age. "Seems sort of sad that they ended up in here. With no one to play with them." I set both aside. "A cigarette lighter? Grown-ups smoke, not kids. Maybe that's part of it? It looks like it used to be a pretty purple color." I held up the metal rectangle, set it down again, unsure. "A white glove like they used to wear to dances, and the envelope with Amanda's name on it. How romantic."

I smiled at Amanda and reached for the last item in the pile, a vintage Disney photo. In touching it, a barrage of images flashed before my eyes: faces, laughter, bright sunlight, the smell of popcorn. Just as suddenly, the images were gone. My vision was so scrambled that I didn't know what to make of it.

"What just happened?" Amanda asked. She knew me too well.

"I think for an instant there I was in this photo. I smelled popcorn, heard laughter. Nothing specific."

"Draw! Right now!" Amanda said.

Taking a deep breath, I pulled my sketchbook from my backpack. "Look," I said, flipping pages, "I didn't tell you guys about this particular dream before, because I wanted to be certain it wasn't just fantasy."

I handed them my book, turned to a sketch of a small campfire. It was a "left over"—a dream I'd drawn and had never trusted. Now, for whatever reason, I thought it probably meant something.

"Those don't exactly look like logs," Mattie said.

"Bones," Wanda said, studying the page. "They look like bones to me. Did you know that for thousands of years, cultures around the world burned bones in rituals?"

"Rituals," I muttered, recalling more pieces of my dream now, "as in rubbing the bones together and kissing them before you burn them?"

Three blank faces stared at me.

"Pass me back my sketchbook, please. I don't want to lose what I'm seeing."

AMANDA

The empty note frustrated me. Jess's sketch of burning bones scared me. I felt completely unsettled. Though tempted to whine about it, I got up and walked around the small room, trying to calm myself down.

"Do you think someone took the note?" I asked.

"No," Jess said. "If someone else found the can, they would have thrown it out or kept it for themselves. They wouldn't steal only the note."

"We don't know that for sure," Mattie said, "but I do think that makes sense."

I wanted to tell them about the heart and the initials carved into the tree, about how Finn had managed to find some old lovers' symbol and had chosen that place to leave his watch. The romance of it cut me through me. Everything he did for me seemed to be unspoken statements and promises. They filled me with such happiness I could hardly think; I would nearly laugh aloud—at nothing.

Now that same rush of giddiness translated to something darker. The missing note tortured me. I wanted to read whatever it was he'd written.

"Maybe he had second thoughts," I said aloud. "Maybe he wrote an explanation, or even another set of clues, but thought they gave too much away. So at the last minute he took the note out. I'm not sure why he would leave the envelope, but he did."

"He was going to mail it," Mattie said. "He had it stamped and ready."

"Okay," Jess said. "Maybe the note was supposed to make sure you found the can, but in the end he didn't think mailing you something was safe, so he was counting on you to figure it out without the hint."

"I like that explanation," Wanda said. "That's something to consider." She hesitated and then spoke quietly, intimately.

"Amanda, how much—if any—of this stuff means something to you and Finn? In other words, is it personal, or is it as strange to you as it is to us?"

"I don't understand any of it," I confessed. "Toys, a glove, a cigarette lighter. As if any of us smoke! I mean, come on! What's with that?"

"Fire?" Jess said, her voice quavering.

Jess had dreamed of fire once before, and the results had been catastrophic—Disneyland in flames.

"At worst, he means to set toys on fire. Nothing to worry about. What we're missing is the larger message," said the daughter of Wayne, a man who always saw the bigger picture. "There's something here. He's gone to too much trouble."

"One thing," I said. "Finn thought they might end up in SBS. Why else leave the note in his pocket, the can on Tom Sawyer Island? He went to tons of trouble to pull this off. That means it's important. But how do all five of them end up in SBS? Let's not forget: Maybeck and Philby were both captured and ended up in SBS. Would Philby risk crossing them all over at the same time on anything less than something super important? But clearly Finn knew they were taking a risk. He prepared for that!"

"So, for now, we'll assume they're on a dangerous mission," Wanda said.

"Which would explain why Joe is freaking out," Mattie said. "He sends them off and no one comes back."

"You think the mission had anything to do with DNA and

the prehistoric bones I heard Joe and the Imagineers talking about at the airport?" Jess asked.

"We aren't officially part of the Keepers or the DHI program," I said. "He can't share stuff with us." I felt chills and a little bit nauseated, like I might throw up.

"Sadly," Wanda said, "this is beginning to make some kind of sense."

"But it doesn't exactly explain the clues he left," Jess said. "Obviously, Finn wants—needs—our help, but we've got to figure out what these things mean, or how can we help him."

Mattie said, "Luowski has plans for Finn, maybe all of the Keepers."

"We stopped him once," I said, "but honestly, some of that was luck. I'm not sure we'll stop him a second time."

Jess, Mattie, and I all looked to Wanda at once, as if she might hold the magical answer.

"I'm thinking," she said.

MATTIE

Wanda was in the middle of explaining the history of the Imagineers when a sharp knock on the door startled all of us. Instinctively, my head whipped around to see who was there, but unfortunately my powers didn't involve X-ray vision. I glanced at an openmouthed Jess and wide-eyed Amanda. They had no clue who it could be. I turned to Wanda, but by the look of it, she was as surprised as we were.

Wanda held a finger to her lips and crept over to the door like a spy. She trained an eye on the peephole, while Amanda and Jess held hands tightly. Yes, it was selfish of me to be jealous at a time like this, but I couldn't help but feel like an outsider. As I tried to push the thought back, I felt Amanda's hand brush on my shoulder. I understood why she would avoid touching anything but my gloved hand—I was still getting used to such alienation.

Before I could dwell further on my personal stuff, Wanda turned back to face the three of us and shrugged. I couldn't decide what was worse: to have someone we knew show up, or someone we didn't. Wanda beckoned Amanda forward.

Another knock at the door, this time more impatient.

Amanda's eye went to the peephole. An instant later, she swiveled to face Jess and me, her face white.

"It's Mrs. Nash!" she hissed.

The name sounded vaguely familiar, but wasn't one I could match a face to.

Jess tensed. "You're kidding me," she whispered.

"I wish," Amanda said.

"Mattie and I can handle this," Wanda said, "Right, Mattie?"

She flashed me a knowing look. She wanted me to read Mrs. Nash. It was nothing new. I simply nodded, slipping off my gloves behind my back.

Amanda and Jess made themselves scarce, disappearing down the hall toward the room where Finn lay, so still, on the bed. Before I could prep myself mentally, Wanda opened the door. A short, jowly woman with accusing eyes entered without invitation. She introduced herself to Wanda, ignoring me.

"A little birdie told me that Amanda was in town," Mrs. Nash said, getting straight to the point. How she'd connected Wanda and Amanda, I had no clue. "One of my girls saw her at the park. You wouldn't happen to know where she is, hmm?"

"I'm sorry, but she hasn't come to see me," Wanda said, and shrugged. "I wish she had told me she was in town."

"Well, I wanted to check in on her. I just miss her so."

Something about Mrs. Nash's tone was off. I could tell she didn't care about Amanda, but then why had she come looking, and for what? Shifting from foot to foot, I waited for Mrs. Nash to acknowledge my existence. But she didn't so much as glance my way.

"Hi, Mrs. Nash, nice to meet you," I finally interjected. "I'm . . . Ma—Matilda, Wanda's niece."

I offered my bare hand, but she didn't return the greeting, preventing me from stealing a read. Her eyes scanned me; she looked unimpressed. What a confidence booster.

"Nice to meet you," Mrs. Nash said with clearly practiced indifference.

The image of the Barracks 14 man from the hospital flashed through my mind. I suppressed a shudder and pushed it away, struggling to figure out the reason behind Mrs. Nash's sudden interest in Amanda.

Mrs. Nash spoke with her hands, gesticulating wildly as she talked to Wanda. I saw a window of opportunity and jumped in. "Oh wow! What an absolutely gorgeous ring!" I forced my tone to be more bubbly than usual. "Can I see?"

Without waiting for a response, I snatched her hand and tried to look as if I was admiring her ring. She clearly didn't appreciate the contact, but it was too late for her to take her hand back without appearing rude.

Images flashed through my mind. I felt dizzy. I let go of Mrs. Nash's hand and smiled weakly.

"Well? Do you like it?" she asked. "It was my great-aunt Mildred's."

My throat constricted. Suddenly there wasn't enough air in the room. "Very nice," I choked out, nearly stumbling back toward the sofa.

Wanda concluded the conversation with Mrs. Nash as quickly as possible. A minute later, she was out the door.

"Did you read her?" Wanda asked.

I nodded, still struggling to catch my breath.

"Amanda! Jess!" Wanda had charged down the hall.

I slowed and controlled my breathing. By the time Wanda returned with Jess and Amanda in tow, I was back to normal—if it's normal to be so scared you're shaking.

"It's worse than we thought," I choked out.

"Worse how?" Amanda said.

"The Barracks 14 guys offered Mrs. Nash a reward for information leading to your capture."

We all looked at Wanda, as if she might have advice. She was as paralyzed as the rest of us.

"That woman will betray anyone for five dollars," Jess said. "We're in trouble."

Wanda searched each of our faces and sighed.

"You'll all have to be more careful coming and going," Wanda said. "We have to assume someone's watching my apartment."

"Great. Just great," I groaned.

"Mattie, I hate to ask more of you, but I'm going to."

The people at Barracks 14 had said this same thing to me any number of times. A power like mine proved too tempting to others. Ironic, since I'd have given anything to be rid of it.

"Sure," I said.

Wanda said, "I think it's time we find out how much some of Dad's old friends know about this. And you're just the person to ask."

AMANDA

Mattie's reading of Luowski had suggested an attack on each of the Keepers on the same night: this night. There was no time to lose. After lunch we Fairlies separated, breaking off on various missions.

I was with Wanda. Together, we sought to move Philby, Maybeck, and Willa to one defensible location: Wayne's fishing cabin, nestled in the trees by the lake on the golf course side of Bonnet Creek, adjacent to Fort Wilderness.

Though I had yet to see the place, Wanda assured us it was the perfect spot, complete with a motorboat for a water escape if necessary—though I saw no way we were going to lug four comatose teenagers onto one small boat. But Wanda's apartment offered too easy a target. So, the decision was made and we took off to rescue Maybeck.

Bess, Maybeck's aunt, met us at the back door of her pottery shop, Crazy Glaze. A round woman with expressive eyes and the kind of smile that melted whomever she faced, Bess (we called her Jelly) looked deeply troubled. The countenance didn't sit well on her. Wearing an apron splattered with dried clay over a colorful but faded skirt, a Tiger Woods golf cap, and a pair of clay-speckled reading glasses around her neck, she welcomed us into her kitchen.

The pantry, its crowded shelves stacked full of clay projects in various states of completion, gave way to the shop on the street side. The kitchen served as overflow for the projects, the counters collecting more art than food. The stove was old, the butcher-block island bowed with age, the entire space neat and tidy as a pin. Two old suitcases stood at the ready by the back door.

"I've spoken with Finn's mother," Bess said. Her low, warm voice made me feel safer already. "From your phone call, and I thank you for that, I understand what it is you propose to do." She focused her full attention on Wanda, her concern like a spotlight. "I want the best for Terry, of course, but you're asking me to turn over my nephew to you, and I hope you'll excuse me, but I hardly know you."

"They're coming," I said. The two women looked at me as if I'd appeared in the room out of nowhere.

"So you say," Bess said.

"Luowski said so," I corrected, "not me. You remember the last time?"

Bess nodded. It hadn't gone well. She'd been knocked unconscious with a Taser.

"I'm not going to argue with any of you. You must know I appreciate your concern and your thoughtfulness, and I know this isn't easy for any of us. But what I wanted to ask, what I hoped, is that I might close down the shop and go with you. I'd like to care for Terry. The others, too. It's just . . . I can't leave him like this; I can't turn him over to someone else in his condition. Not again. I'm afraid my prayers won't be heard if I abandon him."

I felt a lump in my throat. Wanda looked as if she might cry, too. She stepped forward, and the two women hugged. I thought I heard Bess crying; her shoulders shook. The feelings Bess had expressed were foreign to me; I'd never felt that for anyone but Jess. Growing up alone had been a kind of death sentence for my emotions. I'd learned not to have them, not to go there. Only now, watching two grown women fall apart for a moment in each other's arms, did I ache for them.

Closing my eyes, I tried to come to grips with whatever it was Bess and Wanda were feeling. I stretched and pushed myself to feel with them, but the lump went away and I felt only self-pity, deep sadness over never having experienced what they felt now.

Wanda opened her arms and Bess stepped into them. "Of course," Wanda said. "Believe me, we need all the help we can get."

Bess politely shooed away her three remaining customers and put up the CLOSED sign in the window.

The next challenge was how to move Maybeck, at nearly two hundred pounds and six feet tall, from the second floor to a vehicle. Bess arrived at the solution without a second thought; she'd seen part of the technique at a Boy Scout jamboree in which Maybeck had participated.

Maybeck, a former Boy Scout! A smile crossed my face. Philby and Finn would treasure the chance to use this ammunition against their sarcastic friend.

It turns out a ceramics artist has many useful materials lying about. We used the *Boy Scout Handbook*, two lengths of lumber, and a heavy blanket to fashion a stretcher, which we set down on the floor alongside Maybeck's bed. As Bess gently pulled back the covers, my breath caught.

"It's all right," Bess said, misunderstanding my reaction. "I feel that same way every time I see him like this."

Maybeck hadn't dressed himself in all black—a favorite of the Keepers when they were crossing over into DHI. Nor had he donned his typical street clothes: carefully pressed blue jeans, a tight-fitting T-shirt that showed off his sculpted muscles, and his trademark LeBrons. Instead, he looked like a fashion model for the sort of retro clothing sold at a thrift store. I wouldn't have guessed clothes could make a boy look so totally different, but for a moment, I barely recognized him.

With Bess looking at me, I searched for an appropriate response. "It's . . . different to see him so still. Strange."

"Yes, well, hopefully not for much longer," Bess said. "You take his feet, Amanda. I'll hold his head and shoulders. Wanda, from the side. On three." She counted down.

The improvised stretcher worked well. A piece of corrugated cardboard and some patience helped us slide Maybeck down the stairs; a dolly got him from the house to a twenty-three-year-old powder-blue pickup truck with the Crazy Glaze logo on both doors and across the tailgate. The back of the truck was fitted with a shell to protect the truck bed from weather. In our case, it hid a comatose Maybeck from wind and prying eyes.

Wanda left her car at the ceramics shop and, together, we decided to collect Willa and Philby before heading to the fishing cabin. The remote cabin's existence was known to only a few, Wanda said, and to access the retreat, one had to walk five holes of the golf course or ride in Wayne's private golf Pargo, which had a flatbed on the back. We couldn't very well attempt to transport a bunch of kids in comas into the cart at the golf clubhouse, so we'd need to figure out another way. For now, collecting and protecting all the Keepers from Luowski was enough.

MATTIE

Even with Jess keeping an eye on me in case I needed backup, I felt nervous as we arrived at Disney's Hollywood Studios.

I could handle stealth. I'd been hiding from people for months. Hiding was my comfort zone, and my plan to meet with the Imagineers face to face was as far from that as I could get.

But as I arrived backstage, my skin was crawling.

If I played it right, my plan would only require me to innocently shake hands with complete strangers. Awkward! For one thing, the more sensitive people would likely know something strange had happened. They wouldn't know what, exactly; they'd probably think they'd lost something, or maybe missed something I'd said when I hadn't spoken. And if I connected with a Reacher, I'd be in serious trouble. I remained on edge.

Using Wanda's lifetime All Ears Card, given to her by her Disney Legend father, I accessed the backstage area at Disney's Hollywood Studios and took up a spot outside the WDI offices. At first, I just got weird looks, a few tolerant nods. One woman stopped to talk. I shook hands with her, and saw nothing but dinner plans and concern over her daughter's toothache.

Ten minutes later, a younger woman breezed by.

"Hello! I wonder if you can help me?" I made my voice syrupy sweet.

"I can try." She smiled warmly. I made a mental note to keep using the syrupy sweet tone.

"I'm the granddaughter of the Disney Legend, Wayne Kresky," I said, using the exact words Wanda had suggested. "The family is trying to gather signatures and e-mails to help lobby for a Disney Internship called Blue Sky—a think-tank of young creative types that will help us look thirty years into the future."

"Sounds incredible!" The young woman accepted the clipboard and filled out the appropriate spaces. "Not going so well, is it?"

Hers was the first name on the list.

I lowered my eyes. "I can't exactly go in there and bug people."

"No, but I can!" she said. "Come with me."

Over the next few minutes I gathered a string of signatures, and read each person as we shook hands. There was no earth-shattering news. Pixar had a new film in the works I wasn't supposed to know about. A new land was being installed into the Animal Kingdom was slightly behind schedule. *Frozen*'s popularity continued to soar. I filed it all away, unsure what it might mean.

A tall man with steel-gray hair and piercing eyes approached the front doors. Working off intuition, I intercepted him before he entered. He had an air of importance. Wanda would have insisted.

Having won his attention, I rattled off my spiel. He

seemed indifferent, but he couldn't be rude and refuse my extended hand.

"This just isn't how it's done," he said as we shook. "I knew Wayne well. He wouldn't approve."

I heard his words, but it was his thoughts that flooded mine: he was hungry, tired, excited by something at work, discouraged, afraid. I didn't know what to name—to pinpoint—I was adrift in another's mind, not the most stable or reassuring place. But just as I was about to break contact, I saw something unusual.

In the mental image, the charred remains of a small pyre sat in the middle of a dark room. The pyre had been made of kindling and, on top, something smooth and white. Bones? Whatever it was, it gave me the creeps. I knew it was important, so I grabbed the image for my own. The man resisted the attempt, shoving me off the image like he was dumping me out of a chair.

The next image hit me: Finn and Philby in a narrow room decorated in an old-fashioned way. They were moving. This was not how I read people—I saw frozen images, bits and glimpses. Never movement. What was I—?

I felt pushback. Although all of this transpired in a fraction of a second, I'd held his hand too long. Awk-ward! I thought, snatching my hand back too quickly. I thanked the man for helping me out. He looked uncomfortable, though in the end he signed my sheet.

"Let me know how else I can help," he said. "It's a good

idea, but not the best approach. A petition isn't going to convince anyone."

I couldn't tell if he was baiting me or being sincere. If only I'd remained connected just a nanosecond longer. Idiot! I had to find him again. Hopefully, next time I'd have backup.

Another Imagineer walked by, and I had to recite my fake purpose for the twelfth time. After I shook his hand, I thought, I was done for the day. I needed to tell Jess about the drawing ASAP.

I finished talking and reached out my hand to the man, but as our skin connected, something felt different. Regret coursed through me; I should have paid better attention to what this guy was.

A Reacher.

AMANDA

Willa lived with her mother and father (he'd suffered a bad accident that left him with a pronounced limp) in a small but well kept home a few short blocks from Edgewater High School. The front yard needed watering and mowing; the shrubs out had seen better days, but the house itself, a charming yellow cottage, had a welcoming presence.

Wanda went to the door and was shown inside by a woman I guessed was Willa's mother. Bess remained in the cab of the truck, while I sat cross-legged next to Maybeck, whom we'd secured with bungee cords. I opened the shell's overhead vent to get some air flowing in. Time slowed. What was probably five minutes felt more like twenty.

Finally, Wanda came outside and approached the pickup truck. She opened the driver's side door and spoke to Bess as I came up alongside.

"She wouldn't admit to any of it at first. When she finally broke down, though, it was clear how scared she is. They knew better than to involve doctors, thank goodness. But she's resisting the idea of moving her. Willa's father was more understanding. My mention of Luowski and what you and the Whitmans had gone through," she said to me, "clearly affected him. I think he realized he was no match for some young hooligans. He doesn't walk very well. They're talking it over now."

"Does anyone mind if do some praying?" Bess asked.

"Be my guest," Wanda said. "The more help, the better!"

Bess closed her eyes, and moved her lips silently. I met Wanda's concerned gaze with my own. We both felt the seconds dragging by.

"What if they don't agree?" I asked.

"First life lesson: never project. Don't fret about what hasn't happened yet."

I nodded. "Yeah, okay. Easier said than done."

"Yes. But it's important. Otherwise you'll spend all your time worrying about things that may not happen."

Bess, eyes open now, said, "Going to storm later. Storm hard."

There wasn't a cloud in the sky.

This Bess exuded a mystical wisdom I'd not seen before. Sitting there in the cab of the truck, she seemed to possess qualities I'd never associated with the bubbly artist-aunt who cared for Maybeck. I thought suddenly of Tia Dalma, who, despite her evil ways, gave off a powerful air of self-control and ageless wisdom.

It made me think of Terry in a different way. Maybe a deeper well lay beneath the quick-witted, brash boy. Interesting to think about him and Charlene—both one thing on the surface, with something much more interesting kept secret below.

"We'll want to beat that," Wanda said, giving Bess's weather forecast total credence. "We do not want to deal with four kids on the back of Dad's golf cart in the pouring rain."

"And lightning," Bess said. "Winds."

Look at that blue sky! I wanted to say, but I kept my mouth shut.

The front door opened. Willa's mother, Mrs. Angelo, waved us forward, and Wanda released an audible sigh. "We're to go around back. They've agreed!"

Bess looked relieved as well. "Two down, one to go."

"What about Charlene?" I asked. "She's all the way back in LA. What are we going to do about her?"

"Leave that to me," Wanda said. "At some point soon, I'm going to have a talk with Joe. We've entered a new phase in this endless battle. And it's disturbing. We can't do this alone."

"Before you do that," I said, testing my equality with these two, "why don't you let me talk to Jess about Charlie? My guess is she can think of something without involving the Imagineers for now."

"I'll go along with that," Wanda said, "but not for long. We have to protect Charlene, along with the others."

I nodded, hoping Jess could think of something.

JESS

While Mattie shook hands outside the Imagineers' offices, I sat on a bench nearby, preoccupied with thoughts of Amanda's safety. Even with everything that had happened over the past few days, I hadn't forgotten my dream about the Barracks 14 men abducting her.

I wasn't worried all that much about Mattie when backstage; it was inside the park where I'd be needed. Sighing, trying to shake the nervousness out of my limbs, I pulled out my journal.

The ambiguous sketch of Amanda's kidnapping had led me to scout two locations in Disneyland. I now questioned if I'd been on the right track. Was Disneyland a part of anything? I searched the drawing for any detail I might've missed, anything that would clue me in or pinpoint the future event.

Nothing.

Frustrated, I moved on to my second order of business. Amanda had sent me a text about Charlene. I had plan.

AMANDA

Frank and Gladis Philby spoke to us outside, standing awkwardly in the driveway. Philby's dad cast disparaging looks at me and the truck, as if I were the source of all evil and the truck some kind of alien ship.

Philby's mother, Gladis, was a royal pain. She flat-out refused Wanda's request to move their son, and seemed to see conspiracy and treachery around every corner. Frank's military demeanor, which might have simply been his Britishness—I'd never met a full-blooded Brit before—gave me chills. He said he wasn't about "to surrender" his son to anyone else. He wasn't "afraid of some [insert bad word here] hooligans."

To her credit, Wanda remained calm, polite, and caring. Bess played the empathy card: her Terry had once been in SBS, just like Dell had; she understood how difficult this was for them. Even her attempt failed.

So it came down to me. I calmed myself and spoke.

"Mr. and Mrs. Philby, these aren't hooligans. They aren't just a pack of bad kids. Think of them more as members of a dangerous cult. The kind of cult that does sacrifices and hurts people; the kind whose members act like they're on drugs or under spells. Those are the people coming to your house tonight. One of them tried to poison Finn a while back. Finn could have died! Mrs. Whitman and I faced two of them the other night. They broke into the Whitmans' house. They were violent and dangerous. I totally get where you're coming from. Who would let someone take their child away? But one of you could come along, just like Jel—like Bess is doing. You can join us. You're welcome to join us. Just don't push us away. If you do, you and Dell will suffer. Suffer badly. No one wants that."

A warm breeze stirred. Traffic moaned. A dog barked in the distance. Someone had an outdoor grill going, and the smell drifted slowly through the heavy air. No one moved.

I felt as if I'd overreached. Adults don't like being told what to do by kids, even though we're right more often than we're given credit for. I wasn't going to push any harder.

The pain and confusion in Mrs. Philby's eyes spoke to me—it was her husband's stubbornness that was stopping her, I saw. She wanted to release Dell to our care.

"I'm sorry, but our decision is made," she said haltingly. "We certainly appreciate your concern."

"I do not!" said her husband. "This hologram project is out of hand. You realize that, I hope? Dell's aggressive imagination—witches, fairies, sorcerers? It's absurd. This is a grown boy we're talking about, a young man. Enough of this fantasy, I say. Time to move on and face the real world. The same goes for you, miss." He looked at me with dangerous eyes. "The transition to adulthood is not an easy one, but it's time to face the music and grow up!"

He headed back to the house, never looking back. I thought I might cry.

What I heard next was either the wind, my imagination, or Mrs. Philby.

"I'm sorry."

I returned to the back of the truck and kept watch over Maybeck and Willa. Mrs. Whitman was babysitting Finn at Wanda's. It was time to pick him up and move all three Keepers to the cabin at once.

But I was not done with Philby. Luowski was going to attack and try to harm him—or worse. I could not stand by and allow that to happen.

JESS

At Wanda's apartment, I'd seen a photo on the wall of Walt with three other men. Wanda told me they were Imagineers, but that wasn't what interested me. It was the man in the center. I'd seen his face or one just like it. In real life? In one of my dreams? I wanted to figure out who he was.

Still in Disney's Hollywood Studios, keeping an eye on Mattie as she attempted to shake hands with Imagineers in order to read them, I flipped through page after page of my journal, looking for anything like that face. Having left Joe's custody, I couldn't very well go back and ask him about the three men. The Three Wise Men, I named them. Someone not associated with Disney, but an expert nonetheless, would make the best consultant.

But who?

I stared up at the sky, feeling utterly useless. Mattie was out there, working to find answers. I couldn't even locate a Disney expert.

I wished Willa or Philby were here. One of them could figure out how to identify my mystery face.

My more pressing challenge was to make sure Charlene was protected. As we'd discussed, it made sense that at some point the Overtakers would go after her the same way they were the Orlando Keepers.

Right now, Charlene shared an apartment in Venice, California, with her famous co-star from the Disney Channel, Tierra Del Vegro. The superstar's fame made her an easy Web search. Within seconds I had her birthday, favorite flavor of gum, and latest boyfriend, but no contact information. Del Vegro's Facebook page appeared to be managed by a third party, and was full of generic posts about her upcoming roles. Twitter was abbreviated versions of the same posts.

Instagram was different. She had pictures of ice cream and her cat interspersed with standard publicity shots. A little more research, and I found a fan Tumblr that said she even replied to comments on Instagram.

Heart in my throat, I commented on her latest picture: "I need to talk to Charlie about her role in *Sleeping Beauty*."

Quickly, I sent the same message over several platforms, including an e-mail to her publicist. Where possible, I included a photo of me, Amanda, and Charlie. Anyone happening upon the message would assume I was just a fan.

Hopefully, if Charlene was in SBS, her roommate would take notice. If she was okay, then maybe I'd hear from her directly.

AMANDA

Wanda reminded me more and more of her father. She was a woman who thought clearly and quickly, a real problem solver. When no cars were around, she pulled Bess's truck off the road and into the trees. She then left us on foot, and returned an hour later in her father's Pargo, the one with a built-in flatbed.

Carefully, and with a great deal of effort, Wanda, Bess, and I moved Finn, Willa, and Maybeck onto the back of the Pargo.

The forest consisted of tall, thin-trunked pines standing in sparse green grass, some of it knee high. Dappled light pushed through trees, flashing the grass into a jigsaw of fluttering shadows.

Mixed into the birdsong and chitter of squirrels, I could occasionally hear the *thwap* of a golf ball being struck in the distance. The mottled sunlight spread over the faces of our sleeping friends, and the sight brought a lump to my throat. These were perilous times.

"Do we know whether or not they can return from a location that's different from where they crossed over?" Bess asked.

"I don't even want to think about that," I said. "But I bet they've done it before."

"It's important, though, right?"

A siren screeched, and I almost jumped out of my skin. Wanda drove faster; we had to jog to keep up.

"What is it?" I shouted above the electronic cry.

"Lightning warning for the golfers!" she called back.

The gaps in the green canopy overhead showed only blue sky. Bess smiled back at me with an all-knowing grin.

Minutes later, the leaves stirred overhead, the sound like small hands clapping. Wind whistled eerily. It felt like something Maleficent would—

"Oh my gosh!" I blurted out loudly. I had stopped, the golf cart and my friends moving on ahead of me. A thought penetrated so deeply into me that it froze my muscles. Then a rumble of distant thunder shook it away as quickly as it had come.

"Amanda?" Bess said. "What is it?"

"Dragons," I said, pointing to the sky.

"Thunder is all," Bess said, squeezing my shoulder. "Amanda, Terry's on that cart. He needs you."

"Prehistoric," I said.

"Amanda!" Bess spoke sharply.

I broke out of whatever spell was holding me. "I know, I know."

"Let's keep going."

Moments later, a small cabin came into view. It looked so beautiful, nestled in the trees. At the same time, it had a Hansel and Gretel quality I found off-putting. From where we stood, it looked like it was the size of a tissue box. A stone chimney rose from the near side.

More thunder rumbled. The leaves tickled the air overhead. Rain. Fat drops fell randomly.

"We're just in time," Wanda called out. "We'll want to hurry now." She drove faster. We ran. The key was hidden in a fake rock at the base of a nearby tree. As we stepped inside, the heavens let loose.

LUOWSKI

The only books I'd ever liked were horror novels. Stephen King, the master, had once said success was ninety percent hard work, five percent talent and five percent luck. I'd taken that to heart.

I came into luck of my own when one of the three OTKs under me followed Mrs. Nash—the head of the foster home where the Freaks had once lived—to an apartment complex. There, one of my agents, Triana, had seen one of the Freaks. That had enough for me.

I'd staked out the place and, sure enough, more of the Freaks appeared. I followed two of them to Disney's Hollywood Studios.

After entering backstage with my Cast Member pass, I leaned casually against the green metal fence surrounding the character-shaped hedges, watching Weaver make a complete fool of herself in front of the Imagineer offices. From between the landscaping and squat brick buildings, I stalked her, blocking her view of me all the while.

Not like she'd be looking for me anyway. She didn't seem that observant. A sneer twisted my lips. She wasn't going to get away again. Especially not after last time. . . .

I felt the hatred of the Overtakers surge through me, and I shivered despite the heat of the sun.

Icy and rebuking, I heard her orders again, loud and clear. "Stop them! Cause chaos from within. We need them isolated—then we will win. They'll stand no chance."

I glanced around to make sure no one else had heard—and then I realized that it was just a memory, haunting me.

Weaver was at it again. Her squeals about her sappy campaign were loud enough to hear across the square. A tall Imagineer with steel-gray hair was shaking her hand, looking dazed. He attempted to pull his hand away, but Weaver kept hold. The tall man shook his head as if coming to his senses. Blinking, she jerked back, forced a goofy grin onto her face, and thanked him.

I saw her make a move to leave, but then she caught the eye of another Imagineer and started her speech again. I'd been watching for a while, hoping for a chance to nab her in a less public setting. Now I groaned. She'd probably be here a while longer.

Ten minutes later, the rain started, a thunderstorm that would have made Noah proud. I ran for cover, turning my back on Weaver for no more than twenty seconds. When I looked again, I confronted a curtain of gray water so thick, I couldn't see any of the buildings, much less some puny Freak.

Hurrying through the deluge in search of her, I nearly collided with a palm tree. I slipped, skidded, and fell.

I'd lost her.

AMANDA

The cabin had not been designed to serve as a dormitory for comatose teenagers. Log on the outside, the walls inside were varnished knotty pine. Thick green curtains on wrought-iron rods adorned the cabin's four windows—two normal size, on either side of the door; two smaller, one above the kitchen counter, one across from it, above a green couch with flying duck upholstery. There was a bathroom, a tiny bedroom, and a big closet at the back.

The living space didn't feel so much like a cabin as a photo gallery. A hundred or more framed photos hung on the walls, both black-and-white and color. They showed Disney World, people of all kinds, unattributed landscapes.

Standing there, in his space, I wanted more than anything the time to go back into the past and speak to Wayne. But that wasn't possible, and there was work to do. We wanted to get the Keepers settled and keep them safe.

While the adults handled the Keepers, Jess and Mattie arrived soaking wet. While they dried off, the rain quit as quickly as it'd started.

170

Together, we three worked to create a perimeter trip line around the cabin. I was allowed to drive the Pargo to outline our perimeter. Although it was only a few yards, it was the most fun I'd had in several weeks. We strung Wayne's fishing line at knee-height (so small animals wouldn't trigger it) in an awkward circle around the cabin. We rigged it so that it was one long string, which, at its end, turned back and fed through a very small window in the bathroom. On the back of the toilet, we stacked a tower of kitchen dishes: a metal mixing bowl, a tin coffee mug, and an old kettle that filled with knives and spoons. We tied the line to a ring on the mixing bowl, and doubled-checked everything.

By the time we finished, Maybeck and Finn were in Wayne's bed, their mouths refreshed with sponges of water, while Willa rested on an air mattress on the floor. Another window I hadn't noticed was the horizontal one in the bedroom, but it didn't open, so why bother? It was about six feet long and twelve inches high. If you sat in bed you could see the forest through it, and this made the small room feel bigger.

The good news: no one was coming through that window. It was too small. That left only one way for Luowski or the Overtakers to get to the Keepers—through the front door, and then through the bedroom door.

Wanda was running a power drill in the bedroom. With nothing to do, I began to roam the living room's photo gallery. Wayne's collection overwhelmed and impressed me: Disney World before, during, and after construction; Disneyland in the days of black and white; dozens of shots of Wayne in the company of Disney Legends; and so many others I couldn't identify. I considered asking Wanda, but it wasn't the right time.

I'd looked at only a small number of photos when one in particular caught my eye.

"Jess, Mattie? Over here."

The girls joined me. Jess was the first to see it—she and I were so connected.

"Isn't that—?"

"Yes," I said, cutting her off.

"The same photo as the one in the blue can," Mattie said.

"Looks like it to me," I said.

The photo, shot in black and white a long time ago, showed a celebratory crowd gathered on Main Street, USA. You could tell it was from the past: the guests were dressed in more formal attire than a similar crowd would have worn today.

"Why?" Jess asked. "And how? Why would Finn give you a photo from Wayne's cabin wall?"

"It's different from the others," Mattie said. "The ones here, I mean. I'm not saying it's different from the one Finn left. But look at it. It had to have been shot from Sleeping Beauty Castle. Maybe from a ladder or something?"

"A professional," Jess said. "You're right, Mattie. It's sharper than these others. Everything's in such good focus, like they used a better camera."

"Let's say we're right," I said, "and it is a professional, or at least not a touristy photographer. Wayne likes the photo, so maybe it's opening day or something, like we talked about before. He hangs it on his wall. So far, so good. That makes sense, and it isn't all that unusual. But then you're right, Jess. Why would Finn bother to include the same photo, and how did he get a copy of a photo that's hanging on Wayne's wall?"

"We need to compare them," I said. We'd carefully divided up the contents of Finn's blue can between the four of us for safekeeping. I sought out Wanda and returned with the black-and-white photo.

"Why'd you take so long?" Mattie said sarcastically. She was clearly feeling more at ease with me and Jess. She wouldn't have been this sassy back on the Disney *Dream*. It made me smile.

Jess and I had stuck together, solo, for a long time. But while we hadn't been close to anyone else in Barracks 14, we'd made alliances and partnerships, to trade for important information and basic necessities. We'd both liked Mattie. She was trustworthy, a quality that couldn't be underestimated.

I stood on a chair, reached up, and took the photo from the wall. I set the framed photo on the table and took a phone photo of it. Not the best photo, given that the glass reflected back part of my face.

"Check it out!" I said, laying my phone alongside the photo from Finn's can. "Especially the reflections."

"Almost the same," Mattie said.

"So Finn took a photo of this photo," I said. "Finn was here."

"We don't know that. There could be other copies," Mattie said.

"Of a photo this old?"

"I'm just saying."

"I need to get back to the Studios," Mattie said. "The guy I read loves to get an afternoon Mickey Ears ice cream. I want to read him again."

Wanda joined us, overhearing and joked, "Remind me to never shake hands with you."

I told Mattie, "You can catch a bus at the golf clubhouse. I have to say, as much as I'm curious about this video of Finn you saw when you read him, I don't love the idea of you going back there."

"I can handle it."

Jess said, "I'll go with you again. If I get up my nerve to see Joe, maybe he can help with the three men in my sketch."

"I understand your curiosity, Mattie," Wanda said, "but what if you run into whoever touched you in the emergency room? Or worse, what if they run into you?"

"I'll be there," Jess said.

I blurted out what I was thinking before giving it enough thought. "What are you going to do, draw them?" Jess was the least aggressive person I knew.

Her nostrils flared. Her eyes widened. I shrank beneath that glare. "I've been studying martial arts. Remember?"

That won a smirk from Wanda, who hid it from Jess.

"Okay, okay! Just stay together, all right? And be careful! And get back here before dark." I crossed my arms. "In case that alarm we set goes off."

"Yes, Mother," Jess said, making me feel about two inches tall.

* * *

People in charge of me had been underestimating me and discounting my independence for as long as I could remember. I liked Wanda. I respected her. Admired her, even. But I had stuff to do; the girls had stuff to do. I wasn't going to live scared. I'd seen fear chip away at Finn—my Finn!—for far too long.

I wanted Finn and the others out of SBS so badly I could hardly think.

My heart felt broken. I ached, physically ached, for his return.

The Return! The thought hit me like a blow; I stopped, blinking.

I'd been so stupid! There were two ways the Keepers returned. One, the Return itself, was a black key fob Finn carried with him when they crossed over. The other, a manual return, had to be initiated by Philby from his laptop. Surely I could bring them back if I could figure out how to return them manually, the way Philby had.

Did Luowski know that? Had he connected the dots the way I had?

Knowing Mrs. Philby wouldn't let me into Philby's room to steal his laptop, and knowing Luowski wouldn't strike the Philbys until dark, I laid out a plan to Wanda and she agreed it had a fair chance of success. I promised I'd be back before dark or call.

I headed to the home of Bishop Graham.

* * *

Bishop was a geeky friend of Philby's who lived in the basement of his parents' house but acted like a feudal lord, bossing his mother around and calling the shots. Inside, I found myself sprawled out on a horrible lime-green beanbag chair that smelled of candy and popcorn.

His mother, a gorgeous woman with skin like Beyoncé's, delivered hot tea and blueberry muffins, approaching her son with a cowering expression of subservience and terror. I looked away, beginning to wish I'd thought of a different friend of Philby's to approach. Or maybe they were all like Bishop. What a vile thought.

Making the low-ceilinged basement space—with its exposed floor joists, wiring, and plumbing, and two tubs marked EMERGENCY SURVIVAL—even creepier were the dozens of photos of girls in bridal gowns that covered the walls. Some of the girls were gorgeous, a few downright ug-ly, but most were just overly made up, normal girls.

Bishop saw me eyeing the photos and the tubs. "I was on the school yearbook. Photographer. Dell helped us with our computers. Now I freelance as a wedding photographer."

"Well, that explains it," I said, showing him the photo from Finn's blue can. "I was trying to take my own shot of this photo," I added, handing him my phone, "but I couldn't stop the reflection off the glass from getting in the way. Turns out, I wasn't the only one. That's a face, right?"

"There are a lot of faces!" Bishop said. "That's called a crowd."

"On top of that. A face behind what I think is a camera."

Bishop held the photo under better light, squinting. "Ah! Got it!"

"Can you enhance that? The face? The camera?"

"Why's it matter?"

His question struck me as odd. "Facebook has face recognition software now, right?"

"Yeah, so what?"

"So maybe it can identify this face."

"It doesn't work like that."

"I thought guys like you and Philby could make stuff work the way you wanted it to."

"Dell, maybe. For me, I need a little incentive."

"Money," I guessed.

"That works," Bishop said. "I have expenses, you know. Twenty dollars."

"Ten."

"Fifteen."

"Ten."

"Twelve fifty."

"Done," I said.

"Up front," he said, crossing his arms over his chest.

"Not possible. I have to borrow it."

"On delivery, then. I'll keep the photo for now."

"No way. You can scan it, but I need the original."

"I'll need to work with it. You'll get it back when I'm paid."

"Then the deal's off. I have to keep it." I stood up; the beanbag chair puffed out a cloud of dust as I rose. Bishop sneezed incredibly hard, and I jumped toward him and snatched the photo back.

Still sneezing, he tried to stifle the sound in the crook of his elbow. Stuck his whole face in there, until only his chin and cropped hair were visible. I was so used to Maybeck's dreads that a haircut like Bishop's made him seem younger than he probably was. When he lifted his face, I saw that something was wrong with his eye.

He blinked rapidly as I pointed to his face. "You . . . ah . . ."

The words lodged in my throat. At first I thought that he'd blown nose goo onto his eyeball. Then I realized it wasn't that at all—he'd dislodged a contact lens. A brown contact lens that made his eyes the same color as his mother's.

The iris the contact covered was a different color: a deep, horrible green.

Bishop reached up and touched the contact, realized he'd

been exposed. Revealed. He lunged for the photo. "I'll take that."

"No!" I jumped backward, tripped over the beanbag.

Bishop sneezed again. "You shouldn't help them," he said.

He meant the Keepers. I scrambled to my feet, warned him not to come any closer. He wasn't obeying. I scooted onto the washing machine, crouched like an ape. "Stay away!"

"Fat chance."

I warned him again.

"If you join us now, we won't hurt you."

"Join who?" I shouted, knowing the answer but wanting to keep his mind busy.

"You know who."

"Greg Luowski?"

He laughed. "An agent."

"For who?"

"Yeah, right. Like you don't know."

I backed up a step, bumping the washing machine's control knob. It turned on, thumping beneath me. The sound startled me; I raised my hands defensively, and before I knew it, I'd pushed.

Bishop lifted off his feet, the shock on his face worth its own photo. The beanbag flew across the floor, and the two met as Bishop slammed into the far wall and slid down to find himself sitting on it. As he landed, it puffed up more dust. He sneezed loudly.

"Of course I know," I said.

When he looked up again, I was gone. With my photo.

LUOWSKI

The rain had stopped an hour ago and I had left the Studios to go check on Whitless and the others. Even after spying on her for so long, the annoying Weaver Freak had gotten away again. I needed to punch something. I felt like a Ping-Pong ball bouncing between two tasks: first to defeat the Keepers and second to stop the Freaks from helping them. I kept trying to reach both and I was the one getting pounded for it.

Recent visits to Whitless's house had revealed that his parents were very concerned and stayed home from work. They rarely left the house.

But now, before me, the driveway was vacant. No car.

What did that mean?

I headed to Crazy Glaze. Only to find that the window sign read CLOSED and the pale-blue truck that had been parked in the same spot for the past week was gone. My head spun. Two of them. Cars missing in the same hour. What in the world?

In fifteen minutes, I entered the Philby neighborhood, holding my breath. But as I came upon the nerd's house, a car could be seen through the garage window. Someone was home: as in Philby himself.

I didn't know what was going on, but I had to attack tonight, before this house went dark as well.

MATTIE

Having returned to Disney's Hollywood Studios, Jess and I sat on a bench with a view of both the Cast Member entrance the Imagineers were most likely to use and the nearest ice cream cart, nearly in the shadow of Mickey's Sorcerer's Cap. The plaza in front of the cap churned with the action of a street musical show and its captivated guests.

We waited. And waited.

Jess was my bodyguard, I thought, looking briefly over at her. I grinned privately. Jess, a bodyguard?

Hopefully it wouldn't come to that.

JESS

As Mattie and I waited, hoping her gray-haired Imagineer might reappear, a notification lit up on the screen of my phone. A response to my Instagram message! It was from Charlie's roommate, Tierra Del Vegro. *The* Tierra Del Vegro! On *my* phone!

Tierra: who is this?

Me: jessica. i'm a friend of charlene's. has she been getting enough sleep lately?

I waited anxiously for a reply.

Tierra: who are you? what's going on? how could you know that?

Me: you need to move her. take her someplace where no one will look for her. she's in danger.

Tierra took a long time to reply to that one, long enough that I began to worry I'd scared her away.

Tierra: okay. i can do that.

Me: at night. no one can see you do it.

Tierra: i don't mean to be rude, but paparazzi follow me everywhere. as in: everywhere. all the time. it's awful.

Me: then you distract them while someone you trust moves charlie. this is life and death. no drama, promise.

Tierra: i can do that.

I breathed a sigh of relief.

Me: thank you.

Tierra: of course. is she sick?

Me: no doctors. it has to do with her being a dhi.

Tierra: she said they were all done with that.

Me: yeah. we thought so, too.

Tierra: who's we?

Me: did she tell you about the fairlies?

Tierra: now I recognize your name. seriously? you're jess?

A superstar actress, one of the biggest movie stars out there, knew who I was. My fingers wouldn't move. Finally, I typed.

Me: please let me know when she's safe.

Tierra: will do.

I looked up to tell Mattie—but her place on the bench was now empty.

MATTIE

"Hey! Remember me? We met earlier!" I said with a smile. "Madeline. My petition?"

I stuck out my hand. He lifted his ice cream, offering an excuse for not shaking hands with me.

"Yes, of course I do," the Imagineer said, nibbling at a melting Mickey Ice Cream Bar. "And since I'm not a big believer in coincidence, I'm assuming you must want more than my signature?"

He smiled, but it didn't reach his eyes.

"Well, yes, sir. Actually, I've always dreamed of working for Disney myself. I was using the petition to meet Imagineers."

"Well, young lady, I will say one thing: You are imaginative." He paused. "What was it you did to me earlier? Are you telepathic? Something like that? We shook hands and I saw things—things I did not want to see. Things I had not seen. I think it best we keep our distance. I will forget this little exchange we've had."

He started to walk away. I panicked, reaching out and grabbing his hand holding the ice cream bar. He yanked away.

"Young lady!" he shouted.

At the moment of contact, I'd named Finn.

Once again I glimpsed Finn and Philby moving, like in a video. A small apartment.

Fear clouded this man's recollection of the image.

"There are men after you and your friends," he whispered. "They've been in the parks. Probably are still in the parks. They are very well connected. We have no choice but to stand aside in your case. But we are working behind the scene to help you, and all you're doing is lying to me. I've seen the horror you've come through to get here, Madeline. If you and the white-haired girl don't leave right now, you may not make it out of here."

A Reacher for sure: he'd seen Jess's true hair color. He knew she was here. I panicked, unable to speak.

"You must leave now," he said.

I had no choice but to believe him. I raced to Jess.

"We gotta go. Now," I said, pulling her to her feet.

"Because?"

"Just come!"

I heard her footsteps behind me as Jess raced to catch up.

"Mattie, what's going on?"

"Stay with me." I led her around a corner, taking a chance and stealing a look over my shoulder. No one following. Not yet.

Jess and I reached the Transportation and Ticket Center and hurried to the monorail toward Epcot. Getting caught wasn't an option. I wanted to think of the Imagineers as allies, but Amanda kept telling me that Finn and the Keepers were always confused about whom they could trust.

Jess and I elbowed our way through the crowd, angering people waiting in line for the next train. Once on, I breathed a sigh of relief. The moving image I'd read felt like information vital to our cause. But I didn't know how to process it; didn't understand what it meant.

We were about to make ourselves comfortable when I spotted two men in suits in the car next to us.

JESS

"Don't look now," Mattie whispered, "but those guys in the ties are looking at us. And not in the checking-us-out sense. More like watching-their-prey."

By the time we disembarked at Epcot, it felt like an hour had passed. Unable to contain myself, I flew from the train car. Mattie caught up and kept pace with me.

For once, the odds were on our side. Miraculously, there was no wait at Epcot's Magic Band entrance. I had been prepared to run in without scanning and take my chances with Disney Security, but now I didn't need to double our chances of being caught.

Beside me, Mattie was wheezing like a ninety-year-old geezer. Our pursuers showed no sign of slowing. We weren't going to outrun them. We needed a place to hide.

I took a sharp left across a bridge, toward the Odyssey Center, pulling Mattie along. Inside the Passholder help center, we had just seconds to find a place to hide. Something directed me behind the first display on my left.

Mattie, on the other hand, hesitated. She took a second

too long. The men burst through the door as she dove under the nearest display.

I didn't see the rest. I heard Mattie crying out.

In spite of myself, I jumped up and charged, but I slipped at the last second, sliding between two of them.

"Run, Jess, run!" Mattie cried.

My vision blurred with tears, but I did just that: out into the park, racing at full speed, choking on my realization that Mattie was the girl in my kidnapping dream.

Mattie, not Amanda.

Out of breath, with no one following, I leaned against a wall.

A father was explaining Walt's motto to his family. "Dreams really do come true," he said.

You have no idea, I thought, tears spilling down my cheeks.

AMANDA

Fresh off my encounter with the OTK Bishop, I made my way back to Philby's neighborhood. By the end of the bus ride, I found myself on the hate side of my love/hate relationship with the Orlando city bus system. I'd taken three connecting lines, one of which required me to wait forty minutes at the bus stop because of mechanical problems.

Trying to detect a potential spy outside the Philby house was a new and daunting challenge. Deciding where to hide when I suspected others were hiding forced me to consider all angles, the distances and lighting. I settled on approaching from the rear, through a neighbor's yard, which meant trying to stay calm while a large dog growled at me from inside the house. I navigated a backyard with no less than six of those creepy garden gnomes before climbing the fence and dropping into the Philbys' backyard.

Using the plants along the side fence as my screen, I took my time reaching the front of the house. Once there, I hunkered down between two young banana trees and remained stock-still. I had a partial view of the back and a better one of the front. My brain told me Luowski—or one of his gang—would attack from the back, as they had at Finn's. My gut said otherwise, directing my attention to the street.

As I waited for something to happen, I worked over my options. I'd be outnumbered; I anticipated the Philbys being unprepared, despite our earlier warning. Grown-ups had a bad habit of always believing they were right.

Since moving the comatose Finn to Wayne's cabin earlier, his sleeping face had been fresh in my mind and heart. I found it difficult, if not impossible, to suppress my feelings. Whether the result of hunger or fatigue or both, I gave into my worry and felt the tears running down my cheeks.

Without the Keepers, Finn and I would never have met. Yet a big part of me wished the DHI technology had never been invented, that he and I had found some other way of connecting, something that would have allowed us to share unusual experiences without any of them being life-threatening.

Weary, emotionally raw, I wanted whatever could be described as a normal life. Without special powers, I might have had a real childhood. Without Overtakers, I might have had a real boyfriend.

Wiping away my tears, I blinked, taken aback. At the front corner of the house, a garden gnome was facing me. His little Irish green leggings and ginger beard showed clearly in the darkness. I couldn't remember seeing him there before.

I glanced toward the back fence. The only gnomes I'd seen had been in the neighbor's yard. Now four of the ugly little things stood sentry in the garden by the Philbys' back fence. Angry at myself for not paying enough attention, trying to blame it on the growing darkness and my concern about staying out of sight, I wheeled around to study the street and the low bushes—which would provide ample space for Luowski to hide.

The ginger gnome was no longer at the corner of the house. He stood three feet away from me now. Still and solid as a ceramic statue.

I looked left: the gnomes that had been in the back now commanded the bushes along the fence, against which my back was pressed. Same order. Same frozen expressions. But they had moved.

I stole another look: the ginger was gone, neither by the house nor immediately alongside me. I started to shake: the gnomes to the left were now a yard closer. I stretched to the right for another angle. Ginger stood stoically by a red and green succulent. Left! All four, another yard closer; the lead gnome, with a cherub's face and bushy mustache, delivered a penetrating stare from perhaps ten feet away.

Right! Ginger was closer.

Left! The quartet had inched forward.

Something bit my calf and I squealed. When I looked down at my torn jeans, I jumped, crashing into the fence, almost screaming. A small piece of my blue jeans lay at the stubby ceramic feet of the ginger gnome, who still looked perfectly inanimate. His bite had broken the skin of my leg.

And there was the quartet, now spread in a semicircle in front of me. I had yet to see a single one of them actually move.

I shouldn't have taken my eyes off Ginger. Again, he bit my ankle. This time, I managed not to scream—and I *pushed*, hard. Ginger flew straight and fast, burrowing down into the garden's soft earth as if I'd dug a hole for him. I brushed dirt in over his head and stomped it down.

Two more bites followed, like bee stings, on my left leg. I stood, jumped over the gnomes, and dashed to the house. When I looked back, the four gnomes were facing the house perfectly still. Ginger's head protruded from the grave I'd dug for him. All five were still. As long as I looked at them, they did not move. If I so much as blinked, they changed.

My eyes snapped shut of their own accord. Opened again. Ginger was now only waist deep in the dirt. The four had progressed to the edge of the gravel driveway.

At Barracks 14, Jess and I had engaged in staring contests. Sadly, we considered that an exciting form of entertainment—it was all we had. I won more often than I lost. And a good thing, too, because now the bizarre little gnomes and I were locked into just such a game.

It was, of course, an exercise in futility: a ceramic statue with beady black eyes doesn't have to work hard to avoid blinking. An eighteen-year-old girl? Not so much. My eyes watered. They stung. They blinked.

The four gnomes moved closer with eerie speed. Ginger grew from the earth like a well-fertilized plant.

What were they supposed to do, nip me to death? Chew my feet off and then work their way up? That would take what, a week? Two weeks? No, there was something else at play here, and I'd been a fool to miss it: they'd stolen my time and my attention. They were nothing more than a pesky distraction meant to move me up against the house with no view of either the back or front yard.

That meant only thing: the Philbys were under attack!

* * *

Racing forward, heart in my throat, I kicked the gnomes out of my way like a string of soccer balls. One of them broke on the driveway; the others flew into the bushes.

Coming around to the front of the house, I knew what to expect; I'd been through this sort of ordeal at the Whitmans. But there were no preparations to stop the OTKs this time.

Luowski would strike fast and hard, as he'd done at Crazy Glaze, all those years ago. I anticipated the use of a stun stick, at least two OTKs, and a boatload of determination on Luowski's part.

Slowly and quietly opening the front door, I found Mrs. Philby on the floor of the entry, cowering on the other side of the same dark-haired girl I'd seen at the Whitmans'. With her back to me, I pushed, not waiting for discussion or drama, propelling the girl off her feet and along the carpet.

Had Finn or any of the other Keepers been with me, they would have witnessed the change that came over me in that moment. I didn't tire with this push; I didn't waste a speck of my considerable energy. For perhaps the first time, I was in control of my power, real control. It felt delicious.

The girl rolled, aiming a large squirt gun at me—likely filled with some toxic concoction. I waved at her with one hand and the gun went sailing. She looked horrified, and for good reason: I was suddenly a witch.

I thought back to stories of Salem, to my own youth, my body changing, my powers increasing. I'd always used two hands to push, but now one would do. As I soon found that out, I could use my hands and arms independently, too.

For the first time, I pulled, dragging the couch with my right hand while pinning the girl in place with my left. The newfound control of my power exhilarated me! I felt less like a magician with his wand, and more like an orchestral conductor. With a jerk of my fingers, I tipped the couch over on top of her legs; she wasn't going anywhere now. The new freedom to use my push thrilled me. I couldn't stop myself; I was overcome with it. I pulled Mrs. Philby to her feet, slid her back, and set her down gently in a stuffed chair.

This was fun. I felt light-headed with glee. I'd need to learn how to use it properly, to train myself. As the *Aladdin* soundtrack proclaimed, I was in "a whole new world!" Like a sprinter, I'd found another gear, another tool. I was Dorothy with her ruby slippers. Buzz Lightyear with his wings.

And I was practically down the far hallway. I leaped over a conscious but prone Mr. Philby, blasting doors open as I went. A bathroom. A study. A guestroom.

Philby, in bed. Luowski, hovering over his laptop computer.

I pushed Luowski. Furniture moved, including the bed. The bully skidded across the floor and slammed into the wall. I cautioned myself, trying to keep my emotions out of it, to stay focused and clinical with the use of my powers. I'd tasted control; it was time to demonstrate it. In this moment, Philby's computer, not Philby, was the prize for both Luowski and me. Maybe Luowski wanted to hurt Philby, maybe not. Regardless, the OTK had gone first for the laptop, not the boy in the bed.

I used my left hand to hold Luowski. With my right, I directed the laptop to the edge of the desk, bringing it nearly within my reach.

Despite my open palm aimed at him, and despite my considerable intention, Luowski lifted his forearm to screen my force, looking like a man fighting against a strong headwind. To my astonishment, he took a step forward. I increased my power, bringing my right hand up to join my left.

Leaning steeply into the unseen, punishing wind, Luowski marched forward. Impossible! I too leaned in, delivering what felt to me like enough energy to move a truck. And still Luowski trudged toward me, step by heavy step.

It shouldn't have taken me so long to remember that he was possessed, charmed, enchanted. The snarl on his face should have told me as much. His newfound ability was no doubt meant to instill fear in me. To weaken me. It had the opposite effect. I'd been born with my powers; they were part of me. His had been added on; they were a modification.

The closer he got, the more our opposing energies dispersed and swirled around us. Curtains flapped; the ceiling fan whirled at high speed; any piece of loose paper or clothing pasted itself to the walls. Before he took his next step, I heaved toward him—and watched as his face of evil changed to one of surprise. He had not expected that. He opened his mouth to say something, but lacked the energy. His jaw slacked.

I took another daring step. We were perhaps three feet apart. The room and everything in it seemed to spin at the center of a tornado.

Whoever had done this to him had no doubt planned for victory, and in victory, our silence. Philby's computer would be seized; Philby would be harmed. Those who stood up to Luowski would be captured and thereby kept silent. It was late enough that Luowski might have already tried Maybeck's and Willa's.

It thrilled me that I could calmly consider the various strategies set forth against me even as I held this demon-boy at bay with raised palms. Yes, he had put up a good fight. Yes, he had surprised me by doing so. But my newly discovered control, my ability to push and pull ambidextrously, gave me an unrivaled confidence.

Feeling ten times stronger with every passing second, I held him now with only my left hand as I maneuvered a pair of scissors currently stuck to the wall. The scissors pulled away and, as if connected to me with wires, sliced through the powerful wind to fix their blades just below Luowski's chin, pointing at his throat.

"You will go now," I said calmly, wanting to impress upon him that I wasn't rattled. A little white lie. I was terrified. "You will forget about hurting the Keepers. If you don't, I'll make sure you're the next one hurt. Give up before it's too late."

He didn't answer with his voice, but his green eyes spoke volumes. Greg Luowski was not about to give up anything. Being overpowered by a girl had humiliated him; if he could have, he would have punched me in the face. But the scissors at his throat delivered my message more articulately than I could. I pulled and pushed and turned him until I was no longer standing between him and the bedroom door.

But I'd allowed my powers to go to my head. I acted impulsively. And Luowski was waiting.

In an instant, he dropped his arm, his shield. He seemed to be using my power to help him. He slid across the floor like a surfer. He snatched Philby's laptop off the desk, skated out the door, and was gone before I realized I was doing this, not him.

I pulled to get him back, but only swung the door shut with a loud bang, trapping my powers—and me—inside. The thump of the couch sounded; I opened the door and launched into the hallway. I tried to push, but I was too far away; all I could do was break two lamps. I collapsed to my knees, furious with myself for allowing my false sense of control to control me. Luowski had Philby's laptop! With it, the Imagineers might have found a way to return the Keepers. Without it . . . I feared I just condemned the Keepers to SBS for eternity. In my effort to be their savior, I'd messed everything up.

Mrs. Philby reached me, breathless. "Well done!" she called out.

I collapsed to my knees. "I've ruined everything!"

MATTIE

I came awake in what looked like a basement storage room. I was lying on an air mattress. My head hurt. A funky, damp smell clung to the windowless space, the lovely perfume of rot and mildew. It permeated everything, including my clothing.

I had lost my sense of time, but it felt like I hadn't been down here long. I thought it was probably late night the same day the 14ers had grabbed hold of me. Jess knew I'd been taken. She'd be looking for me.

Knowing I had a responsibility to escape, I conducted a quick sweep of the small room for anything that might serve as a tool or weapon. The most promising item, a locked closet door, presented both an opportunity and a challenge.

I had no idea how to get it open, but if I could . . .

I tried not to think about my captors, or my friends, or the Keepers. Instead, I focused solely on my mission.

Get out. Get free.

JESS

Working on a lightning-never-strikes-twice strategy, I'd returned to the Odyssey Center and had hidden there following Mattie's abduction.

Crouched down, out of sight, I'd stayed hidden for hours wanting to get out of there and try to help Mattie. But every time I tried to leave I'd see a Cast Member or Disney Security outside and retreat back to my hiding place.

I committed myself to getting Mattie back, no matter the challenge. Mandy and I had coaxed her into escaping the Barracks in the first place. We couldn't let them take her back there.

On one of my attempts to get out of there I passed a collection of Disney paraphernalia that caught my eye. Inside the display case were old photos—boys in khakis and button-down shirts, girls in skirts and white socks—old fashioned toys, a harmonica. And older women in high heels, thick lipstick and white gloves.

White gloves.

When combined, the items nearly matched exactly the contents of Finn's mysterious soy protein can.

I took a handful of phone photos before hurrying out into the warm evening. I walked with my head down, my heart racing. Maybe I'd just cracked Finn's puzzle.

* * *

I used my phone as a flashlight to reach the cabin, carefully avoiding the tripwire we'd installed.

Greeted by a openly worried Amanda, Wanda, and Bess, I was wild with a mixture of panic and excitement. I described for them Mattie's abduction at the hands of men I presumed were Barracks 14ers. I briefly related my discovery of the display and showed them my photos. But it was Mattie's rescue that held our collective attention.

"What are we supposed to do?" I said.

"We're supposed to calm down," said the ever-calm Bess. Wanda nodded.

"It's my fault. I feel horrible. I should have left sooner."

"They were looking for you, too. You did the right thing," Wanda said.

Bess said, "What's done is done, child. We have to remain positive. There is a solution to everything."

"How can you say that?" I shouted.

Bess never raised her voice. "Because it's true, child. You will see."

AMANDA

We spent the night making plans. Wanda, who didn't for a minute believe Joe was in league with Barracks 14, woke Joe and told him about the missing Mattie. He said he'd make calls. The Imagineers would try to pull security video of the Transportation Center to identify the culprits. While the adults worked to save Mattie, Wanda wanted me and Jess to continue trying to make sense of Finn's cryptic message.

"We can't allow the Barracks 14 men to distract us from saving the Keepers," Wanda said. "That would be travesty."

Reluctantly, Jess and I agreed; it was one of the hardest things I'd ever done, leaving Mattie to others, but I knew Wanda was right.

I met Mrs. Angelo, Willa's mom, at Downtown Disney's Once Upon a Toy, where she worked part-time. She looked frail and exhausted.

I felt sick, seeing her like this. I had a bad headache, and every muscle was sore, a result of the confrontation with Luowski. All hope of manually returning the Keepers had been lost along with Philby's laptop. I couldn't get over my own role in that.

I fought against increasing sense of failure, but there was no escaping it: we were losing on every front.

I sat next to Mrs. Angelo. "Willa has always bragged about how tech savvy you are."

"Does she?"

"Says that's where she got her abilities." I showed her the photo from the soy can. "Well, I could use some help."

Mrs. Angelo took the photo from me. She extended her arms, then searched her purse for a pair of glasses and put them on. "Old," she said.

"Can you see the reflection off the glass?" I asked.

It took her a moment. "Interesting," she said. "I think you're right. Older man or woman—and in color, no less."

I hadn't noticed that, and I said so now.

"Phone camera. Probably printed at one of the big drugstores."

"I think I know whose face it is, but I'd love to be sure," I said.

"A real detective you are. Is that it? Is this going to unlock the secret of bringing my daughter back?" Her words dripped with sarcasm.

"It's part of the solution, yes," I said, trying to overcome, but I won only her skepticism. I kept going, though I still had little idea what I was talking about. "I was thinking—some of the social media sites have face matching. You put in your high school class photo and it scours the Internet for current photos of your friends."

"Old news," Willa's mother said.

"So what about this photo? Could we match faces in the crowd with their counterparts today?"

"It's black-and-white."

"Duly noted."

"Faded."

"Yes."

She fingered the photo. I watched her slowly come alive, lifted out of her funk and all-consuming worry about her daughter. "The resolution may not work."

"But we could try?" I asked. "You could try?"

"Do you have the original negative?"

"No. But there's a better photo at the cabin. You could use that one for the faces, except . . . it doesn't have this ghostly looking thing." I pointed out what she'd already seen: the vague color image of a partial face. It was like looking at yourself in the mirror after a hot shower. "Maybe you could work with both?"

"If the other image is sharper, there are some enhancement tools that might help. It's an interesting proposition," she said, smiling at me. "Bringing the past forward into the world of social media . . . I'd be happy to give it a try."

"Wonderful!" I said, and thanked her profusely.

She looked at me with a troubled face. It occurred to me then that she had not been sitting here brooding about her daughter. She was worried about something else entirely. Mattie was the one who could read people. I had a lot to learn, it seemed.

"What?" I asked.

She shook her head and looked at her shoes.

"Please."

"I spoke to my husband just now. He said . . . the thing

is . . . we aren't supposed to say anything." She sounded like a little kid. The change shocked me. Her eyes darted toward mine, then away. "My husband. Late last night, two government types came to our front door—"

I inhaled sharply, stopping her.

"You know them." She made it a statement.

I nodded. "They aren't government. They claim to be, but we no longer think they are. Some big corporation, maybe, with a lot of money, connections. And a lot of nerve."

"I wasn't . . . We weren't supposed to speak of it."

"We know all about them," I said. It seemed to mollify her. "Your house isn't the first place they've come looking. Jess came east because of them. She traveled with Disney people. Disney knows about them, too, you see."

"It gets worse," Mrs. Angelo said.

I swallowed dryly.

"My husband told them you and your sister had taken our daughter to a cabin. A secret cabin."

I tried to speak. I couldn't.

"Thankfully, my husband has no idea where the cabin is or who it belongs to. I know this, because he told me that he said it was, 'Walt's cabin.' He didn't make the connection to Mr. Kresky. But still . . . it's not good."

"No," I finally croaked out, "it's not good at all."

DAY 8

MATTIE

The door to the basement creaked open, accompanied by the heavy footsteps of one of the men. I scrambled back to the air mattress, leaving my recent findings in a box in the closet. I could only hope he would fail to notice the missing hinge pins on the closet door. The hinge pin is the nail-like shaft that holds the two pieces of a hinge together; I first learned how to open a door by removing them when Susie McGowen locked herself in the Barracks 14 furnace room.

With the approach of my captor, I hadn't had time to restore the hinges properly, but the door itself was in place, and only a careful eye would discern the pins' absence.

The man entered my jail cell. My heart felt like it was going to pound out of my chest. As he offered me yet another bag of fast food, I worried he would hear it. I must have been flushed as red as a radish, but I accepted the bag with a phony grin—and made sure to brush his hand in the process of our exchange.

This was the third time I'd targeted one of my captors,

trying to find a means of escape. I'd learned from my closet exploration that we were likely in a former spa, probably in an abandoned strip mall. Now, thanks to my gift, I knew I'd been wrong about the basement: I was being held in storage room or office at the back of an abandoned store.

Two of the men missed their families; the other one missed his dog and weekend hunts along the Chesapeake— Barracks 14ers for sure! Today, this guard had a phrase in his head: "Superata Society." I tried to remember it.

The man pulled his hand away, shaking his head. My attention wasn't on the food. When he let go of the Happy Meal bag, it dropped into my lap. Awkward.

If I'd read him correctly, a delivery entrance immediately to the left of my room's only door led to the outside. He was here alone. They took turns watching me. Others were off trying to find Jess and Amanda; I couldn't read how many.

Alone, locked in my cell, I wolfed down the burger and fries. Then I went to work.

Of the varied items in the spa supply closet, the most promising were a box of hair coloring chemicals, a half-dozen electric curling irons still in the box, some rolls of aluminum foil, and two dozen aprons carrying the spa's logo and name: SPA-CIALTY YOU—HAIR CARE AND BODY WORKS. The terrible pun might have explained why it went out of business.

Originally, I'd planned to climb out a tiny trapdoor in the ceiling of the bathroom, but I'd broken the sink off from the wall by standing on it to reach the ceiling, and the access door was screwed shut—not to mention way too small for me. Regrouping, I used the hideous bathroom as a staging area, creating my trap out of sight in case I was subjected to yet another random visit.

From years of hiding, I was no stranger to dying my hair. Still, I loathed the burning chemicals, my last resort but a major asset.

I constructed a welcome mat out of two layers of aluminum foil with a skim of shampoo sandwiched between them. I deconstructed four aprons for the ties used to secure them around the waist. Finding an outlet above the vanity, I plugged in a pair of curling irons and set them to high.

Back at the locked door—its hinges were on the outside, or I'd have already been free as a bird—I hollered loudly, "The toilet's overflowing!"

I pounded on the door as hard as I could. "Hey! Come on! The toilet's overflowing!"

The key clicked in the door. I checked that the mat was in place, my weapons ready, my backups in place on the floor behind him.

Come and get it, I felt like saying.

As the door swung open, I stood to the side, back to the wall. The man took one step onto my welcome mat and slipped, legs swinging wildly, like he'd hit a banana peel. He tried to use the doorknob to steady himself. I took care of that by burning his hand with the hot iron. He screamed. As he fell to the floor I squirted the hair color into his eyes—something the label warned against in bold lettering: AVOID CONTACT WITH EYES.

Snapping two of the strong apron ties around his head, I gagged him. He raised his burned hand blindly to fight me and I let him grab the hair curler a second time. He screamed out some combination of bad words I'd never heard before and hoped I'd never hear again.

Last important chore. I used the backup curling iron—nice and hot—on the side of his neck and the palm of his other hand. This threw him into the defensive posture I'd hoped for—he curled up. Daring to draw close to him, I snatched his cell phone from his belt clip and added a liberal squirt of hair dye to one of the fresh burns for good measure. He howled like a coyote.

Whirling, I pulled the door shut, locked the door, then removed and kept the key. I ran.

Fresh air never tasted so good. Even better: I was the proud owner of a new iPhone.

JESS

"Epcot," I mumbled, dumping the contents of the soy can onto the cabin floor. It felt like the hundredth time. I studied the photo—the mass of excited people. "Anyone wearing gloves?" I asked, thinking more clearly. "Find a woman wearing white gloves."

Amanda snatched the photo from me. I didn't complain.

Instead, I moved over to scour the photos on the walls.

"Why gloves?" Amanda called out as she continued to study the photo of the crowd.

I said, "Finn wouldn't leave us a bunch of random messages. He'd leave us one."

"Agreed."

"And so far, we've missed it."

"No doubt."

I passed a small table. On it sat a picture of a very young Wayne with a younger Walt Disney and another man, presumably an Imagineer.

A closer look at Walt—and it clicked. I hurried over to Amanda, shoved the picture in her face. "Check it out! Walt Disney's wearing the same clothes here as he is in the shot of the crowd."

She looked at me, eyebrow raised. "Right. Look, we're all tired, Jess. And hungry. When was the last time you ate?"

"The same clothes! As in: the same day!"

"Ooookay. And I care because?"

"It's obviously a big day. Look at the crowds! Walt Disney is there. Photos are being taken."

"Opening day," Wanda said. "Disneyland's opening day. We talked about this, Jess. We've been pretty sure about that all along."

"Do you know what that ball is?" I said. "It's called a Super Ball. It's from the 1960s. Jacks? That's a game played during the 1950s and well before. "

"You're a historian now, Jess?" Amanda said caustically.

"No! That's the point! Finn is the historian."

Slowly, Wanda picked up the white glove. "The cigarette lighter. Also from that era. You're right, Jess. The time period is what everything has in common."

"They're all vintage, like the display I saw in Epcot," I said. "It isn't about each item! It's about everything together."

"Like the Keepers," Amanda said. She was speaking to herself, but we all heard it. "Finn wanted us to see the whole group."

"It isn't a scavenger hunt," Wanda said. "We know Dad's picture with Walt was taken on opening day. Now Jess realizes Walt's wearing the same clothes in both shots. So the big crowd is opening day, like we thought."

Wanda was repeating herself, but no one was going to stop her. I could feel her building to something. Not one of us dared interrupt. Transfixed, we listened. We watched.

She squinted her eyes closed. "Come on . . . Come on . . ."

I was so tempted to say something. I literally bit my lower lip to stop myself.

Her eyes popped open. She looked elated, surprised, and terrified.

"Vintage!" she barked. "Jess, you're absolutely right."

"I am?" The words escaped me.

"Finn left us a calendar. We were so stupid! Take a look at the stamp on the envelope. The reason there's no note is so that we'll pay more attention to the stamp. Somebody do an Internet search for a U.S. stamp called Atoms for Peace!"

"A calendar?" Amanda croaked out.

I grabbed my phone and took to the Internet. "Oh my gosh! The three cent Atoms for Peace stamp was issued on July twenty-eighth, 1955."

Wanda smiled widely. "Yes, Amanda, a calendar. Opening day at Disneyland was July seventeenth, 1955. Finn left us a time capsule!"

MATTIE

The fresh air lifted; it boosted my spirits as I made my way on foot toward the church. My abductors had emptied my pockets, meaning I had no money to take a bus. I had no phone numbers memorized, and the only friends I could think of who might help me were the people in the Alcoholics Anonymous group that met at the church. Someone there would certainly lend me money. They might feed me something other than fast food. They might even drive me the half hour to Disney World.

Stretching my limbs felt nice, and it gave me more time to think about my reading of the Imagineer in Disney's Hollywood Studios and the unusual moving images in his mind. This man had seen Finn and the Keepers in Walt's apartment. Walt's, not Wayne's. And it wasn't just from any angle: it was like he'd been standing on a chair.

I couldn't see how that was possible—and yet, I'd seen

it! I racked my brain for a possible explanation. And then I had it.

A place as important as Walt Disney's apartment would have security cameras. Security cameras were often mounted high up in a room.

As tired as I was, my feet started to carry me faster. Soon, I was moving at an all-out sprint.

This guy had seen a security video of the Keepers doing something in Walt's apartment—something important enough that he carried it in the forefront of his mind. That made it important to me. To us!

My knees practically hit my chin, I was running so hard. Finn and the Keepers had been spied on. Observed. They were now comatose in SBS.

What if the two were connected?

AMANDA

"How? When?" I asked Wanda as she and Bess prepared breakfast in the small cabin.

"An ambulance arrived to the Philby's home. The driver claimed they'd been dispatched by 911. Mrs. Philby recognized Greg Luwoski. He took off."

"What about Mattie?" I pleaded.

"No word, but Joe is on it. He threatened the people in Baltimore he'd call the police if he didn't hear from Mattie immediately."

"The Philbys have given us Dell," Bess said. "He's in the back room with the others. We now have all the Keepers but Charlene. Snug as a bug in a rug." She was pouring pancakes. I was starving.

Jess reminded us that that Charlene's TV star roommate had agreed to move Charlene. "I told her to keep her hydrated."

I asked Wanda and Bess why they looked so worried if everything was going better.

Maybeck's aunt flipped the pancake. "There's something troubling us, it's true. Last night I was on watch, maybe two or three in the morning. I'd dozed off. I come awake and the room's all glowing-like. Flashing. My Terry and Willa are looking like a lightbulb that's not screwed in right. Going on and off. Sputtering." She hesitated, not wanting to say anything more, but Wanda nodded at her. "Finn did the same thing not long after. Going in and out—"

Wanda helped Bess put it into words. "We think they were flashing in and out of DHI."

I tried to process what I was hearing. "I don't think that's possible."

"My Terry was all there one minute, then he was . . . I don't know exactly . . . humming. And I don't mean his voice. His whole body was vibrating. Same with Willa and Finn."

"We should ask Joe, if we can trust him," I said.

Wanda had never looked so serious. "Of course we can trust him! Besides, keeping secrets is nothing new for the Imagineers."

Thoughts sparked in my head. It happens like that for me sometimes. Random ideas colliding, sticking. "You know what? We're the problem. Jess and me. We have to leave."

"What on earth are you talking about?" Bess said. "You are not any kind of problem. Neither of you!"

I explained what Mr. Angelo had told the men posing as government workers about a cabin. "If we hide here, they're going to find this place eventually. Us, and the Keepers. What then?"

"You know how many cabins there are around here?" Wanda asked. "Needle in a haystack. They'll never find it."

"On Disney property?" I challenged. "Where would you start looking if you were them?"

Wanda looked the same color as the pancake batter.

"If Jess and I leave and if we make sure they know we've left—Joe, Brad, Barracks 14—the pressure's off. Luowski might still be out there; he might even try to follow one of you. But as long as you're careful not to let that happen, the Keepers are safe."

"But you three are not." Wanda was having nothing to do with my suggestion. "At that point you're homeless, vulnerable, and prone to capture."

"On our own, yeah, that's probably true." I waited, drinking in the aroma of the food being prepared. I was tempted to eat off of Wanda's chopping board. "But since when are we ever alone? We've got Mickey on our side."

LUOWSKI

It all started when Mr. Philby dialed 911. I knew I had to get out. While everyone was busy in the house, I jumped into the empty ambulance and turned the key in the ignition. The engine revved and I floored it out of the Philby's neighborhood faster than I'd ever driven in my life.

On the highway, traffic slowed my getaway considerably. Where should I go? I hadn't really thought that far. Where could I go?

I passed a minivan with two young kids in the backseat. The little girl's eyes bugged out, and the boy looked frightened. I scowled at them, causing them to duck down beneath the window, out of sight. Focusing my attention back on the road, I grinned. People were afraid of Greg Luowski. Terrified.

Forget being a high school bully, I was an unstoppable tank!

I was feeling pretty darn good about myself when the sudden sound of a siren twisted my gut. I glanced in the rearview mirror. No police in sight. I shook my head. I must have imagined it—but there it was again!

I re-checked. Nothing. Swallowing, I hunched lower over the steering wheel.

A kid in the car ahead of me turned back. He had glowing green eyes and an evil grin. I blinked. No, the boy's eyes were brown; he stared blankly at me.

A second later, I nearly hit my head on the ceiling of the

ambulance when I saw a billboard for the DVD of the new Maleficent movie. Every sound I could hear was an Overtaker laughing, a cop car's siren.

"Get out of my head!" I roared, jerking the steering wheel to the left.

Cars honked and drivers shouted angrily.

The church! That rat hole where the freaks had stayed. They weren't there now, and it'd be a convenient place to hide.

Hide from what, Greg? The cops? The Overtakers? Their orders?

An uncharacteristically cold wind for Orlando in summertime prickled the hairs on the back of my neck and arms. I glanced back at the mirrors, even stuck my head out the window to make sure I wasn't being followed. In my mind's eye, I could see it as though it were happening right now. All of them crowded around the fire, burning bones and other unrecognizable substances, cackling, planning. I needed to get the information, or I'd be in for it. They'd kill me.

Driving down the off-ramp and into the older suburban area, my heart thumped so hard inside my chest that I was sure it would bore its way out. I drove around to the back of the church and parked, out of sight of the main road.

I must have fallen asleep. I had no idea for how long. Using the impending darkness as a cover, I ran through the parking lot and took the church stairs three at a time, delivering fisted blows to the air and wall on my way up. As though it were responsible for my problems.

In the creaking hallway that led to the rooms above the church, I heard muffled voices. Some sort of meeting seemed to be going on below me.

The first unlocked room was empty, except for a few milk crates and sofa cushions. Curtains were drawn over a window on the right wall. Good. I had multiple ways out.

As I paced the little room, my shoes kicked up the dust that had settled in the Freaks' absence. I felt ready to breathe fire. I'd nearly had my hands on Philby for the second time. But then his stupid dad had to call the police.

The floorboards whined *we—eak we—eak*.

"I am NOT weak!" I roared, and with the last syllable I punched a hole through the wall. The old drywall crumbled away; it was no match for my inhuman strength. I glared at it furiously, wishing I could burn a hole through the wall with my eyes.

"I just don't want to be their puppet anymore," I whispered.

I sat down on one of the overturned milk crates with a thud. My weight almost broke it.

I hated the Keepers, especially Finn, and I didn't mind doing the dirty work if it meant getting rid of them, but I hated Disney more. The most. That hate was engrained in my mind; it flowed through my veins, and yet, it felt like it didn't belong to me. Like a virus taking me over, making it hard to think straight . . .

I turned my head at the sounds of footsteps crunching on gravel in the parking lot below.

Something snapped inside of me. Fear. Hatred. Revenge.

We-eak! We-eak! People coming up the stairs.

I braced myself for them.

The door swung open.

Oh, this was getting good.

MATTIE

There were no AA people in the basement meeting room, only an ambulance parked out back. No explanation as to why it was there. Not knowing how to drive, having no keys, and not wanting to steal an ambulance, it didn't help me. Neither did my new phone, which was locked and basically useless.

Desperate, I searched around a found a landline that the AA group meeting room that they must keep for emergencies. I called the number on the AA sign. The man on the line gave me Joyce's info. She answered the phone in a groggy voice. I explained my predicament, leaving out the part about being abducted by impostor agents who ran a fake boarding school on an abandoned military base outside of Baltimore. No sense getting too cozy with a relative stranger.

Joyce responded as if we were sisters who'd been separated at birth. We were in the middle of making plans for me when I happened to make a snide remark about the ambulance out back.

"Yeah, that showed up as we were leaving," she said.

"You mean someone just parked it there?"

"I guess. I thought he was a friend of yours. He must have used your entrance."

"Which one? The window or your door?"

"The window. One of our girls was outside catching some air, she said—she meant having a cigarette, but she doesn't want to talk about things like that with me—and caught a look. She was all hot and bothered because he was a big, boyish guy with red hair and stunning eyes."

"Green eyes?" I said dryly.

"No idea. Why? You know him?"

I looked up at the ceiling involuntarily, imagining who was up there. Knowing who was up there.

"Actually," I said, "I'm not so sure you need to come over, but I sure appreciate the offer. Do you think it might be possible for you to send an Instagram message to a friend of mine with this phone number? I don't have Internet."

She agreed without asking a single question. "But you call me right back if you need anything, okay? I'm here for you."

My throat knotted. That wasn't something I was accustomed to hearing. I tried to thank her, but my voice cracked.

When Amanda finally called, I cried. So did she, though she said they were happy tears over my escape. She caught me up on everything that had happened, told me to keep an eye on the ambulance and sit tight.

She had a plan.

AMANDA

Arguing with one of the lead Imagineers as an eighteen-year-old girl who'd already benefited immensely from his kindness and generosity proved far easier than I'd expected.

"It's too dangerous," Joe said.

"Trusting you is dangerous," I said. "Bringing Jess with you seemed like such a nice thing to do . . . until it occurred to me that it made catching the three of us in one place that much easier."

"That's ridiculous!"

"I know that now. But it took Mattie reading about a dozen Imagineers for us to realize that you're still on our side."

"Of course I am! We are!"

"Then why aren't you telling me about finding the burned bones with DNA that tested as reptile?"

Joe's attempts to keep the shock off his face were very good, but not good enough. I'd hit the bull's-eye, and I had Wanda to thank for the theory. Throw a bunch of women together in a small cabin and watch what happens. Wayne's daughter was able to connect the DNA testing Jess had heard the Imagineers discussing in the airport terminal with the other bits and scraps of information we'd collected. I'd thrown the idea at Joe, not knowing what might happen—and here I was, celebrating.

"We will talk about that another time. Don't go jumping to any conclusions."

"The OTKs are coming after the Keepers. The Barracks 14 guys are coming after us. We can change all that tonight if you just agree to help us."

"We'd need agreements with the parents."

"I don't think you'll encounter any resistance. They, we, all of us, are exhausted. And scared. It's time we come together as a team."

Joe thought so long and hard that for a moment I was sure he'd dozed off with his eyes open. I'd seen a cat in Baltimore that could do that.

Then he snapped out of it, and he looked straight at me. "Your plan is not for the faint of heart. You girls will need to show a great deal of courage."

I took that as agreement.

* * *

Not long after my meeting with Joe, Jess, Mattie, and I celebrated our reunion with a quick group hug. Then we found ourselves tiptoeing up the church stairway in the bluish light of night, whispering nervously about our plans.

We passed a window. I unlocked it and opened it quietly.

"How am I supposed to read Luowski for what happened in the past?" Mattie asked.

"You're the expert," I said.

"That's not very nice, Mandy," Jess said, chastising me. "Mattie's asking what she should focus on in order to get a clear read."

"Greg's the only one we know who's connected to all of this. I don't think you read him for the past, I think you read him to find out who's pulling the strings. Essentially: who is he working for? If we're going to fight an enemy, we have to be able to see him."

"Or her," Jess said.

"Jess and I are here for the sake of numbers. Three against one, if we're lucky."

"But if the girl's here with him?"

"We've still got them three to two. Jess and I will distract the girl while you get a read on Luowski. Whatever it takes. Jess'll get a hand on him, too, and maybe she dreams something about it or because of it. He's all we've got."

We stopped on the upper landing, looking at each other in the strange light, and we felt something collegial pass between us. I nearly giggled, I felt so giddy. Or maybe it was nerves.

"Ready?" I whispered.

Jess and Mattie nodded, though with something less than outright enthusiasm.

Holding hands, we entered our old apartment.

* * *

A brooding, evil-spirited Luowski sat unmoving on an inverted plastic milk crate with a pillow on top. Dressed in an EMT medic's uniform shirt, he looked official—entirely different from the bull-headed ape I knew he was.

"Bad timing," he said, making no effort to stand. "I need a private moment."

Mattie's eyes quickly searched the few places the girl might have been able to hide. Then she returned her gaze to us, shaking her head. He was here alone.

"We heard about it," I said.

"Shut up."

"You could have hurt them, overpowered his parents to get to Philby, but you didn't."

"I said shut up!"

"You made a choice. The right choice."

"They called 911, you idiot."

Jess spoke up. "You had time. The thing is, Greg—if Greg Luowski is anywhere in the boy I'm talking to—you're not a kid who hurts the innocent. You pick on kids, sure, but that's different."

"What do you know about it?" Luowski's face was beet red.

Jess said, "I know you're in trouble now—with them. You're scared, like we are."

"You three have more to be scared about than I do. They have plans for you."

They, I noted. But I said nothing.

"That may be true," Jess said. "But I bet failure's not tolerated very well by the Overtakers. You had your chance. You know it. We know it. You're here because you wanted a place to think it out. What's next, Greg? What did you figure out?"

"Shut up and get out of here."

"That's not going to happen," I said. "We're going to the Central Plaza in the Magic Kingdom. The Imagineers are going to help us. You can join us, Greg. They'll help you, too."

The sound of slamming car doors won our attention. All of us, including Luowski, turned slightly toward the windows.

Mattie worked her way toward the window, toward Luowski's side.

"Keep your hands off me," Luowski said.

No effort to attack us. I wondered if he might actually be afraid of me. It gave me a little rush of adrenaline: Greg Luowski, afraid of me, afraid of another pair of scissors at this throat.

"Three guys," Mattie said, looking out. "Suits. Someone must have called them."

"No way!" I said. "We'd better hurry. It's Central Plaza for us, Greg, ASAP."

"Who are we talking about?" Luowski asked. "Who's out there?"

"Our former jailers," I said, "from a long time ago."

"Return of the Living Dead," Mattie said.

"Your doing?" I asked him, keeping my gaze steady.

"Yeah," he said sarcastically, "My best friends. Didn't you know?"

"You could have taken a plea bargain. Maybe you want to turn us in, exchange us for leniency."

"So I magically attracted you here," Luowski said. "I mean you came to me—or am I missing something?"

"A bug," Jess said. "He could be wearing a recorder."

"Take off your shirt," I instructed him, "or Mattie's going to do it for you."

"Nice try," Greg said. "That girl is not touching me." Then he added, "Nice job with the Imagineers in the Studios, by the way."

Mattie snarled at him.

"Those three guys are coming up here," Jess said.

"So? Let them." He didn't sound too concerned.

"You could say we aren't here," I suggested.

"Why would I do that?"

"So that when they take you away, there are three of us here to rescue you."

"No one's taking me anywhere."

"They may feel differently about that, Greg." Lifting my palms to him, I asked again for him to unbutton his shirt.

He reluctantly undid the top three buttons, then untucked his shirttail to confirm there was no wire. "Satisfied?"

Mattie was. She had used the distraction to sneak up behind Luowski and place her hand on his neck. Luowski jerked up, waving his arms wildly, barely missing Mattie as she jumped away.

"Out that window," I informed him, "is a ledge. Where it meets the church roof, you can slide down and grab the pipe that's sticking up. It's a drainpipe; it'll get you to the ground. Jess and I had to use that a couple of times. Believe me, it works."

"You first," Luowski said. The sound of footsteps climbing the stairs was louder now. "This type of guy always leaves one man on the ground. I'd be walking right into their net."

"If you insist," I said. Mattie climbed out, then Jess. Luowski looked troubled; he thought I was bluffing or trying to trap him. I hesitated in the window, just long enough for the door to open. Long enough to be seen. Luowski jumped up—but I was blocking the window. I slipped out, ran along the ledge, slid, caught on the pipe, swung to the drainpipe, and climbed down. The part I hadn't told Luowski about was simple: use the open window halfway down. I climbed through the window I'd opened on my way up. Back in the stairway, I met Jess and Mattie. We slid the window shut and locked it.

The next step, leaving by the AA meeting entrance and bypassing any "agent" waiting by the cars, was made easier by the fact that Luowski had taken our route, but had ridden the drainpipe all the way to the ground, falling straight into the hands of the waiting Barracks 14 man at the bottom. The man saw us running; I made sure of that. Preoccupied with Luowski, he had no choice but to call for his partners.

The trick now was to make sure we got caught—and this part of my plan required Joe's help.

Halfway up the block, the back doors of a white van swung open, and the three of us piled in. Joe shut the doors behind us.

"Are you sure about this?" he asked. "You have to be absolutely certain."

The woman on the seat beside him wore purple surgical gloves; there was a tackle box open at her shins.

"We're sure," I said, speaking for the three of us.

Joe gave a signal, and the van drove off.

MATTIE

When I placed my hand on Luowski's beefy neck, I wasn't sure what would happen. I had never read an individual four times. But it was easy. I had Luowski mapped out. I channeled his thoughts to the Overtakers and the orders he was following.

Immediately, memories of Tia Dalma that didn't belong to me filled my mind. Luowski's impressions of her were clear: furious and sinister. He was afraid of her because she had threatened him.

Even after Luowski jerked away, the strand of words that haunted him and held him so tightly to his task remained fresh in my mind. It was as though Tia Dalma had spoken them to me herself.

"I must know their secret. If you do not bring me de secret, you will die. We all will die."

I felt like a cavern, empty, her threat echoing in silence. This seemed terribly dangerous. What secret was so important that it would put someone's life on the line? So important that the Overtakers were worried, too?

I slipped out the window, Jess following, wondering if

"they" could mean the Keepers. Finn and the others obviously knew something that they hadn't told us.

Halfway down the drainpipe, I angled myself through the second-story window we'd left open.

Luowski's thoughts had to have something do with the Keepers being trapped in SBS. Or information that Finn had known before he'd gone comatose.

Amanda slid through the window behind Jess, and slammed the window shut, locking it. From the hallway, we watched Luowski ride the drainpipe to the ground and get caught by the Barracks 14 guy waiting at the bottom. I laughed.

Lost things often hide in plain sight. Maybe we were making this out to be more complicated than it was.

Maybe the answer was staring us in the face.

DAY 9

AMANDA

By the time Jess, Mattie, and I arrived at the Magic Kingdom's Central Plaza, the end of the extended hours had pushed tens of thousands of weary guests toward the front gates. It was past midnight.

We sat together on a bench facing the Partners statue, the area ringed by bronze figurines of famous Disney characters. People watching, one of my favorite things to do in Disney parks, hit new heights of amusement; strollers seemed to be pulling the parents trailing them, and young children bounded and bounced, not wanting to leave.

"How much longer?" Jess asked. "You think they'll make it?"

"I'm sure," I said. "I have no doubts. If there's anything we can trust, it's that they'll get here before we're thrown out."

"If you say so," Mattie said.

"I do. Joe knows what he's doing." I paused, and then said, "Are you both afraid?"

"Yes."

"Me, too," I admitted. "Good! Hold on to that fear. We're going to need it."

"What if this is the last time we see the park?" Mattie asked. "What if that happens?"

"One thing at a time."

"But if it does?"

"Then we'll consider it a success," Jess said slowly. "We'll have provided the necessary distraction to make the move. What choice do we have?"

"I'll miss the music," Mattie said. "I'll miss it the most. I like having a soundtrack in my life. The parks are great that way."

"Yes, they are," I said. "The parks are great in every way."

"You're worried about him, aren't you?" Mattie asked.

"I'm worried about all of them," I answered. "All of."

"Uh-huh." Mattie's cynicism was beginning to annoy me. Or maybe I was just stressed. Either way, I snapped at her.

"You think I only care about Finn?"

"I think you care more about him. Of course."

"She doesn't." Jess jumped to my defense. "In her heart, maybe, sure. But not in her actions. I've never seen you favor Finn that way," she said, looking at me.

"Uh-oh," I answered, looking beyond her. "Company."

The three of us rose at the same time. Four men in suits, men who did not belong in the Magic Kingdom, approached us. Two of their faces were eerily familiar.

Two more blocked us from behind.

"Does that scare you enough?" I asked my partners.

"Um, yeah!" answered Mattie. "They're the ones that got me."

Jess said nothing.

The man directly in front of me shook his head as he saw my eyes wander from side to side. "Don't make a scene," he said softly. "The company knows we're here, and it knows why. All you'll do is damage their reputation. Not ours. We have no reputation. We don't exist."

"We're supposed to just . . . what?" I asked. "Walk out of here?"

"We won't be joining the others. We're headed for the parade route gate by Splash Mountain."

"The Imagineers would never let this happen," Jess said.

"Don't be so sure," the man said.

"We're no longer minors," Mattie said. "Taking us against our will is kidnapping."

"We will be happy to have our attorneys explain it you, Madeline. But that's for tomorrow. Tonight you will be our guests on a flight to Baltimore."

"No," I said, trying to hide my nervousness. "Tonight you will put us up in a Disney hotel on property. Tomorrow morning we will meet with the lawyers. Only then are we getting on some plane."

"You are hardly in a position to make demands."

"Seriously?" I said. "What do think we've been doing while

we've been away?" I raised both arms, each aimed at one of the suits. I clapped my hands. The two men slid, standing up, like they were on ice, and smashed into each other at high speed. In seconds, they lay groveling on the asphalt. Then I used my left hand to knock the stun gun from the leader's hands. It broke into pieces on the concrete.

"Should we go again?" I asked. "If one of you so much as lays a hand on me or my friends, we will not go willingly."

With four men surrounding us, it made sense that I couldn't actually win a battle. But I could inflict significant injury, starting with the leader.

The two on the pavement climbed to their knees, stood, and brushed themselves off. I wasn't good at making new friends.

"Fine," the leader said. "It will take us some time to make the arrangements."

"And we will sit here until you do."

"I'd rather we all get into the vehicle."

"I'm sure you would, but that's not going to happen. You wouldn't like it anyway. My power in a closed space like that? No fun for anyone."

We negotiated a bit longer, but I surprised myself—and Jess!—with my lack of compromise. All the while, I kept an eye on the leader's wristwatch, tracking the minutes as they ticked past. At one point, Mattie allowed a wiggle of a smile to sneak out, but she bit it back just as quickly. I winked at her.

Grown-ups can be pathetically slow. Rather than just

booking a few rooms himself, the leader assigned the task to someone at the other end of a phone call. It was probably beneath him to carry out such menial labor. Thankfully for us, putting a middleman into the logistics and reservations meant killing more time.

The minutes slipped past. The flow of departing guests was down to a trickle. Soon the security guards trying to clear the park would notice us. That would give me a chance to test how honest the leader had been. I had my doubts about Disney's complicity in our detainment.

Luckily for the leader, confirmation came before security.

"The Polynesian. One room, two beds. We will be in the rooms on either side of you and across the hall."

"Show us to the car," I said. "But as a reminder, if any one of you touches one of us, even accidentally, I will flatten that man and anyone else within twenty yards of me."

For the first time, the leader didn't have a response.

LUOWSKI

I ran from the church, wanting to distance myself from the feeble guy in the suit. I had no idea what might have happened if he'd caught me for real; I had no desire to find out.

Giddiness swept through me as I pictured the look on the man's face when I easily fought him off. Whatever had happened to me after I'd become part of the Overtakers, I now possessed the ability to deflect an opponent's strength. It wasn't like I could bench press four fifty, but just try taking a swing at me.

Two miles to the bus stop.

Despite my internal revelry, the near-capture had warned me that nowhere was safe. I had no idea who the suits were or what they wanted. That didn't help me feel any more secure.

I wasn't being followed. Maybe the Freaks were telling the truth. Maybe the men were actually after them.

A series of bus rides and I ended up at Downtown Disney. From there, I'd have to wing it.

"We'd better hurry. It's Central Plaza for us, Greg, ASAP." Amanda's words echoed in my head. Philby's stupid laptop was proving impossible to crack, so the Freaks seemed like the only way to find and take out the Keepers.

At eleven forty, I approached Central Plaza in the Magic Kingdom. Keeping my eyes open for the Fairlies, I headed for shadow. I loved shadow.

Ten patient minutes later, I thought I spotted Amanda's brown hair. She stood, arms akimbo, shaking her head at a small group of the suits. They looked like the same men from the church. I inched closer, trying to hear what they were saying.

"Show us to the car," Amanda said. "But as a reminder, if any one of you touches one of us, even accidentally, I will flatten that man and anyone else within twenty yards of me."

It's true! I thought wryly.

I followed the group toward the Jafar row of the Magic Kingdom parking lot. As they walked, Amanda almost seemed to sparkle in the lamplight.

I'd liked her for a long, long time. She knew it. Whitless knew it. And still, they'd treated me like scum for two years at school. Payback time.

The suits led the girls to a black SUV.

I had no way to follow.

Looking around the backstage parking lot, I saw a Disney transport van idling with the lights on. It was used to bring Cast Members to distant parking lots. The driver was busy talking to a Cast Member, both drinking coffee. I had no choice.

I hurried across the lot, ducking low, using cars to screen me. I slipped into the passenger door, and climbed behind the wheel.

The SUV was nearly out of sight.

I shifted and hit the accelerator and the back tires squealed. In the rearview mirror I saw the driver drop his coffee.

As the SUV came back into sight, I slowed to keep my distance as I smiled, deeply satisfied.

So far, so good.

* * *

Fifteen agonizing minutes later, we pulled up to the Polynesian, a tropical themed resort with eleven longhouses set up like the eleven islands of Polynesia. I parked the van out on the street and crossed through a parking lot to reach the hotel.

At the lobby entrance, one of the suits went inside, probably to collect room keys.

I didn't know if it was my own thoughts, or a voice speaking to me, but I knew suddenly that I couldn't stay. The Freaks weren't the answer. The person who knew what was going on was the Head Imagineer. I knew—or I was told—where to find him. Maybe I'd overheard someone talking about it. Maybe it was the jet flying overhead. Regardless, I knew I had to wait outside the backstage gate to Disney's Hollywood Studios—the Imagineering offices. An answer would come.

I headed back to the van through the valet parking lot.

I saw an amber flashing light through the bushes. Disney Security had found the van.

Panicking, I spun, trying to think of what to do.

When one of the valet dudes in the stupid costumes parked a car and began to trot back toward the hotel, I caught up to him and clipped him from behind, dropping him to the pavement with a single punch. Then I took his wallet and keys. I didn't have to use the key, just have it in my pocket. One push of a button, and I was rolling in a red Buick with black leather seats.

Sweet.

* * *

When I was right, I was right. Shortly after I parked near the Studio's security exit, a white van pulled out—the interior light on!—and there was the Head Imagineer, Joe, riding shotgun. I followed, giving them a good distance.

A half hour later, they turned off the highway toward the Orlando Airport. The van caught me by surprise, exiting before the final turn. I drove past, got caught in the loop that circled the terminal. I'd lost at least ten minutes.

When I finally made the turn I'd missed, I was on an access road that led along the vast area containing a string of companies and hangars. I slowed at each driveway, looking in. Just past the entrance to a place called JetPort, I saw the van on the tarmac beside a fancy jet with the Disney "D" on the tailfin. A number of stretchers were being lifted by a device and rolled into the jet. *The Kingdom Keepers!* The Imagineers were moving the Keepers out of Orlando!

To avoid making a scene, I drove on and doubled back.

Judging by the cars I saw parked nearby, JetPort was a private jet terminal used by rich businessmen and major companies. I went on foot to the front door, but turned around immediately. The Imagineer was talking to someone at the counter. I didn't want him seeing me. I felt like a dog on a short leash.

Only after the Disney jet taxied away did I enter the JetPort terminal. The place looked like a country club, all padded carpeting, heavy formal furniture, and an abundance of huge flat-screen televisions. There was a help-yourself refreshment area. I wolfed down two chocolate chip cookies before approaching the counter.

Glancing at my reflection as I passed a steel post, I realized with a jolt of surprise that I was still wearing my EMT uniform. It occurred to me that I had to play a role. There was no turning back.

The lady smiled, "How may I help you, sir?"

"Well," I drawled, "the Disney group that just left? They asked me to air freight some equipment they didn't have room for. They're going to need it. I'm supposed to send it to the terminal there, where they're landing." I patted my various pockets. "Trouble is . . . and I hope this can stay between us . . . I've lost the address for the place."

"Sir?" She bit her lip.

"I can arrange it down at FedEx, but heck, not if I don't have the right terminal!"

She hesitated. "The thing is, sir, we have a strict policy about customer privacy. Very strict."

"It's not as if I can call Mr. Garlington." I thought using Joe's name might help me. I was right. She stared at me, unsure, but I could see her face softening.

"Look, I messed up," I said. Words that didn't come easily. I sighed for effect and looked down. "But my mess up shouldn't cause someone's health complications."

"All right! Okay!" she said. "It's an FBO at Burbank called StarFlight. Their flight plan is to Burbank, California. But I didn't tell you that."

She lowered her head as if I were no longer in the room.

* * *

Soon I was in the Orlando Airport at the ticket counter, buying a red-eye flight courtesy of one of the parking valet's many credit cards. I hadn't gotten much sleep in the past few days. The night flight would do me good.

AMANDA

Blinking awake, I felt a soft tremor beneath me, as if I was on the floor of an apartment near a passing train, or maybe on a ride in the parks. Above me I saw the gentle curve of off-white fabric. My neck was sore and tight; I fought back a bad headache in an effort to look to my left. Last thing I remembered was the Barracks 14ers in the Magic Kingdom.

Joe's face, a knot of concern and worry, loomed above me, as big as a hot-air balloon. Slowly, he blinked, his eyes watery. I watched his troubles melt from his face like Olaf dissolving near a fire. A tear spilled.

"You're all right," he said.

My dry mouth and throat prevented me from speaking. He called out something I couldn't hear, and a water glass and straw arrived.

"Don't sit up yet. It's the drugs," he said. "They affected you badly."

"Drugs?" I choked out. I hated even the idea of the things. Had never done any, would never do any.

"Medications. The sleeping aid you agreed to? You all agreed. The nurse, remember?"

I did, vaguely. The idea had not been entirely Joe's. We'd worked out the legalities before heading to the church, which I also remembered.

"The van," I said, the water tasting delicious, cooling the back of my throat. "The back of the van."

Joe nodded. "We put you to sleep and crossed you over as DHIs into the Central Plaza. That way the men from Maryland were only collecting holograms. You must have done a good job convincing them not to touch you. If they had, they'd have known."

"We allowed fear," I said. "Being version 1.6, that made us more solid. But yes, I tried to let them know we wouldn't tolerate being handled."

"I'm glad you remember. It must have been a shock. On this end you were supervised and monitored the whole time. We returned you just now. You're all three coming awake. Sure glad it worked."

I saw the nurse; a couple other people I took to be Imagineers on Joe's team too. Mattie was on a couch across from me, with Jess farther up.

"Where am I?"

"The Disney jet. Remember the plan? We're heading back to Burbank. It's a little past three in the morning. We've brought the four Keepers along with us for safekeeping. Their continuing dormancy is disturbing and potentially dangerous. But mostly this is about you." He grinned devilishly, like a boy who'd played the ultimate prank. "If your captors are keeping a close eye on you, well, you just disappeared. Otherwise, someone is in for a big surprise tomorrow morning. I doubt they know much about DHIs, so they're going to wonder how three girls escaped from a locked room. Let them try to figure that one out.

"I guarantee you," Joe continued, "those men have no idea where you've gone or how it happened. They'll likely be fired. And I've got another trick or two up my sleeve when it comes to you three. A way to protect you, to keep you safe and sound in the School of Imagineering for a long time to come."

Overwhelming joy and relief left me speechless. I sniffled, and Joe told me the nurse would get the three of us some power drinks.

"We've got work to do," he added. "I got the security video, as requested. We have it with us."

* * *

Mattie and Jess came through the return well. Joe had not wanted to induce sleep, but he knew he had to cross us over into Central Plaza in the short span of a car ride. So the nurse had given us something mild, and we'd drifted off. Joe crossed us over, fooling the Barracks 14ers long enough to get us onto a plane and out of Orlando.

Mission accomplished.

Halfway into the long flight, our stomachs full, our heads cleared, Joe got down to business.

238

"Wanda requested security videos of Walt's apartment in Disneyland," he said.

The jet's window shades had been pulled. A flat panel TV hung on the wall by the cockpit. The screen had been showing our flight path a few minutes earlier; currently, it broadcast video blue.

"We found it interesting, since our DHI team had been reviewing the same tapes this week. Can you explain why she made that request?"

He looked directly at Mattie.

MATTIE

Joe stared directly at me. My eyes drifted around the jet. My cheeks were on fire.

"We needed answers. You guys, the Imagineers, always seem to have them," I said softly.

No one spoke. My stomach dropped.

"I'm sorry," I said. "It's just we were desperate—are desperate. And there was this one guy . . . he has grayish hair. He'd seen the apartment surveillance videos. Because he saw them, so did I."

Joe's face darkened. I hoped he wasn't considering opening the door and throwing me out of the jet without a parachute. He kinda looked that way.

"No one can fault you for creativity. As long as you don't share what yo—"

"Never!"

Jess, Amanda, and I did not move. Did not breathe.

"Well, then," Joe said. "Let's get to work."

JESS

The screen flickered to life, revealing grainy footage shot by a security camera. I immediately recognized the room: Walt Disney's private apartment in Disneyland.

The small space was decorated like something you'd see in a grandma's house: two couches and a handful of chairs; faded floral pillows; the signature lamp in the window—lit, as always. A large wooden box on legs looking like an extremely old jukebox stood in the corner.

As we watched, five figures entered the room. Amanda tensed as Finn came into view, followed by the rest of the Keepers. They gathered around a chest-high brown box and carried on an animated discussion. But we couldn't hear them. The camera lacked audio.

"That object is a vintage music box. Some of the furniture in the apartment are reproductions, but the music box is original. Walt loved his music," Joe said. "The tapes show us that the Keepers visited the apartment *and* the music box several times. Then this, a few days later."

A new video played. This time Finn and Philby stood by the music box. Philby moved to a photo on the wall and removed it. His body blocked any view of what he did before returning the photo to the wall.

"We are assuming he found a key on the back of the frame," Joe said.

Philby again blocked the music box. A small drawer popped open below the glass window. Philby took a disc over to the ancient phonograph, and the boys listened.

"We lost them after that. I'll play another."

The screen flickered. Finn, alone in the apartment, in front of the music box. He leaned to the side, stared in at the workings of the machine, and then quickly left.

"Not a big help, I'm afraid," said Joe.

"Can you please replay that last part?" I asked.

Joe politely did as I'd asked.

"His leg!" I said, a little loudly. "Back it up and watch his leg."

A moment passed. We all watched for a third time. Finn's leg passed *through* the cabinet.

"It's a hologram," Amanda said. "It's a DHI, not the real Finn."

AMANDA

I studied Finn intensely.

No Philby, no Charlene. Just Finn, up there on the screen. Uncontrollable, adorable Finn. The boy who had no idea how cute he was. The quiet, brainy kid with a smile that could reach across a football field and stop you dead. That Finn. My Finn.

"Did you know?" I asked. "A DHI?"

"No. No clue. I'm as shocked as you are. It would appear they came several times as themselves, and then returned as DHIs."

"But why?" Jess asked. "Why as a DHI?"

"It changes things," Joe said.

"How?" Mattie asked.

"I wish I knew the answer to that," Joe admitted. "It took an effort. A plan. Clearly they must have had their reasons."

"You're angry," I said, hearing it in his voice.

"They were only to cross over with our knowledge. They went behind our backs," he said.

Joe pushed pause on the remote. He might as well have had a button for his facial muscles, too, because he froze.

"You know something," I said, cutting off whatever he was going to say next. "Those are our friends up there. We've fought OTKs, had garden statues threaten us, and been run down by a bunch of guys in suits. All to save them. Don't we deserve the truth?"

Joe sighed. Nodded. He seemed resigned to be truthful with us, though it clearly pained him.

* * *

Jess spoke up. "I saw you with a woman in a wheelchair. I'm guessing the videos are the last known record you have of the Keepers. Did Philby discover the camera at some point and shut it down?"

"Incredible," Joe said, his face drained of color.

I didn't know if he was complimenting Jess's logic, or if she was so completely wrong that it made her incredible.

The other two Imagineers came to their feet, exchanged a long look with Joe, and entered into a silent conversation. It went on so long it almost felt comedic, though with Finn in my thoughts, I wasn't laughing.

"Your juvenile assessment—" said one of Joe's colleagues.

Joe stopped the guy with a raised hand. "No, Alex. No more keeping them in the dark." He spoke solely to Jess: "We have suspected the Keepers were crossed over, but none of the parents would acknowledge this. Now, thanks to you, we know they are not only crossed over, but in trouble. We don't know where they may have gone, or why."

"You have ideas."

"Hear me out," Joe said. "Objects inside the park have been doing strange, unexplainable things, like moving by themselves. We consulted Disney Legends as well as experts with the Archives, and others, to get a handle on what's been happening, but it remains unclear. We have encountered certain . . . atmospheric anomalies. This is just one of many curiosities over the past several weeks. Jess's pointing out that the Keepers had gone into SBS came late.

"Then, the threat to you—all three of you are part of the team, an important part of the team. You should know that. Now, here we are. We have the videos, but they're as worthless as everything else. Too many dead ends. You run out of gas."

"You can't quit trying to find them!" I said.

"Of course we won't! We are responsible. Believe me, we live with the full weight of that reality."

From the glum silence, Mattie raised her voice. "You looked at videos of Wayne, too."

Joe and his colleagues did not like being spied upon by a mind-reading teenager, and each reacted with his own expression of indignation.

"In Wayne's apartment?" I asked. "Or in Walt's?"

If Joe could have punched something to relieve the stress, he would have. "I can't comment on that."

"You won't, you mean," I said.

"We certainly never had security cameras in Wayne's apartment," he said. "We installed video in Walt's for obvious reasons. At times it's like the whole world wants a look inside."

"So Wayne was in Walt's apartment. Did you know that before?" I asked.

"We did not. It was an accidental discovery, when we went looking for videos of the Keepers."

Jess spoke up again. "What's with the music box? They all headed straight to it."

"We don't know," Joe said.

"Wait!" I said. "You guys are the Imagineers, and you don't have any ideas?"

"Correct. We are but mere mortals," Joe said. He might have meant it as a joke, but it missed its mark.

"You've looked at the music box?" Jess asked. "Studied it?"

He nodded. "The word *computer* has come to mean a laptop or tablet. Fifty, sixty years ago, a computer would've been something mechanical. The code machines in World War II were strictly that—gears, springs, wheels. We did not try to open the music box. It was wisely suggested that we scan it first.

"Well, wait for it. What we found inside was anything but a music box. It's a primitive computer—in the way we'd use the term today. We don't yet know how it operates, because our scanning revealed booby traps. It will be rendered inoperative if we try to open it."

"Self-destruct," Mattie breathed.

"Exactly."

"What made your colleague think to scan it in the first place?" I asked.

"I beg your pardon?"

"Who would think to do that?" I said. "You'd just open the thing. So why didn't you?"

I was pushing Joe to say things he did not want to say. "Very well, young lady. Have it your way. From what we can tell, the back of the box does open. But carved next to the release, very faintly, my colleague saw the initials N.T. That stopped him. And it prompted us to scan the music box."

Mattie voiced what I was thinking. "Why would a pair of initials stop him?"

"N.T." Joe repeated. "In our line of work, we pay homage to a few geniuses besides, of course, Walt: Leonardo da Vinci, the greatest of them all. Zhang Heng, the amazing Chinese sage. And Nikola Tesla."

"Like the car," I said.

Joe and the other Imagineers laughed, making me feel stupid. I didn't like feeling stupid. I wished I'd said nothing.

"Like the car," Joe said. "An extraordinary mind. Tesla was an older man when Walt Disney started to reveal his own genius. There's always been speculation—never proof—that the two not only admired each other, but may have met, may have even collaborated."

"Tesla built the music box," I said, in awe.

"Speculation."

"But what you found inside . . ."

"Clearly the work of an extraordinary mind, yes. And nothing to tamper with."

"But how would the Keepers know about it?" Mattie asked.

"Wayne," Joe said.

"And how would he know about it?"

"Walt." Joe spoke softly, with an air of reverence. "As a young man, Wayne was a technician in the early construction of Disneyland. He interacted with Walt on a regular basis."

The hum of the jet filled my ringing ears. The resulting silence meant something different to all of us. I was thinking of Finn. Joe of Walt Disney, I imagined.

"We, the three of us, would like to get into Walt's apartment," I said. "We promise that we won't open the music box.

You can watch us on the security cameras. But we need to be there."

I expected push back. He would refuse me and I would have to fight to get Jess and Mattie in there to try to "read" the apartment.

"Yes," Joe said, stunning me, "I know. We've already made plans."

DAY 10

AMANDA

The following day, led by a Cast Member, Jess, Mattie, and I climbed the backstage steps to Walt's historic apartment. I felt apprehension beating in my chest. Given what we knew, this was likely the last set of stairs Finn and the others had climbed or descended before entering SBS. Wayne had trod these stairs. So had Walt Disney himself.

Now three girls with exceptional abilities followed in their footsteps—but with trepidation. I knew that each of us individually, as well as collectively, felt like we were the last great hope for the Keepers, the only hope of saving them from whatever they'd gotten themselves into.

I'd asked Joe for a list of anyone who'd visited the apartment since the Keepers' disappearance, along with their pictures. Jess could occasionally get a "daydream" from something as simple as a picture. We weren't leaving anything to chance.

On the list was a rock star, two movie stars, a film crew, a Disney archivist, a U.S. senator, and a historian from the

Walt Disney Family Museum. Singling out the senator and the historian, I'd inquired about the purpose of their visits.

The senator's father had worked for WED Enterprises, the group that eventually became the Imagineers. The historian from the Walt Disney Family Museum had made the request last minute. She was interested in certain historical documents relating to our early adoption of technolgy.

Ghosts! Had to be.

Climbing the stairs toward the old apartment reminded me that even the old is new. The apartment was over fifty years old, and I was excited to see it once more.

The Cast Member let us in, saying a polite good-bye.

Inside, the doilies and old furniture reminded me a little of Mrs. Nash's, only a lot classier. Mattie gawked at the antiques, the artwork, and the view of the park past the glowing lamp in the window. Jess took a meditative moment to let the space surround her. I'd seen her do this before, but I marveled at her ability to relax and disconnect from what was going on around her.

My heart was sailing as I stood facing the music box. I could feel Joe and the others watching us over the restored surveillance system. But I knew from the videos on the plane that they could only see us, not hear us.

JESS

My best chance for a daydream would be to connect with the places in which people slept and *dreamed*. Gently, I sat on the edge of the sleeper sofa to the left. The apartment had the feeling of a museum, and I didn't want to disturb anything, materially or psychically.

A sense of calm washed over me as I closed my eyes. The room remained present in my thoughts; I could see it before me, empty and charming.

But alarming, too: the light in the window was not illuminated. No music played; the only sound was muted chatter from Town Square.

There was a noise at the edges of my consciousness. It started as a few faint notes of carnival music, light and playful. Circus music? I wondered.

It steadily grew louder; as it did, I realized it wasn't coming from the window, as I'd thought. I opened my eyes, but only slightly, trying not to lose the moment. I must have mumbled something because Mattie and Amanda were staring at me. The music began fading, and I squinted my eyes shut. Slowly, carefully, I suspended all thought and concern.

The music returned, like a flighty bird reversing direction. It swept past me, now coming from my right. It grew louder and louder. Too loud! I pressed my hands to my ears, trying to shut it out, but it was inside my head. I'd only made matters worse.

I popped open my eyes. The music stopped.

I sat staring at the music box.

"I think I may know what drew them to the music box," I said to the room at large.

It would turn out I was wrong.

MATTIE

I found the apartment living room's crimson theme both beautiful and relaxing. It was the kind of feeling I wanted to capture if I ever had a place of my own. I'd lived my life in tiny rooms in houses not of my choosing. The dream of having my own place helped me in my darkest moments. A kitchen with food I liked. A cat. Books.

Now I concealed my excitement as I looked around the tiny room. I hoped I didn't seem childish, but then I honestly didn't care. My favorite spot, the view of the park seen through the window where the antique lamp shone so steadily, allowed me to imagine Walt, right there, looking out over his kingdom.

The space filled with a tingling energy. The last time I tried to read an inanimate object was a total flop, but at that moment, the apartment seemed like a living, breathing entity. Something otherworldly. I crossed the room and placed a hand on the door.

Nothing. The wall, also nothing.

For whatever reason, I felt dropped to my knees. I placed both hands on the carpet and felt a hum or vibration in my wrists. I yanked my hands back before slowly applying them again.

This time, the hum traveled up my arms. I wanted to release my touch, but found myself compelled to lean forward more heavily. The spreading sensation was not Walt Disney wonderful, but a dark tremor, like a crack in the earth opening to consume me, overtake me. Whatever I felt, wherever it came from, it did not originate in this room. It was nothing of this world.

I pulled back. My hands were stuck.

"Help," I moaned weakly. "Help . . ."

Amanda and Jess came to my side. They spoke, but I barely heard. My vision was filled with a deep burgundy smear of horror, my ears with wailing. My body succumbed to pain.

Somehow, they tore me loose and got me to my feet. I bent over, breathing hard. Terrified. Ready to throw up.

"We have a problem."

AMANDA

Mattie settled into a chair, pale and scared. Her experience was a clear warning, and I approached the music box with reservation. I wasn't so much scared or nervous as I was apprehensive. I didn't know what would happen, and I wasn't sure I wanted to find out.

"It looks pretty basic," I said. "A metronome and some kind of switch on the side."

"I agree," Jess said, kneeling beside me. "Not really anything else to it."

"You must be able to switch discs," Mattie said weakly from her chair.

"I suppose. But we don't want to switch discs. We want to know what they were listening to before they left. Maybe it's a voice message."

"Joe would know," Jess said. "Maybe he wouldn't have told us, but he'd know."

"I get what you're saying, Amanda," Mattie said. She seemed to be slowly recovering her strength. "But we can't be sure that the disc in there is the same one. All the people who've been up here since, including the senator and the historian—anyone could have changed it. The camera hasn't been working."

"Why would anyone change the disc?" I asked.

"How should I know?" Mattie cried. "I'm just saying!"

"Yeah. Okay. I get that."

"It doesn't mean we shouldn't try," Jess said.

I reached for the controls, but my phone rang, stopping me. I didn't recognize the number, and with my full attention on the music box, I was in no mood to take a call, so I sent it to voice mail. It didn't buzz in my pocket, which meant the caller hadn't left a message.

Back to the music box. We didn't count down. We didn't make it dramatic. I pulled on the small brass pin sticking out below the metronome. Music played.

Circus music. A calliope.

Jess muffled her gasp.

I took a step back from the machine.

"That," Jess said, "note for note, is the same music I just heard in my head."

Over the odd-sounding pipe music melody came the flutter of wings.

"Check it out!" shouted Mattie, pointing.

On the other side of the window behind Walt's lamp, perched on the sill, flapping its tattered wings to remain balanced, stood a black raven. It had seen better days. It was so scraggly and disgusting looking that it almost seemed as if it had been set on fire.

"Poor thing," Jess said. "It looks sick or something."

"Mattie," I whispered harshly. "Get close enough to see its eyes, but do not touch the glass. Do not get any closer than you need to."

"You don't think—" Jess said sharply.

"Think what?" Mattie asked.

"An Overtaker—a dead Overtaker—had a raven called Diablo. That's why I need to know—"

The bird flew away.

"—the color of its eyes." Too late. Mattie hadn't had time to get close.

Mattie turned. "But isn't Diablo—"

"Yes! Let's not talk about it, please." I couldn't bear the thought of the burning bones being part of some dark ritual. Fear poisoned my good thoughts far too often. I wanted away from fear and trouble.

"Don't go all Harry Potter on me," Mattie said. "'He who shall not be named.'"

"I'm telling you," I said, "it's not the worst philosophy. Some words conjure up bad thoughts. Emphasis on *conjure*."

The music stopped. Thankfully.

When the three of us focused on Walt's lamp and the window—not to mention the raven—we had turned to face Town Square. This, along with the eerie calliope music, helped explain why we didn't hear the unlocked back door open.

"Quaint."

Greg Luowski, looking about eight feet tall and as angry as a starved wolf, stood closest to Jess. I was next. Mattie, across the room by the window, said something she shouldn't have. I needed Jess out of the way if I was to push.

But Jess being Jess meant trouble for people who surprised her. Jess did not take kindly to surprises.

JESS

I'd never taken kindly to surprises. I didn't enjoy them as a little girl; I didn't enjoy them at Barracks 14; and I certainly didn't enjoy these appearances of evildoers now.

When Luowski walked through the door of the apartment, I reacted with the instincts of a dog under attack. Perhaps my protectiveness of Mattie and Amanda and the desire to get the jump on Luowski fueled me. I'd heard of blind rage before, but now I was living it.

Standing before me was an agent of Maleficent, the woman who had taken away the first freedom I'd ever known. At least in the barracks, I'd had my thoughts for myself. The 14ers could keep me locked in a room and run tests on me all day, but they couldn't take away my imagination. Maleficent could. She put ideas, her voice, in my head. She'd nearly ruined me. If it hadn't been for the Keepers, she would have.

Luowski had gone willingly to her side. Perhaps a spell had kept him there, but he made the initial decision to follow her. Mercifully, his mistress was finally dead. But he was still here, still a symbol of everything she'd put me through. Put *us* all through.

All this ran through my head in a matter of seconds, and I snapped. Not knowing what I was doing, I rushed him. The shock was evident on his face—I had never been much of an action figure; I'd even played the damsel in distress, captured by the Overtakers until the Keepers came to save me.

Not today. As I balled my fists and threw blows at his head, I found an internal power I'd never known I possessed. At first, the oaf deflected my attempts. He saw my punches coming before they could land, blocking them with bizarre and supernatural speed.

But I had powers of my own—six years of pent-up anger toward the Overtakers and all they stood for. For every blow he deflected, I returned more. It was as though all the anger I'd bottled up had finally burst, giving me power and speed. My arms and legs blurred. Luowski couldn't keep up—and in my adrenaline-fueled rage, I was just getting started.

My blows began to land. I wasn't practicing any longer, I was doing what I'd been trained to do. I drove Luowski back as he threw two roundhouse swings. I jabbed him in the ribs. Luowski buckled.

Before he could process what was happening, I kicked

under his knees, knocking him off balance, and delivered an uppercut to his jaw, smiling as his head snapped. He stumbled backward, in full retreat now. Terrified, he was at the door and fumbled for the handle.

As I watched, I realized he was terrified of *me*. He'd abandoned his mission; his only objective was to make it out of the apartment in one piece.

But I had different plans for him. I stood at the end of the short hallway, not backing down, just waiting. I felt dangerous. Looking at Luowski's wide eyes, a thrill went through me. I was dangerous. Finally.

He got the door open and backed out onto the small landing, unwittingly positioning himself for my grand finale. I took a running start and cartwheeled into him, copying a move I'd once seen Charlene do. My foot connected with his chest and sent him tumbling over the guardrail. Luowski landed in a heap at the bottom of the stairs.

AMANDA

Unexpected as it may have been, I knew Jess had it in her. I'd witnessed her thrashing in her dreams, her dedication to working out, but it was her watching all those YouTube martial arts videos while we lived at Mrs. Nash's that should have tipped me off.

Jess had been through more than any of the Keepers, more even than me or Mattie. Being kidnapped and under the spell of Maleficent had affected her psychologically and physically. Once freed by Finn and the Keepers, she had quietly dedicated herself to never allowing that to happen again.

I considered myself her closest friend, but she didn't talk about her time with the Green Queen, even with me. I discovered the YouTube videos by accident and kept it to myself; I watched her get herself fit, strong, and capable of endurance, felt her sift through the destructive elements of her captivity and resurrect herself, sensed the anger and rage building, just waiting for the right outlet to unleash it upon.

Greg Luowski walked into that storm.

At first, his apparently enchanted body deflected her attempts. It was like a force field surrounded him, stopping her blows. But that force lost power as this newly wild Jess continued to aim blows from her legs and arms at him in a dizzying display. He took a pair of roundhouse swings at her—blows that should have knocked her unconscious—but Jess ducked them like she was seeing everything in slow motion.

With Luowski's arm raised to punch her, she jabbed him in the ribs, caught his chin, kicked his legs. The beast of a boy, green eyes and all, was drained of the power of whatever spell controlled him; he staggered back toward the open door, stunned and powerless.

It was as if Jess had four arms, four legs, and no intention of stopping. Greg Luowski was just a boy in retreat now. And he might have made it had Jess not executed what looked like a cartwheel, turning herself into a human wrecking ball that spun toward Luowski like a pinwheel, connected, and sent him plummeting down the stairs, head over heels.

As he on the pavement at the bottom, he saw the six shiny black shoes aimed at him.

JESS

I waited for a pang of guilt as he landed two stories down, but it never came. On the contrary, I felt great. Suddenly, I understood the appeal of sports: this must be what it felt like after a victorious soccer game, winning a swimming meet. After a lifetime of playing defense, I had stood my ground and won. I had single-handedly beaten the unbeatable. I was no longer a damsel in distress, but a fighter.

Standing at the top of the stairs, I was ready to take on the world. Including the three pairs of shiny shoes that I now saw standing at the base of the stairs.

MATTIE

Seeing Luowski beaten at his own game felt good, but the adrenaline coursing through my veins stopped cold when I spotted the black shoes. I had a sinking feeling in the pit of my stomach, but I told myself to wait, that I needed to know for sure whether or not they were Barracks 14ers.

My gaze connected with the same men who had held me captive in that abandoned spa. His eyes were not amused.

I wanted to cry out, but I inhaled sharply and willed myself to keep it together. I scanned the area, but couldn't see any way to escape.

This was it. The three of us were headed back to Baltimore.

AMANDA

My head spun. It didn't make sense that Luowski had somehow followed us, but he had dark magic on his side. That was obviously enough. We knew that we'd tricked the Barracks 14ers with our DHIs back at the Polynesian, so their presence here made absolutely no sense.

Until I saw Joe standing to the side. He was smiling.

My heart sank, all hope of finding out what had happened to the Keepers lost. The Head Imagineer had betrayed us.

I dropped to my knees. Jess looked over at me, her elation dissolving into despair. Her eyes darted to the open door, and I knew she was considering escape. But how far would we make it in the park if the Imagineers were against us?

I shook my head, lowered my chin, and fought off tears. My sorrow wasn't mine alone. It was for Finn, Philby, Maybeck, Charlene, and Willa. It was for Wayne and Wanda and all they had striven for. It was for the Kingdom itself, because clearly something bad was under way—and without the Keepers to defend it, I saw little hope of good prevailing.

My gut turned. I envisioned the Keepers in the Syndrome. What if it hadn't been their plan? What if the Overtakers had put them there? If that was true, then the Keepers were in the hands of the very power we thought had been defeated.

The burning bones. Prehistoric DNA.

I nearly fell down the stairs myself.

* * *

My heart began beating again as I saw the three Barracks 14ers drag the fallen Luowski to his feet. Either the pain of the fall, the disgrace his defeat by a girl, or the frustration of restraint turned Luowski wild and vicious. No longer himself, what he his eyes blazed that hideous green. He growled and struggled.

But the 14ers had him. This time, he wasn't going anywhere.

I didn't know what Mattie and Jess were thinking, but I'd resigned myself to defeat. It went against everything Finn and I had talked about over the years, everything Jess and I lived for. But just the sight of the suited men proved too much for me.

Still, Jess, Mattie, and I didn't move.

The 14ers engaged Joe in brief conversation. Then the men shook hands all around, and I thought I might vomit, seeing Joe acquiesce to them. I couldn't imagine what had driven him to quit on us. I briefly entertained the idea that he was the DHI, that Joe had been replaced with a virtual puppet.

He waved us down the stairs. No one moved.

"Come down!" he hollered. "It's done."

With the 14ers looking up, with Luowski slumped between his two captors like he'd passed out, first Mattie, then

Jess and I descended the stairs. We all held our heads high. Not like brides, but like condemned prisoners on their way to the gallows.

Before Mattie reached the pavement, the 14ers started off, dragging Luowski along behind them. My spirits brightened slightly; I imagined the 14ers were giving us time to say good-bye to Joe, and in my case, it wasn't going to be pretty.

Jess reached ground level before me. I joined her, Mattie, and Joe.

"How could you?" I said.

Joe smiled, which made me nearly as mad as I'd ever been.

"Greg Luowski asked questions about our flight after we'd taken off. Thankfully, I was notified."

"You just allowed him to come after us?" Jess sounded incensed, as if she might try her martial arts out on Joe.

"There is a cost to nearly everything," Joe said, "business, friendship, loyalty. Even love. We're all practitioners in the art of negotiation, Jess. We win, we lose, we compromise. Most of all, we compromise."

"You compromised *our lives!*" I protested. "We love the School of Imagineering. We've dreamed about finding a home in the company, of belonging to something."

My voice broke. I hated myself for it.

"Which is exactly why I had to negotiate," Joe said.

Mattie said, "What kind of negotiation is it if you put us back into that place? It's like a prison?"

"I didn't," Joe said. "I convinced the . . . gentlemen to

observe Luowski's powers more closely over our security surveillance system. One of them had encountered the boy at the church, and could not believe his strength. I reminded them that they had observed you three for several years. There wasn't much more to get out of you. Luowski's enchantment was new to us, new to them. A worthy candidate for study. I traded him for you."

"You what?" I felt like an idiot. "You traded?"

"We encouraged Luowski to be here during your visit—the right place, the right time for the gentlemen to observe him. The way he deflected Jess's early blows looked like a special effect. It fed their curiosity. It was a gamble, I admit; I might have lost you three. But we needed to end this."

"Thank you," Jess said.

I thanked him as well. Mattie remained indignant. "You think that will stop them from coming after us? They lied to you. They lie to everyone."

"I'm not naive," Joe said soberly. "But I think I've bought us some time. Come on; you heard me. Compromise. Negotiations are always two-sided. No one wins. You just try to get what's workable for your side in the short term. For the time being, the immediate future, you have your lives back. And we at Imagineering hope that will include us."

I was the first to throw myself forward and hug him. Jess followed close behind. Mattie stayed where she was, and Joe spoke directly to her.

"If you'll give us a chance, Ms. Weaver, we would be happy to find a place for you on our team."

"I'll take it under consideration," Mattie said.

Recalling the horrible prospect of the Keepers being put into SBS by the Overtakers, I concentrated on making my request sound like a demand.

"With that figured out, Joe, we need another look at all the videos. I think there's a possibility we haven't considered."

JESS

Joe relocated us to a Cast Member break room behind Main Street, USA. Some Cast Members came and went, but mostly we were left alone in the somewhat funky smelling cafeteria, with its worn tables and plastic chairs.

While in the midst of an animated argument with Joe about her theory, Amanda's phone rang. Pulling it out of her pocket, she glanced at the screen and let out an annoyed sigh. "Same stupid number! Keeps calling me."

Joe continued, "I'm telling you, we can trace the manual crossover to Philby's laptop."

"But Luowski got hold of that," Amanda said.

"We're aware. We also know Philby's machine is encrypted, which lessens but does not eliminate our concern. Obviously, Philby should not have had that software. Water under the bridge, I guess. We're working to disable access from his laptop. My point being: the Overtakers did not cross over the kids. Philby did. This is of their choosing."

"The Overtakers," I whispered, "You said, 'the Overtakers.'"

Joe froze. Considered and turned to me. "So I did." He sounded crestfallen.

"The Overtakers," I repeated. "Who are supposed to be dead."

"The bones," Amanda muttered.

"The fire," said Mattie. "I saw the bones in a fire."

"Oh dear." Like me, Joe was struggling for air.

MATTIE

The room was spinning so fast I could hardly breathe. Everything was finally making sense. The images I had seen, of bones in fire, flashed through my mind. Bright, blinding flames and blackened bones—but there was something else too, something that hadn't been there before.

I didn't believe it at first, because my readings weren't usually accompanied by audio. But the more I focused, the more I heard it. A voice, soft at first, but definitely feminine. I struggled to discern what she was saying, but her thick accent made it difficult. I narrowed my focus, but just as quickly as the voice had come, it ebbed out of my consciousness.

JESS

At the mention of the Overtakers and the fire, the room faded away, and a vision took hold of me. The tune from the music box rang in my ears, accompanied by an image of a gold-toothed horse. I watched as its head raised and lowered.

Galloping? Nodding? I wasn't sure. Its stiff mane stayed still, somehow, not moving even as the horse's head bobbed.

The conference room snapped back into place as the vision ended. Immediately, I clicked open a pen and sketched what I'd seen on the napkin in front of me.

MATTIE

The image of the burning bones sparked a marathon of memories, all the ominous readings I'd collected while in Orlando flooding back in a rush. Among them, most clearly, was my reading of the tall, gray-haired Imagineer at Hollywood Studios. Compared to the security footage shot in Walt's apartment, what he'd seen was different.

"Wait!" I held up my hand. "The videos the Imagineer saw are slightly different. Is that possible?"

My focus was solely on Joe's reaction. He looked worn out, like the rest of us. More than that, with our words about the Overtakers, he seemed to have lost the certainty we took for granted. When he spoke, he did so reluctantly.

"Look, anything's possible. Right?"

Something fluttered in my chest; a new energy filled me. A sudden hope.

"I'd be up for reading him again," I said. "But he's there, and we're here." I made sure to lock eyes with Joe. "What if I read you?"

Joe laughed. "You mean for a second time?"

I gulped, not answering. I didn't have to be specific. He had Reached into me that first time, whether he'd known it or not. He obviously knew something strange had happened.

"I can target my read to something specific. I promise I won't invade your privacy. Maybe you saw something you didn't pick up on right away. But the other Imagineer did."

I didn't mention that my powers were growing. I could now recall bits and pieces of my readings, even days later. That was new. I picked up more, faster—it was like I had a faster processor. I noticed things I hadn't before, like the eerie voice that accompanied the burning bones.

"I'm not sure we have much choice," Joe said. He extended his hand.

I slipped off my sticky glove.

AMANDA

Joe moved us all by Pargo to an office building behind Toontown. He offered us power drinks and protein bars. I ate and drank eagerly. Then I washed my hands and face in the restroom, and felt half human again. I needed sleep, but didn't have any time.

Joe being Joe, he organized the video viewing quickly. Together, we watched them again. We watched Wayne, the Keepers, and Finn.

And all the time, Joe watched Mattie with an eagle eye. Since allowing her to read him, he'd acted deeply troubled.

MATTIE

As Joe worked with the security footage, I could feel his eyes occasionally burning into me. He'd reacted poorly to my reading. Most people didn't realize it was happening, so it had to have been creepy to know a nineteen-year-old girl was prowling around in your thoughts and memories.

I'd targeted the read for anything to do with the videos. As often happened, I got more than I expected.

For one thing, Joe's mind operated on a whole different level from most people. His was a mind where I could have lingered for hours, a treasure trove of Disney lore, history, park attractions, and insider information concerning the Imagineers. Films and music occupied him, as did details about the Disney cruise ships, a new Disney Channel TV show, and more. I could hardly tear myself away. At a time like this, I loved my power to read.

As the video started to roll, I paid attention to every detail. We had a puzzle to solve.

JESS

Joe didn't seem worried to me—he seemed sad. Everyone had private thoughts. Letting Mattie roam the library of his mind had bothered him. I totally got that. I certainly had my share of secrets, and I wanted to keep them to myself. They were mine and mine alone. I wasn't letting Mattie anywhere near me.

Joe called up the security video on his laptop and angled the screen so all of us could see. Once again, we watched Finn walk into the apartment, fiddle with the music box, and leave. Joe rewound it. We re-watched. Same thing.

"Wait." I called out. "Rewind it, please. There's a tiny bump."

Joe rewound. We watched the video for a third time.

"There!" I said.

Two more viewings of the same few seconds.

"I see it! It's like the camera moved," Amanda said.

Next to her, Mattie nodded. "But the camera can't move, can it, Mr. Garlington?"

"I see what you're talking about, but it looks more like a digital speed bump to me," Joe said.

"Something causes speed bumps," I argued.

"Look. We—the Imagineers—have watched more footage than what you all are seeing, and we have it boiled down to just these important pieces. I wouldn't worry about it."

"You would if you were us," Amanda said brazenly. "Anything unusual has to be studied carefully. Is there a time stamp on the original?"

Joe looked impressed. "I'll tell you what: I'll check the master. No stone unturned."

He left the room. The three of us didn't say much. Not with our voices. Amanda's eyes showed fatigue and worry. I studied sketches and random pieces of paper in my journal, hoping to find a clue. At some point, I lost track of time, caught up in my attempts to dream or imagine what we'd missed on the video.

I didn't get anywhere.

Joe returned. I looked up at the wall clock and realized twenty minutes had passed. It shocked me.

"You were right! You won't like it, but here we go," Joe said. "Your missing two minutes." He pushed Play.

My throat caught. Amanda gasped.

On the computer screen, a figure entered the camera frame. A short woman. Seen in black and white, she was dark, her feet bare, her head a wild mass of hair. She wore multiple earrings and necklaces. She had tattoos.

"That's Tia Dalma," Amanda said, barely audible.

The creepy figure followed the route Finn had taken earlier and made a beeline for the music box. Reached around the side. Then, almost as if she sensed she were being watched, Tia Dalma turned and threw a spell at the camera.

The screen went black.

"I almost wish we hadn't seen that," I croaked out, my throat constricted and dry.

AMANDA

Joe ran from the conference room, leaving the freeze-frame of Tia Dalma on the screen. Mattie, Jess, and I exchanged glances.

Jess said, "The voice. The bones burning. That was her. I just know it."

"You're scaring me," I said softly.

"You didn't hear this from me," Mattie said. "But my reading of Joe didn't go exactly as planned. I saw stuff I'm sure he wouldn't have wanted. Not on purpose! I want to make that clear. It just happened. I don't know exactly what this means, but I think I can guess: the DNA test on those fragments of the burned bones came back as belonging to some prehistoric lizard."

I shook my head. "What does that even mean?"

Mattie lowered her voice again. The air duct was louder than she was. "The word in his head was *dragon*."

I clamped my hand over my mouth and let out a muffled yip of terror. Then I cast a look at Jess and saw her eyes rolling back in her head. I reached out instinctively, caught her as she fainted. Mattie helped me get her onto the floor. We put her knees up, and Mattie put Jess's head in her lap.

Jess continued to breathe steadily. After a moment, her eyes fluttered open, and she sat up.

"I don't know that I can face her again. If that . . . thing . . . comes back, comes for me, for us, for the Keepers, I have no idea what I'll do."

Mattie stroked her hair. "It's only some burned bones. That's all."

"She got them from Mexico. It's a spell of some kind."

"Conjuring," I said. "Technically, it's conjuring."

"You're a big help," Mattie said, scolding me.

Jess took a deep breath. "Whatever Finn and the Keepers

are doing, wherever they've crossed over to, she wants to follow. That's the only thing the missing video can mean. We
have to warn him—them!—somehow."

"Good luck with that," Mattie said. "They're holograms,
right? Lost holograms."

"It also means," I said, heaping more fears on our pile,
"that an Imagineer, or someone even higher up in Disney,
edited the security tape."

Mattie went white. "If that's true, that's horrible."

"Why do you think Joe took off like a rocket?" I said.

"He must be freaking out."

"I know I am," said Jess.

We both consoled her. My phone fell out of my pocket,
and Jess picked it up. "You have two missed calls from Willa's
mom."

"Willa's mom?" I said. I remembered the calls. "I was a
little busy when she called. How do you know it's Willa's
mom?"

"Duh! Because I know the number from calling her house.
You know me and numbers. So call her back," Jess said indig-
nantly.

"Yes, ma'am."

"No fighting, you two!" Mattie's outrage echoed off the
walls of the soundproofed conference room.

"What is it with us lately?" Jess sounded heartbroken.

"We're just stressed," I said. "I'll try harder."

"Me too."

I called Ms. Angelo back, and told her she was on speakerphone with the girls. As she spoke, her voice sounded a little desperate. My skin flushed.

"I did what you asked. The imaging work on the photo of the crowd. Putting whatever faces I could up onto Facebook and trying to face match. I got a surprising number of hits. Surprising to me, anyway. Always on the kids, the younger faces. Sadly, not on many on the adults. Are you there?"

"I'm not sure any of us are breathing," I said.

"Front row. Well, first or second. The head is clearly visible, and because it's close to the front, there's more image to work with. Past about the fourth row, there's no way to work with those images in terms of Facebook matching. I improved the resolution throughout, but that's the best I could do."

"I'm serious," I said, "I'm not sure we're breathing."

"It's a teenage Wayne Kresky," she said. "The face recognition program doesn't discriminate for age. Wayne Kresky is definitely front and center in the second row. His daughter's Facebook page has all sorts of pictures of him, and it was a solid hit."

"Opening day," Mattie whispered.

"I'll text you a link to the enhanced image. It should come through on your phone. If you can get to a computer, you'll see more. It's improved a great deal."

I thanked her and we ended the call, promising to be in touch.

Joe entered and shut the door brusquely. "My team is in

agreement," he said, not allowing us to speak. "Tia Dalma's presence in the apartment can mean only one thing."

"She's trying to follow Finn's crossing over," Mattie said.

He looked at us as if we weren't there, as if he must be dreaming.

LUOWSKI

I couldn't tell if the Suits were the same guys from the church, but either way, I glowered at the thought of them defeating me. No one touches Greg Luowski! I was unbeatable! A tank.

And yet . . .

Looking around, I realized I sat in a van decked out like a military-like vehicle. Suits to my left and right, and three positioned across from me. My chest, as I inhaled, met with resistance. Metal restraints held my arms and legs to the side of the vehicle, while crossed heavy-duty polyester belts strapped my upper body to the wall and my legs to the seat.

I could imagine her cold, unforgiving laughter before it turned to rage over me allowing myself to end up like this.

I had to get out of here. But how? I could barely turn my neck to the left, let alone take on the Suits in the back of the van with me.

We'd been driving for hours. I'd heard the Suits mention Baltimore more than once, but I hadn't done great in geology, or geography, and couldn't remember if that was the capital of Idaho or where or what that was.

Apparently I'd been traded for the Freaks, which threw me into yet another tantrum. One of the Suits threatened me with by displaying a Taser, and I calmed back down.

The guy said, "Take it easy, kid. Where you're going there'll be other kids like you. Not exactly like you, but close enough. Most of the testing is easy. It hardly hurts at all."

I grunted. That didn't sound too reassuring.

Then a bolt of terror sent shock waves through me. Sweat prickled my skin. Did they consider me a freak like the Freaks? Seriously?

I tried to explain it to them, but they had a gag on me. *They had to listen!*

I had to get out of here, now!

I wouldn't make the mistake of trying something as soon as they took me out of the restraints. They'd expect that. No, I'd play along for a time. Greg Luowski didn't take to the idea of imprisonment lightly.

While they listened to the radio and looked at me like I was some kind of stray dog they'd collected from the side of the road, I made a plan.

DAY 11

MATTIE

"I'm supposed to try to *reach* him," I said, disbelieving, "not *read* him?" Jess, Amanda and I had slept in. I felt half-human again. We were assembled with Joe in a bland room inside the Burbank studio lot that held all three comatose boys on cots. We were told some Imagineers were currently across town collecting Charlene.

"We're thinking that between his crossover and immediately after Amanda's kiss, there ought to be some kind of mental gap for you to slip in," Joe said. "You pass Finn the image of Tia Dalma. Not that I know what I'm talking about."

We all chuckled.

"I've never tried to reach."

"I understand that."

"What if I can't?"

"We go to Plan B."

"Which is?" I asked.

"To *B* determined!"

Amanda groaned, making Joe laugh aloud at his own joke. An instant later, he apologized.

"Seriously, though," he said. "Guys, at this point, what's there to lose?"

JESS

My job in all of this was to "dream" what was going through Finn's head when Amanda kissed him. "I don't know if I can force a dream. I've tried it before, but it's pretty unreliable," I warned.

Forcing a future dream of *mine* was difficult enough. Forcing a future dream for someone else? I wasn't even sure it was possible. Forget doing it on cue.

Besides, I wasn't positive I wanted to see Finn's half of a kiss with Amanda. The thought of eavesdropping on something so personal made me uncomfortable at best.

AMANDA

Joe used his phone as the countdown clock. I watched the screen without blinking, which gave me an excuse for the tears that formed. Wherever Finn was, he needed me, needed us. At least for the next twelve hours, we had only this one chance.

Being a professional, Joe hid his concern well, but there was no denying the truth. The presence of Tia Dalma in Walt's apartment altered everything. The Keepers were no longer just missing; they were at risk. Not from a former school bully, but from a witch doctor capable of horrific crimes, including the murder of Dillard Cole and, as one of the leaders of the Overtakers, Wayne Kresky.

It didn't take a lot of imagination to wonder who would be next.

Eleven fifty-nine.

Memories, I often felt, were my friends. I could sometimes select which ones to view and which to ignore. But tonight, my memories of Finn and me became a stew of fun and fright. Every time I would think of something pleasant, Maleficent, Judge Frollo, or a tiger would jump into my brain and scare me half to death. All of the Keepers' stories lived inside me.

Joe's plan, for my kiss to "shock" Finn at the moment of crossover, filled me with hope and dread in equal measure. For one thing, I had no idea whether or not it could possibly work. More worryingly, what if it did work, but I shocked him at the wrong moment? If we'd had the slightest clue as to where he and the other Keepers had crossed over, things would have been easier. But in that moment, I was terrified.

Ten . . . nine . . . eight . . .

I leaned over and hovered my lips above his. Not long ago, it would have made me nervous—the idea of kissing him—but now it was different. I thought about *Sleeping Beauty*. I thought about Disney. I thought about "true love's kiss."

Our lips barely touched. I felt a small shock, almost like electricity.

His eyes came open.

I screamed.

MATTIE

As Amanda leaned in to kiss Finn, I grabbed his hand, summoned my strength, and reached.

I envisioned Tia Dalma and thrust the image out of me, like shouting a word. Finn's fingers moved. I screamed, dropped his hands, and nearly passed out.

Then, taking a deep breath, I cracked an eye open just in time to see Finn's body twitch. I had no idea if I'd caused that or if Amanda had, but I liked what I saw.

A twitch. And if I wasn't imagining it: a scowl on his otherwise placid face.

DAY 12

JESS

As the clock struck midnight, a flash of light flooded my vision. I was vaguely aware of Mattie muttering "Tia Dalma"— and then I was swallowed up in a flood of images.

Wayne, but a young Wayne, the young man we'd seen in the picture, stood in front of some kind of submarine, which filled the background behind him.

That image was replaced by Amanda's face. Then nothing.

AMANDA

"I think it worked," Jess told Joe. She described a flash of light and what she'd seen, including my face.

"I didn't see any submarine," Mattie said. Her voice told me she questioned Jess's report.

I didn't say anything. Finn's eyes opening and closing had dropped me to the floor, bawling. I felt horrible for being so emotional. But in that moment, he had seen me, and I'd seen him, and I didn't care what anybody said about it. I knew what I knew.

Joe sounded put off as he addressed Jess. "You're saying you saw young Wayne and a submarine?"

"Yes."

"Can you draw it? The submarine?"

"Of course she can draw it," I answered for her.

"I need paper," Jess said. "A pencil or—"

Joe extended a pen. "Right there on the sheet. That's fine."

"Seriously?"

"Please."

Jess began to sketch.

JESS

I sketched out the image on the sheet, narrating as I drew. "It was like a tube, but with a bulge on the top. And little circles along the sides. Windows, I suppose." I completed my sketch. "I think it's a submarine."

Joe came around the side of the bed. Disbelief spread across his face as he took in my sketch. "That's impossible! That hasn't been around in forever."

I shrugged. I realized long ago that nothing was impossible.

AMANDA

Joe's mention of "forever" prompted an image not of submarines, but of the blue soy can and its contents. *Time.*

"The time capsule!" I whispered. Then, more loudly, "I'll be right back!"

I took off running. Downstairs. Along the empty streets of the backlot. Into our temporary dorm. I found my backpack. I dug out the soy can.

Though tempted to dump its contents, I held myself back, repeating the Keepers' credo to myself. *Team first.*

More stairs. The same empty street. Climbing, out of breath, gasping. Finally, I burst into the Keepers' dorm. Dropping to my knees, I spilled the contents of the can onto the floor in a messy pile and fished out the photo.

"What's going on?" Joe said.

"Mandy," Jess said, "we've looked at that stuff a hundred times."

"Reading glasses," I said, addressing Joe. "Do you wear reading glasses?"

"I have a magnifying app on my phone," he said.

So there we were, the four of us, on our knees around a bunch of ancient toys and a cigarette lighter, looking at the photo through Joe's phone app.

"Amanda," Mattie said, as my eyes filled once more with tears. I wasn't seeing anything new. But I'd been so *sure*! "The one Willa's mom sent. Remember? She said it was higher resolution?"

I felt like a bell had gone off in my head. I had my phone out and the photo open within seconds. My hands shook so badly Joe took it from me.

"She said to use a bigger screen," Jess reminded us.

"This screen is fine," Joe said.

With the image greatly expanded, only a small piece of it showed on the screen. Joe moved it carefully from right to left, and then dragged it up.

Screen by screen, we examined the photo. When we reached Wayne, we paused. At this resolution, you could actually see a vague resemblance to the older man we'd known. Joe stayed there a little longer than expected, perhaps flooded with his own memories.

"More," I said gently. "Maybe Wayne's the only reason Finn gave us this, but I don't know . . . the minute you said forever, something told me we were supposed to study every inch of the photo."

And so we did, with no complaints. Screen by screen. Carefully. Scientifically. Joe in control. For ten or even fifteen minutes I felt frozen.

A long time ago, Wayne told us that the best place to hide things is out in the open. We'd looked at the photo too many times to count, but never at this resolution, this definition.

Joe wasn't moving the screen anymore. He'd landed on a spot well back in the dense crowd. Children waving. Adults posing. American flags. Mickey Mouse ear hats.

The Kingdom Keepers.

There was no questioning it. This was them. Side by side. Cheering.

Joe mentioned something about Photoshop, but his voice

gave him away—he didn't believe that any more than we did.

"July seventeenth, 1955," Jess whispered. "It's not possible."

"A time capsule," Mattie said. "Finn was telling us all along, don't you see? A time capsule! He wanted us to know they'd gone *back in time*."

"As DHIs," Joe gasped. "Tesla. How could . . . ? It's impossible."

"If you can dream it," I muttered.

The three of them looked up at me. I could feel their gaze without actually meeting their eyes.

"Nineteen-fifty-five," Joe repeated. "You understand: there's no way this is possible."

I nodded faintly. "I know. But then . . . explain this."

Carefully, I widened the image slightly, zoomed in on the space between the heads of Finn and Willa, who stood shoulder to shoulder. The picture became grainy again.

"What is that?" Mattie breathed.

Jess answered. "It's Finn's right hand. He's holding something. He's looking right into the camera and he's smiling and he's holding something."

I wasn't going to claim he was looking right at me. But I knew what I knew.

Joe had figured it out, too. You didn't get much past Joe. He fished the empty notecard envelope out of the pile of stuff on the floor.

In the photo, in the space between the two heads, in Finn's

right hand, was a rectangular piece of paper. It had been written on, though we'd never be able to read it.

My note. The note that belonged in the envelope addressed to me.

Joe spoke aloud the truth that was haunting us all.

"They were in Disneyland on Opening Day, 1955."

"With Wayne," Jess said.

"And Walt," Mattie added.

"Finn," I gasped through more tears. "What are they doing there?"

"Perhaps not even they know," Joe said.

"But Wayne knew, or he wouldn't have sent them."

"Wayne is there with them," Joe said.

"We solved it!" Jess said. "That's what's important. We can project them now. We know where they are and that at least for now they can't return."

"Or don't want to," I said, feeling my throat knot.

"We don't know what they want, but hopefully they know Tia Dalma's part of it now."

"I miss them," I blurted out.

"You saved them," Joe said. "All three of you."

"And you got rid of Greg Luowski for us!" Mattie chimed in. "Thank you for that."

"Good riddance," I said.

"You should be proud of yourselves," Joe said. "For now, the Keepers are safe, and you've warned them of potential trouble. Not bad for a trio of Fairlie Humans."

Jess started to laugh first. Then Mattie. Finally I joined in, though the tears I shed were not tears of laughter. I looked at the grainy black-and-white photo and the card held in Finn's hand. A card meant for me.

I wonder what it said, and I wondered if I'd ever find out.

Don't miss the next adventure:

THE RETURN—BOOK 1
DISNEY LANDS

READ AN EXCERPT

CHAPTER ELEVEN

"PHILBY CALLED," AMANDA TOLD JESS across a lunch table bearing two orange trays from the Team Disney commissary. As they spoke, Jess squeezed a piece of packaged California roll between disposable chopsticks; Amanda wolfed down penne pasta with rotisserie chicken and Parmesan.

"And?" Jess asked, knowing by Amanda's tone that it was something important to the Keepers—and nothing personal. If it were personal, Finn would have been the one to call Amanda.

"He needs our help. It's for Finn, he said. Research."

"Spying?"

"I don't know exactly." Amanda shook her head, brow furrowed in confusion. "He wants me—us?—to dig into the early work of the Imagineers' involvement with television. He says it's not stuff the Archives would have. But he thinks we'll find it here. White papers, they're called."

Here was the Disney School of Imagineering, which operated out of the Team Disney building, located just behind a towering wall separating a backstage area from Disneyland's

Toontown. Few of the Team Disney Cast Members knew of the school's existence. It had its own entrance, and the college-age students coming and going from within were easily mistaken for Cast Members or kids in Disney's College Program. Those associated with the Imagineering school called it "DSI," which sounded enough like the name of a popular TV show to be confusing.

Enrollment at DSI never exceeded two hundred, and usually hovered around one hundred and fifty. With many of those in the field or studying abroad, daily traffic in and out was usually fewer than a hundred. The DSI students ate lunch in two shifts in their own commissary, on a floor that required a special card embedded with an RFID chip to operate the elevator.

Amanda Lockhart and Jess Lockhart, two of the newly enrolled students, were sometimes thought to be sisters despite their differing looks. Amanda, olive-skinned and vaguely Asian around the eyes, stood five-foot-eight and full figured. Jess was pale, white-haired (not blond), and could have used both a few inches and a few pounds. Both pretty in their own right, the two girls put on airs of mystery and self-confidence, having learned the art of survival at an early age. Jessica had adopted Amanda's last name after the two escaped a secure research facility posing as a boarding school, in which they'd been used as guinea pigs by a shadowy organization.

Though each girl possessed unusual "gifts," neither liked the term *paranormal*. It was those gifts that had landed them in the Baltimore "boarding school" in the first place. Barracks

14, as its young residents nicknamed the research facility, was a school for kids thought to be freaks of nature. Getting out was the best thing either girl had ever accomplished.

A few key Imagineers knew about the girls' past at Barracks 14. They had negotiated Jess's and Amanda's current enrollment in DSI, and were helping keep their location confidential.

"He needs the full history of television in the park and in the company," Amanda said now. The more fiery of the two, she displayed great passion for things that interested her and paid little attention to the rest. She'd helped the Kingdom Keepers rescue Jess from the clutches of Maleficent by deploying her "special talent," telekinesis. She could physically move almost anything without touching it. A simple "push" of her arms, driven by a focused intention—anger, fear, hatred—and she could move chairs, close doors, break windows.

"Well, at least he's not asking for much," snapped Jess, emitting a high-pitched hiss like a tire losing air. "The full history of TV? That sounds like a PhD thesis."

"Philby says the Imagineers keep a stash of files off site in the dorm. It's the stuff they don't want students to find or others to see. Old exams. Legal stuff."

"What happened to him coming here himself? He's already been accepted. He can do it in a couple weeks."

"I think it's about timing at this point. He needs us. Finn needs us."

"Mandy, I wouldn't trade our time with the Keepers for anything. You know that. But it's over. I'm not going to keep battling villains that don't exist anymore. Finn . . . since Wayne . . . he's paranoid. He has issues, Mandy. This kind of thing is not going to help."

Amanda sat back in her chair, set down her fork. Jess knew her well enough to see she was withdrawing into herself.

"He needs me," she said softly.

"I like it here."

"It's Philby asking, not Finn. Doesn't that mean anything to you?"

"Of course it does. But this school is by far the coolest thing we've ever done, or ever could do. Wrap your mind around that: we're being paid to learn about all the coolest stuff Disney has ever done. Why risk it?"

"Wrap your mind around this: why are we students here? Because we helped the Keepers. Because we're their friends. And because of them, we happen to know a lot of important people in the company. That's why we were offered this in the first place."

"I just . . . I don't want to be the oddball anymore," Jess said, her voice growing soft. "We've been called witches, spooks, freaks, and aliens. I'm not naive, Mandy—the other students here will eventually realize what we can do. But I don't want to do anything—anything!—to make that happen faster. I want to just start over as a normal girl. We've talked about this, Mandy. You want it as much as I do."

"I do," Amanda confessed. "It's true. I want all that and

more. Friendships that last. A room I can actually call mine. A chance to go to movies and malls and do the stuff we've never done."

"DSI is going to make that stuff happen."

Amanda nodded, sadly.

"One phone call from Philby changes that?"

Amanda's pained expression cut at Jess like a knife. "He needs us, Jess. He saved you. Now we've got to save him."

"Do not guilt-trip me."

"They found a message in Wayne's apartment. Finn crossed over and weird things happened to him. Philby won't say exactly what, but he obviously thinks it has to do with the Imagineers' early experiments with television. It's a couple of folders. That's all he needs."

"I will not get myself expelled, even for Philby or Finn."

"He's our friend."

"Of course he is! I'm not arguing that. I love them all. Really. As in, love them. Finn, too. But you're in deep with him, way too deep. We're moving on here, Mandy. I'm not saying we can't have them as friends. That's always and forever. But we can't risk this chance that's been given to us. We jumped ahead of thousands of kids on a list. Kids who would do anything to be Imagineers. Do not mess this up."

"Philby said Becky Cline told him about the Imagineer stuff. She mentioned the dorm library."

"The Tower library?" Jess sat back, her face thoughtful. "That's different. Getting in there is no problem."

"That's all I'm saying."

"You know it's not. It always starts with something like this," Jess said. "Right? A message. A clue. And it gets out of hand. I'm not going there. I will not lose this chance."

"We're not going to take anything. We're not going to steal or . . . whatever. We're just going to study in the library."

An older girl crossed the commissary, heading toward them at a brisk pace. Both girls took notice. Her dark hair was pulled back tightly, stretching skin riddled with acne.

"Which one's Amanda?" the girl asked, giving them a bright smile.

Amanda raised her hand cautiously.

"Peggy wants to see you."

"Peggy?"

"Victoria Llewelyn. Don't ask me why she's called Peggy! She's the first year adviser. All first years get reviewed. It's kinda random when it happens. You'll like her."

Amanda looked over at Jess. Her eyes said, *Please.*

Jess nodded, but a frown contorted her face.